DEVILS RIDGE

STACY N. HAWKS

DISCLAIMER

Devils Ridge is set in Alleghany County, NC in the early 1930s. Certain long-standing institutions, agencies and public offices are mentioned, but the characters involved are wholly imaginary.

We would like to thank the real-life members of former Sheriff Irwin for letting him be portrayed in this novel.

Certain names, characters, places, dialogue, and incidents are the product of the author's imagination or are used fictitiously to build a believable historical world. Any resemblance to actual events, locales, or persons, living or dead, is entirely coincidental.

<u>The Blue Ridge is on fire this morning</u>
from the blazing sun
there's nowhere that I'd rather be
than right here on this run
With nerves of steel
tight wrapped to peel
the gravel from this road
my pedal's floored above the roar
of moonshine coming home

- G.W. Plain -

PREFACE

*I*n the early 1930s North Carolina and the nation itself was undergoing great economic strain, but prior to the Great Depression much of the South was in its own agricultural depression.

The prices of tobacco and other crops fell drastically low, and farmers struggled to make ends meet. The solution in some cases in these states was the very thing that was challenged by the passing of the 18th Amendment to the U.S. Constitution.

The Amendment prohibited the production, transportation, and sale of intoxicating liquors.

In the mountains of Appalachia moonshine had many purposes, the first being to feed one's family. The second, medicinal, and the third, was for the love of drinking itself.

It is the latter reason that on August 18, 1920 the 19th Amendment passed, giving women the right to vote. This reform having been born of the Temperance movement also gave women more of a voice in their home and family life.

Despite the law, many moonshiners took risks hauling illicit liquor across state and county lines in the dark of night.

Of course, no heist, or bootlegging operation, would be complete without the proper horsepower. With recent innovations in transportation, cars made

1

it possible for the business of bootlegging to thrive as mechanics learned ways to outrun the law. While successful, at times it was also dangerous.

There is no denying the fascination with such legends who rose up from the dark corners of mountain communities to become truly notorious outlaws. Those whose stories still captivate and endure even today.

This is the era when Bonnie and Clyde reigned as the Queen and King of fugitives. A time period when mobsters were the anti-hero in a civilization thirsty for a sense of financial security.

CHAPTER 1

Spring 1932

D eputy Walter Irwin ascended the newly constructed stone steps sliding his hand along the iron rail banister of the Alleghany County courthouse. A year earlier, the town had been all but destroyed.

The courthouse that had stood there since 1910 had not been immune to the flames as they ravaged all except a portion of the Clerk of Courts office. The small community banded together to ensure a crisis of this type would not impact the town again, or so Irwin and other town officials hoped.

Hardly able to reach the landing without being within inches of another individual, he quickly became aware that the newspaper prediction of a large crowd was at that moment a reality.

Gazing as far as he could through the double entry doors that were propped open Irwin saw few vacant seats, in what was soon to be standing room only.

There were voices rumbling and echoing about the newly built space so prominent he nearly missed the one that had become familiar over the last several months.

"Hope you have had your coffee," BOI agent Frank Lincoln approached extending his hand, "It's about to be an interesting morning."

Lincoln was six-foot-four, broad-shouldered, with a faded scar on the left side of his face and a more recent one that had was starting to fade just below his left ear.

"Had three cups already. Have you spoken with Higgins?" Solicitor John Higgins, a well-known and well-respected prosecutor was seated at one of the tables before the judge's bench going through a file.

"I did, and in addition, McCann arrived this morning just before seven, he has settled in and they both have expressed their gratitude towards you and your involvement deputy."

Before Irwin could respond the bailiff shouted, "Ladies and Gentlemen, take your seats please!" The courtroom started to quieten, the creek of the floors lessened as individuals began to file in. This included the Defendants wife and mother.

"Follow me," Lincoln kept his voice low as he led Irwin to the bench directly behind Mrs. Robert M. Gambill, Editor of the *Alleghany Times* and his boss, Sheriff Dean Henson. Mrs. Gambill waited until the door beside the bailiff opened before putting her pen and pad to the side. "All rise! The Honorable Judge Steven McClain presiding!"

"Please, be seated," McClain motioned after he was positioned behind the bench. Irwin wondered if Higgins was as anxious as he was.

The man seemed calm, collected, and there was no reason for him not to be. All the evidence was there. Every piece of it—*well almost every piece*, Irwin thought to himself.

Mrs. Gambill glanced over her shoulder and gave him a supportive nod as the judge shuffled around a paper or two on the stand.

Raising a thin pair of glasses to his face McClain, a wiry man himself, stared down at the defendant as if in complete disbelief of what he was reading and cleared his throat, "Mr. Higgins I presume your council has shared all documentation with Mr. Warren of the Defense?"

"Yes your Honor," Higgins said without skipping a beat. "And I presume that this is a *complete* list of charges against the Defendant?" "Yes your Honor," Solicitor for the state Bennett McCann answered this time, "If it pleases the court we would also like to add another charge."

McClain raised his eyebrows, "And what more would you like to add counselor?" "Impersonating an officer your Honor," McCann answered without moving from his chair. Irwin glanced over at the Defendant. Part of him hoping to see some remorse for what had happened. Another part of him knew it would never come from someone like Connor Ridge.

"Says here Mr. Ridge you have stolen multiple vehicles both in and around Alleghany County ran a bootleg operation to which the Sheriff and Deputy of this County have rendered useless and costed several hundreds of man-hours to our state authorities in the search for these vehicle parts, not to mention the damages incurred by the county due to arson."

Irwin kept his eyes on Ridge, who did not even bother looking in his direction, but was quite content staring directly at the judge as he spoke.

Taking a breath the judge then stared at Mick Warren, second chair of the defense, "One, in particular, belonging to the Honorable Judge Carico of the great state of Virginia to our north. Mr. Warren, how does your client plea?"

Mick Warren buttoned his jacket as he stood, turning on his charm as Irwin had often seen him do in similar cases, "Your Honor, if it pleases the court, a plea agreement was reached in this matter." Judge McClain glanced at Ridge, "And you accepted this agreement Mr. Ridge?" "Yes, your Honor."

Higgins slid his chair back causing Mrs. Gambill to look up from her pad and take notice. "With all due respect your Honor, we are objecting to bond at this time."

McClain pushed his glasses up the bridge of his nose, folded his hands and nodded quietly in agreement.

"My client is not a flight risk," Warren started to argue.

Higgins shot the man a look much like a British Naval caption would when firing across the bow of an oncoming enemy ship, warning him to tread water—lightly.

"Mr. Warren, in light of the evidence I was able to review last evening and the sum total of these crimes, I am going to have to rule in favor of Mr. Higgins at this time. The state will remand Mr. Ridge back to the Yadkin County jail until sentencing June 18th."

A flurry of excited voices carried from the front left of the courtroom all the way towards the back. A visibly upset Mrs. Ridge sat nearly on the edge of her bench just across from Irwin on the opposite side, her hands folded in her lap but squeezed tightly together. "Order!" McClain bellowed bringing down the wooden gavel so hard it sounded like thunder echoing around the voluminous room.

"Is there anything else Mr. Higgins, Mr. Warren?"

"No your Honor," Warren answered, pausing just in case Higgins had any further comments.

"Not at this time your Honor," Higgins replied, his voice showing no lack of confidence.

Having no further business, Judge McClain picked up the papers he had been examining and then motioned to the bailiff who opened the door. As McClain exited the chambers, everyone rose to their feet except for Mrs. Ridge and Connor Ridge's mother. "Nice work," Lincoln said as Higgins turned around, a look of satisfaction on his face as he shook Lincoln's hand.

"I could use a drink of water," Higgins replied coughing slightly, "And don't thank me. It's the agencies here who did all the work, and of course our Sheriff's office." Sheriff Henson shrugged off the supposed compliment, picked up his hat, and acknowledged Irwin's presence for the first time that morning, "Deputy, what happened to Darrel Joines?"

"Same thing, he will be tried with Ridge," Mrs. Gambill interjected without looking at the Sheriff, "They had him here earlier."

"I'm sure we will learn all about it once the newspaper comes out?" Irwin said with a crooked grin trying to ease the tension. Mrs. Gambill gave him a slight shrug, "You never know." He watched as she headed off to the back offices of the courthouse. Her printer and assistant just beyond the doors. Her return to the close proximity of the Sheriff's Office and Court could easily be both a blessing and a burden.

"Excuse me," Irwin stepped away from the conversation between Lincoln and the others to check on Mrs. Ridge. "Ma'am," Irwin approached. Connor Ridge's mother looked up first. It was clear she did not wish to speak to him, but Irwin had to try anyway. "Ma'am I know this is hard, and I am very sorry for your daughter-in-law and your son's family. If there is anything I can do—."

"Nothin' you can do now is going to get him out, is it?" Connor Ridge's mother snapped, her voice a low hissing whisper, "My boy wasn't doin' a thing other than providin' for his family." Connor's wife cleared her throat, stood up, and stared directly at Irwin, "I know you was just doin' your job deputy," She paused, her breath catching momentarily, "But you know the strain we've been under. Why punish a man for doin' somethin' the law should stay out of in the first place?"

Irwin let the women proceed out of the courtroom without responding. However, he was reminded of the argument he had read in a newspaper some months back. Moonshiners were running illicit liquor to Chicago from West Virginia.

The journalist who had covered the story made mention of moonshine being illegal at least so much as according to man's law, but God's law said every man had the right to provide for his family. Walter Irwin looked up at the county seal over the judge's bench for a long moment and thought, *"But God never intended man to do so if those actions would hurt others."*

Late Spring, 1929

Looking down he surmised he was a mile up, straight up. The hills and valleys below were encapsulated in their signature sapphire haze as the July sun began to peak over the ridge. Reminding himself of what his Pa used to say Connor quickly averted his eyes back towards his final ascendant and steadily planted his worn boots on the rocks.

For days, no weeks, he had been planning this moment. A way to better the life of his family and those of his friends. No one had ever done anything as bold as what Connor was planning before, not in this small corner of Appalachia.

No one had yet dared tempt man or his law. No one had dared to claim back what was rightfully theirs, or as Connor saw it, what should have been his to start with. A decent wage. A way to pay for his children to have shoes, a way for his wife to get a new Sunday dress, a way for him to own a car of his own someday. Or a truck.

Standing atop the precipice Connor turned to admire the place that would be his. The sound of birds mixed with the warm summer breeze as it passed through the forest of poplars, dogwoods, and laurels all around. Off to his right he could hear the main reason he had chosen this spot.

With careful eager steps he proceeded towards that sound. The faint rush slowly evolved into a roar the closer he got, and the ground had a vibration that touched his very bones. As it came into view through thin poplar saplings, Connor could not help but to stare in amazement.

Ahead of him lumbered a waterfall gushing gallon after gallon of water onto the rocks below. His gaze followed the water watching as it wound its way down the mountain until it disappeared from his line of sight.

Fresh water. High ground. Dense trees. A perfect spot to set up his first still. Before he could celebrate Connor felt something heavy pass over his left boot. His eyes shot downward realizing instantly that he was standing dangerously close—or rather the danger was close to him—to a cottonmouth moccasin

The snake slithered quietly, carefully, across the top of his boot and then down the hill nearer to the water's edge to bask on the warm rocks. Careful that he was not in the presence of more than one cottonmouth, Connor slowly backed away into the woods.

When he reached a small clearing a few feet away he spotted them, a whole nest of them. With his heart racing Connor made the decision not to disturb the creatures.

The thought suddenly occurred to him that a place this secluded needed a name to keep others from venturing to it. A name that could only be derived from the very thing Connor planned to do. Quietly he smiled to himself, *That's it, this will be my Devil's Ridge.*

Summer of 1930

Darrell Joines wiped off his hands stained with grease, his faded coveralls smelling of a mixture of gasoline and wood. The old shop had held up well despite the past winter's storms and the recent heavy downpours that often-accompanied sweltering humidity in the foothills of North Carolina around mid-July.

His father sometimes worked in the garage with him when the tobacco did not need tending. Their family farm was a few sparse acres and would require harvesting by early August. Unlike his father, Darrell had started to see more of a need for vehicle repairs than for picking crops.

As a result, at the age of twenty-eight Darrell planned to make the most of it. He had been saving up to build his own business, yet there was no denying he was still a long way off from making his dream a reality.

Just as his father did on the farm, Darrell worked hard to cultivate a relationship with new car dealers and neighbors to drum up business. Some days he was so busy he hardly got a bite to eat until the sun went down. Other days he would spend reading about car engines or repairs learning new ways to make vehicles efficient or faster.

The sound of a car coming down the driveway near his home caused Darrell to push away from the coupe he had been working on and head out onto the lot.

"Morning," A stranger dressed in a pair of khakis and light gray shirt greeted.

"Morning, what can I do for you?"

"You work here?"

"Yes sir," Darrell answered with a smile. "The boys up at the house on the street sent me here. It seems my tire is low, the front one, do you mind checking it?"

"Sure, no problem," Darrell walked over examining the tire with his eyes first and then with his hands. The smooth rims told him the man would need new tires sooner rather than later. Darrell paused as his hand graced over something that felt rough, not smooth like the rest of the tire and he cocked his head just under the wheel to take a better look.

"What is it?" The man asked. "Here's your problem," Darrell tapped the tire, "You ran over a nail."

The man's frustration was visible in his expression as he placed his hands in his pockets, "Can you fix it?" "I'll get the nail out and patch up the tire so you can get going. But," Darrell added as he rose to his feet, "You may want to consider getting new tires soon." "Thanks, I will. How much do I owe you?"

"Twenty-five cents."

"Thanks," The man took out his wallet and handed Darrell a dollar bill.

Figuring he would get the change before the man left Darrell went to work on the tire. While jacking the car Darrell noted there was a certain weight to the midsection that he had not seen in that model of Plymouth. "How long have you had this car mister?" Darrell inquired.

"It's not mine, I picked it up for a friend, heading home."

"You ain't from around here?" Darrell could hear the slight variation of the man's accent, his words a bit quicker than those of him and his neighbors.

"You could say that," The man replied, "Are you?" "Born and raised right here in North Carolina." "Ever been to the coast?" The man inquired. "No, but I tell you what if you go hiking up these mountains, you'll see the prettiest blue sea in all your life, better than any ocean in my opinion."

Without any further conversation Darrell lowered the car from the jack hearing what he thought were glasses chiming. "I'll get your change," He said, noticing the look on the man's face as he stood opposite him near the driver's door.

"Don't worry about that. "Keep the change. You've saved me a great deal of trouble."

"I couldn't do that—," Darrell replied but the man came around the hood of the car.

"Don't believe I got your name." The man spoke in a way that was both friendly but also daunting.

"Darrell, sir."

"Darrell, are you always this good at fixin' cars?"

"I like to think so," Darrell answered carefully.

"How much you make a day doing this?"

The man waved his finger around at the garage while his eyes wandered a bit from the tools to the beat-up gasoline cans.

"Depends. Some days it's five bucks, others I make nothin'."

"Are you okay with making nothin'?"

"Not really." Darrell responded.

"You have plans for this garage?"

"Savin' to build a better one," Darrell answered.

"How much have you saved?" Darrell's expression told the stranger all he needed to know.

"What if I told you I knew people who could help you make more money?" Darrell wrinkled his forehead in concern as he felt the stranger's intense gaze and came to the realization of what was in the car, and what the man was actually doing.

"What do you say to ten percent of my business if you are my repair guy between here and Tennessee?"

Staring at the man with gold rimmed eyes Darrell felt only slightly conflicted. On one hand he knew what the man was doing was wrong, but on the other he knew it also put a lot of food on people's tables. Darrell understood his neighbors made moonshine and even his own cousins had been arrested for bootlegging once or twice.

Moreover, bootlegging afforded some luxuries others struggled to afford like shoes and coats in the winter. If the tobacco crop did not turn out, Darrell also grasped he would have to pitch in to help his family survive the winter and that could mean abandoning the garage for good.

Slowly raising his right-hand Darrell made the decision. "Then I'd say we have a deal." The stranger's grin widened into a smile as he shook Darrell's hand firmly.

"Good. My friends call me Connor, my workers call me Ridge. You can call me whichever you prefer," His gaze fell to the vehicle, "but can I count on you to forget I or this car were ever here?"

Placing his hands in the pockets of his overalls Darrell felt the crisp dollar bill, and nodded, "Sure thing."

"Then I'll see you Saturday Darrell," Connor informed before climbing into the coupe disappearing in a screen of fine dust as its wheels found the road.

CHAPTER 2

January 1931

He whispered as he walked. A silent prayer that tonight would go smoothly. No setbacks. It was a hope that could only be washed away with the drizzling rain as it dotted before him. The last few moments of the already dark day dimmed in the distance over the bare mountain ridge.

With the advent of motor cars, the roads had slowly begun to form, winding their way up and through some of the steepest terrains, just as he was doing now except on foot.

Like the early settlers, and his ancestors, who first stepped foot in Appalachia all he was trying to do was survive.

Whispering as he walked, the prayer faded at the sound of a steady motor. Up ahead through the barren trees, came a Chevy coupe. The driver jostled around as the rubber wheels worked their way up a long gravel path. Folding his coat around him he looked back ever so slightly to ensure no one had spotted him.

Headlights cut through the curtain of precipitation almost aiming him in the direction he needed to head. The vehicle slowed, coming to a crawl as it reached a large two-story home with a dark shingled roof, and a wrap-around porch.

A couple of rocking chairs near the eastern windows were gently being pushed by the cool evening breeze.

From his place among the trees he could see a woman standing just behind the lace of the screen door, the light inside outlining her silhouette. The man who climbed out of the coupe opened his umbrella and proceeded to remove a briefcase and a jacket from the passenger side of the vehicle.

Hearing the car door close, he watched and could hear just faintly what the man was saying as his wife stepped out onto the covered porch with her arms crossed.

"Fine evening for a walk," The woman could be heard saying as she observed her front yard watching her husband approach up the steps. "Don't you mean a swim?" Her husband lowered his umbrella as he reached the porch and kissed his wife on the cheek.

"Dinner is inside, and the radio is on," The woman informed, taking her husband's coat and briefcase in her hands.

He held the door open and they disappeared inside. This was the easy part. At least for him it always was.

Minutes lingered feeling more like hours. By ten o' clock in the evening the rain was starting to lift along with his patience.

Unable to wait any longer he walked quietly across the open field approaching the coupe. Every window was dark now, not a single light had been left on. The home's occupants had turned in calling it a day, while his was just beginning.

Lowering himself on the driver side near the back door he slowly reached out and touched the handle. Holding down the metal knob he heard a click. A rush of adrenaline mixed with relief flooded his system as he slowly cracked the door open sliding inside while being careful to keep himself low.

With one eye on the house and the other searching for the intricate wiring needed to start the coupe, his fingers instinctively found what was needed to create a spark.

Carefully, holding his breath, he let the two ends touch, waking the six-cylinder engine. As he closed the door he half expected to see movement, or lights coming on inside the house. However, in that moment a crack of thunder shattered any chance of discovery, urging him to move.

Putting the car into reverse he slowly backed out of the driveway, careful to leave the headlights off. As the rain began to pick back up, steadily hammering the windshield in front of him, he could not help but think, *"Just how fast can you go?"*

Bouncing and rocking from side to side the Chevy coupe made its descent onto the rough gravel path towards the body shop, and garage. Leaning back a bit, relaxing his foot on the clutch he let the vehicle slowly roll into the back lot of Darrell Joines' warehouse.

It was here he deposited stolen cars, or their parts. Their engines, carburetors, and everything right down to their tail pipes and fenders were often sold or used on other vehicles.

Climbing out of the front seat, the closing of the door announced his presence.

On the other side of the warehouse was a tiny brick home with a back porch freshly built, and a woman the size of a whippoorwill leaning over the railing grinning like a Cheshire cat.

Her long dark hair draped over her pale freckled shoulders setting off her emerald colored eyes, "Afternoon stranger!" She smiled curiously.

"Afternoon," He acknowledged, "Darrell around?"

"Up there, talkin' to one of those Shepherd boys." He noted a hint of annoyance in the young woman's tone.

Proceeding to follow the path toward the garage Darrell could be heard interrogating someone, as he usually did, "Where exactly did you get this rattle trap?" The Model-T Ford with a half-rusted fender sat idling as Darrell was bent over examining the motor.

"Never you worry about that," The Shepherd boy answered, "She's a fine piece of machinery. She'll get the job done." "Maybe," Darrell's thick accent was filled with doubt. From his spot at the entrance he interrupted, catching both men off guard, "*Maybe* what you really need is a Chevy coupe."

Darrell wiped off his hands, a look of sheer surprise on his face as he locked eyes with the man standing in the opening of his garage, "Connor Ridge is that you?" Zane Shepherd pushed away from the nearby pile of tires he had been leaning against, "Thought we wouldn't see you for a while, not after the last haul."

The last haul had been a run through Tennessee who had offered any bootlegger a hefty price just to get their shine into Nashville. It had been smooth sailing until some patrolmen tried to pull Connor over.

When the bootlegger didn't relent the patrolmen proceeded to pursue Connor. Accustomed to the curves and mountainous terrain of North Carolina Connor easily maneuvered the vehicle he had been given, topping off at some fifty miles an hour at times. However, the patrol cars nor their drivers were as well equipped.

Mid-chase one flipped, rolling down the side of a steep embankment into the darkness below. He did not bother to look back, or stop. Instead he managed to get the haul to its destination, and his money for making good on his word.

"Home is home," Connor replied, shaking Darrell's hand firmly, "No place like it."

"A coupe you say?" Darrell stepped back and folded his arms clearly skeptical, "That would be ideal, but we don't have a coupe here."

Connor grinned, the gold rings around his green eyes shimmering light that began to show itself through the cracks of the garage roof. Knowing his partner and friend all too well, Zane remarked, "You have a coupe, don't you?"

"I just might," Connor stared at Darrell who looked at Zane, "Well where is it?" "Out there," Connor motioned with his head towards the driveway.

"Is it yours?" Darrell asked, knowing the likelihood of a Chevy coupe belonging to Connor Ridge was slim to none. "Not exactly, but it's in fine operating condition, unlike the Model T here," He kicked the back tire, feeling the soft rubber with the toe of his boot.

"Let's have a look at it then."

Connor led both men outside and stood in front of the coupe, "Here she is." Zane Shepherd touched the hood of the car and ran his left hand all the way down the length of its body, "Where—Never mind I don't want to know how or where you got it. Just tell me how many cylinders."

"Six, this is the Master Chevy Coupe, latest remodel since '29, if I recall correctly," Connor took out a cigarette from his shirt pocket and lit it. "Indeed, she is," Darrell walked along the opposite side of the vehicle and opened the passenger door inspecting the interior.

Letting out a low whistle Zane continued to stare at the car, "They upped the horses too, right? By what?"

"Sixty to eighty," Connor took a drag on the cigarette, his arms folded, his eyes fixed on Darrell. "She's a beauty Connor."

"What do you want to do with her?" Zane inquired curiously, "Run shine?" Connor shook his head snickering, "Actually, we need her for another reason."

Darrell closed the passenger side door, staring towards Zane who did not appear in the least surprised.

"What job?" Zane asked. Smoke formed from Connor's nostrils as he leaned on the hood of the Coupe, his cigarette still burning, "Whitehead Grocery. They have a new shipment of sugar coming in at the end of the week and we need it if we're going to survive the next few months. We got a special order to fill."

Zane laughed slightly, "Sugar? That's all you want to haul in this car?"

"For this job," Connor replied, "And maybe we'll get lucky and there will be cash in the register too."

Zane looked at Darrell, "Seriously, in your opinion when we need to run the liquor, how many gallons can this baby hold?"

"I could outfit her to haul at least fifty gallons, possibly seventy." Seeming pleased with the answer Connor looked at his friend, and partner, "Does that mean you're in?" Knowing there was no better way to make money Zane nodded, "I'm in."

CHAPTER 3

January 1931

January 1931 had proven to be one of the coldest starts to winter Thayer Whitaker could recall since being a kid. Both he and Zane had been ordered by Connor they would be the one's breaking and entering. *After all,* Thayer thought with some provocation, "*He calls the shots.*"

Thayer had learned over the years to be ever-so-careful to keep thoughts about Connor Ridge to himself, especially in the presence of Zane Shepherd. However, this had not stopped him from expressing dissent to members of his family, mainly his brother Erick.

It was the very thought of members failing to comply with any of Connors' plans that shook the participants of his gang to their core. Most of the boys had found out through Jeb what Connors' wrath could look like, and none of the stories had ended well for those who had crossed him.

The vehicle was idling just a few seconds away from the Whitehead Grocery store in Laurel Springs part of the county just inside of an old dirt road. Looking in the rear-view mirror he saw Zane Shepherd blowing into his hands, "Think they'll close any time soon?"

"It's nearly five now," Thayer tried to sound encouraging, "Just a few more minutes." "It's freezing out here Thayer, and in case you haven't noticed, I do not have any gloves."

"Whose fault is that?" Thayer replied in his dry tone. Zane gave him a nasty look from the mirror but said nothing further.

When the lights finally went off and they could see old man Bare head to his vehicle Zane instructed Thayer to slowly pull up to the side door of the store.

Thayer waited until old man Bare was well out of view before nudging the car forwards. He parked as close as he could to the side of the building without drawing attention.

Zane, a rather burly man stepped out of the backseat holding his coat close to his chest, his hands stark white and his face flushed red as he followed Thayer.

Taking out his lock picking tools; Zane quickly worked the lock of the store's side door. There was a slight click as Thayer saw his partner grin, "We're in." Moments later they were standing inside the warm store, their hands slowly regaining feeling as they wound their way towards the front.

"Can you get it open?" Thayer's eyes were locked on the cash register, but he could tell from Zane's hesitation that opening the register may not be possible.

"It could take a while and we don't want to be here any longer than we should."

"How long would it take?" Thayer asked.

"An hour, maybe more," Zane sounded slightly irritated at the prospect, not wanting to get caught. Thayer sighed, "You know if we come back with nothin' but sugar Connors gonna have somethin' to say. You know there has to be money in here."

Zane snickered, "That old buzzard keeps more money in his pockets than he does in this store."

Thayer's expression as he lifted one of the bags of sugar was a friendly reminder of his words. In Zane's experience he knew Thayer was right, Connor would *not* be happy with sugar alone.

When Thayer returned, his hands empty, Zane reached beside the cash register and tossed him a pack of Lucky Strikes, "Keep 'em for yourself, I'll see what I can do to get this thing open."

Tucking the cigarettes in his back jean pocket Thayer proceeded to load the car with sugar. Staring at the cash register Zane knew he had a few options. The first, crowbar, the second lift the register to see if he could trip the release to open the drawer, or three, take it with them.

"You figure it out?" Thayer asked as he made his fifth run to the car and back inside. "Maybe," Zane took his left hand and pushed the cash register upwards, leaning it back towards the aisle. "What are you doing?" Thayer asked, lifting another sack of sugar. "Just get that sugar in the car," Zane instructed as his eyes searched for a release somewhere. There wasn't one.

"Thayer!"

"Yeah?"

"Crowbar," Zane shouted back. A few moments later, returning from the car, Thayer handed him the rusted crowbar from the back of the car and Zane went to work prying open the drawer. When it was finally given, the two men stood and looked at its contents. "That's gotta be what?" Thayer asked quietly.

"Close to three hundred dollars," Zane answered as he took the money and placed it in his pocket. Thayer grinned as he held up a cigarette, "Looks like you could use one of these."

Zane might have protested if it weren't for the fact he had not had a good cigarette in a few weeks.

"Let's get the rest of the sugar and get out here," Zane replied as he stuck the cigarette between his lips and proceeded towards the storage area.

The last bundles of sugar had proven to be much heavier than anticipated taking both men to haul them into the trunk of the car laying more than four in the floorboard of the vehicles backseat Hurrying they managed to grab a few extra loafs of bread just before the last trace of sun slid behind the mountains.

Mrs. Robert M. Gambill walked through the door of the Twin Oaks grocery store just in time to see a couple of store hands stashing a large metal machine into the storage room off to the side of the store.

If one had not known better, they might not have seen that the machine had a lever on the side. However, Mrs. Gambill, like most who lived in the county the last few years, had learned all about them. Whether most approved or not the nickel play vending machines had their purpose.

"I had no idea those were still being kept," She said as she walked up to Samuel Walker, the store's owner. At the sound of the woman's voice, Sam turned, scrambling for an answer, "Well—uh—you see…"

"No need to explain to me Sam. I imagine there are still a few around. Do you have any extra butter?" Quickly the manager made a beeline for the back of the shop and reemerged holding what appeared to be a pound of butter, "Twenty-four cents Mrs. Gambill."

Opening her purse, she held up ten cents, "Can this tide me over on credit until next week?" Sam nodded and put down the remaining amount owed on a ledger with most of his customers' names, "Are you going to make a cake or something?"

"Our church is havin' a revival this week and the ladies thought we would make something special afterward. You and Audrey are invited of course." "I do love your lemon cake," Sam smiled, "I bet you'll be needing sugar for it too."

He reached over and pulled off a bag of sugar, only one of three bags he had sitting on a nearby shelf. "I can't possibly—." "Say nothing of it, if I get a cake it'll be worth this bag and more." Mrs. Gambill shook her head in disbelief, "I will pay you for it, and no arguments." Sam Walker knew better than to argue with Mrs. Gambill, she was as independent and as stubborn as any newspaper reporter dared to be.

"Speaking of sugar," Sam leaned over the cash register whispering, "Did you hear about Whitehead Grocery last night?" "No, why? Did something happen?" Sam glanced around to make sure no one was close by, "Rumor has it a couple of people broke it through the back and stole around two thousand pounds of sugar."

"Two thousand…?"

"And cash from the register," Sam added as he opened his own with a tap of the button placing her ten cents in its tray, "Talk to Mr. Bare he'll tell you all about it."

Taking her butter and flour from the counter Mrs. Gambill steadily walked to her car.

Once seated behind the wheel she turned on the engine, deciding to head over to Whitehead Grocery for herself. Her first few weeks at the *Alleghany Times-News* as the Editor had been slow. Because of this stagnation she had come to the realization that if it were to survive, it would have to generate sales through stories. And a robbery, however unfortunate, was just the ticket.

The Alleghany County Sheriff's Office was notified a little before six in the morning about a robbery at Whitehead Grocery by its owner Mr. Bare.

Standing in front of the checkout counter and a row of bread, deputy Walter Irwin listened as Mr. Bare, the owner of the store, spoke with the Sheriff's right hand deputy, James Debord.

The assailants had broken in through the back door and had taken two thousand pounds of sugar, bread, some cigarettes and just about three hundred dollars in cash from the register.

"One thing is for sure, they made a mess of things," Mr. Bare asserted. Irwin noticed the items strewn about the check out counter, the fine grains of sugar against the wooden floor, and the open side door. He headed over and examined the lock, noting that the jam had not been pried open or kicked in.

"Whoever they were, they know how to pick a lock," Irwin replied, turning to the owner. "Do you suspect any of the boys who work here?"

"No," Bare answered quickly, "They're good kids, hard workers, never took nothin' from me without askin' first."

Deciding that no one was off limits Irwin proceeded outside. Experience with theft had taught him when someone was desperate enough, they'll do anything, even steal from employers. Farmers in the area worked hard, supported their families, but like most they too were struggling to get by.

The sound of a vehicle approaching caught Irwin's attention, turning around just in time he saw the 1929 Chevrolet series pull into the parking lot.

"They're not opening for another hour," Deputy Debord stated holding a cigarette, "Someone needs to tell the lady." Part of Irwin wanted desperately to tell Smith to put the cigarette out and go talk to the lady himself, but the other part of him knew he was not Sheriff. His only job was to contain the scene until they had what evidence they needed.

Slowly Irwin started towards the vehicle and greeted the woman who emerged. She was in her mid-to-late thirties, dark hair, professionally dressed in low heels and a dark skirt that nearly reached her ankles. The blouse she wore was a dark blue, matching her eyes.

"Ma'am," Irwin tilted his hat respectfully, "Good morning." "Good morning deputy," She held out her hand, "I'm Mrs. Gambill from the *Alleghany Times-News*."

Irwin shook the woman's hand firmly, but his stare continued to question her statement. Smiling, Mrs. Gambill took out a card from her coat pocket to show her credentials, "I heard an interesting story this morning out at Twin Oaks."

"I bet you did," Irwin chuckled knowing full well Sam Walker had already heard about the robbery.

"Unfortunately, I cannot comment, but you may speak with the Sheriff if you want."

"Irwin?" The journalist noticed his name on the badge, "As in Zora Irwin?"

"Zora is my wife," Irwin answered, "Do you know her?" "She is an absolute sweetheart, and yes we met a few months ago, back in the summer. How is she?" Before he could answer, Sheriff Henson called out.

His voice carried through the parking lot drawing Irwin's attention. Mrs. Gambill silently hoped she had not caused the deputy any trouble on the job. "Sheriff," Irwin turned, putting Mrs. Gambill in view.

"Oh," Henson paused, "Good morning ma'am, shopping for groceries?"

"No, not quite, thank you."

"Something we can do for you then?" Henson inquired.

"Your deputy was telling me I should be speaking with you regarding the supposed robbery last night. I understand they took sugar?"

Henson shot a glance at Irwin before addressing the question of the journalist whose five-foot-five-inch frame was encased in his shadow. "And what is your name ma'am?"

"Mrs. Gambill, *Alleghany Times-News,*" She offered her hand, but Henson hesitated.

"The *paper?*"

"That's right," She smiled.

"You're doing a story on this?"

"What else does one cover for the local paper?"

Irwin fought back the urge to laugh instead choosing to look back at the store as the other deputy seemed to be wrapping up with Mr. Bare. "Come by the office this afternoon when we've completed the reports. I will have more information then and you can write a brief story for the paper."

"Our deadline is at six this evening," Mrs. Gambill informed, "Should we say three?" Henson nodded although reluctantly and finally shook Mrs. Gambill's hand before turning to leave.

"How long have you been with the newspaper?" Irwin asked when the Sheriff was out of earshot.

"For a while."

"Have you written for the paper before?"

"Yes, for a few years, but I was appointed Editor just a few months ago."

Reaching for her car door Irwin helped to hold it open, "Thank you deputy. I suppose we'll see each other around."

"I suppose we will," Irwin closed the door watching her head off in the direction of town. Something in his gut told him that perhaps the newspaper would be key to learning what had happened at Whitehead Grocery.

Sheriff Henson had provided Mrs. Gambill with the usual list of details about the robbery. Among those details were the presumed time of the robbery, presumed merchandise stolen, and the fact the cash register had been broken into.

However, what the Sheriff failed to mention was why anyone would do all that damage for petty cash and a few loafs of bread. Standing in the rear of the courthouse she watched as cars and horses plotted up and down the single back road between Main Street and a clearing that was probably better described as a park.

Hearing the voices of people from the front she looked over her shoulder to see the deputy from the grocery store walking north along Main Street.

Midway towards Four Oaks he stopped to say hello to a man and his wife, probably friends, and Mrs. Gambill saw this as her window of opportunity.

Not wanting to interrupt, she stood close enough that he could see her. When the couple went on their way the deputy glanced in her direction, "Mrs. Gambill, am I right?"

"You are," She replied, "Deputy Irwin, correct?"

"That's me," Walter Irwin answered, "What may I do for you?" "Satisfy my curiosity," Mrs. Gambill said as she folded her arms, "The Sheriff left out some details about the robbery."

Irwin removed his glasses, "That right?"

"Look, I have a job to do, same as you," She replied, "All I'm askin' is for a little help. Why would Sam Walker tell me about two thousand pounds of sugar havin' gone missin' from Whitehead Grocery, but the Sheriff never mentioned anythin' about it?"

"You'll have to ask him," Irwin stated.

"Or I could ask the deputy."

Irwin shook his head, "I'm not about to confirm or deny Sam's story. If the office has decided not to share certain details of the case there is good reason."

"Fine, then, don't—just give me a nod if I'm on the right path." Irwin gave a soft laugh, "You're truly a journalist aren't you? Just after the story."

"Like I said, I have a job to do and if the story sells papers..." Clearing his throat Irwin shrugged, "Tell me what you suspect Mrs. Gambill and I'll let you know if you're right."

"Really?"

"Sure."

Skeptical Mrs. Gambill slowly stated what she believed to be fact, "Two thousand pounds of sugar, money, and sure, a few other items were taken, but the sugar was taken for a specific reason otherwise Henson would have mentioned it."

Irwin who had his hands on his jacket pockets rocked back on his heels. At that moment the newspaper Editor realized that Deputy Irwin's silences could speak volumes.

Even though his expression betrayed nothing, his inaction was everything. "Thank you deputy."

"Don't thank me," Irwin said, "And..."

"I know, keep your name out of it," Mrs. Gambill grinned, "Got it."

CHAPTER 4

January 1931

The robbery of Whitehead Grocery had not gone unnoticed or unpublicized by the local newspapers. From Sparta all the way to Hillsville, Virginia people had read about the remarkable heist of 2,000 pounds of sugar.

2,000 pounds of sugar Connor Ridge knew he needed in order to keep operations going and satisfy a customer looking to pay for over 100 gallons of white whiskey.

There were two things Connor knew made all men equal. Money and moonshine.

"Did you hear?" Jeb Dalton, Connors oldest and perhaps closest friend in the moonshine business asked. Jeb had been a boy when his father taught him how to make moonshine, how to tend to stills, and how to hide them. Now in his late seventies, the old man had passed down much of what he knew to Connor and his still overseers.

The smell of cigar smoke hung heavy in the air whenever Jeb was near. He had one lazy eye and looked as if he had not slept or taken a decent shower in days. His old blue and black plaid shirt was missing a button or two near the bottom and his jeans were faded until they were nearly white down the legs.

"Hear what?" Connor implored as he lowered himself onto a nearby stump placing his elbows on his knees and leaning forward. The smoke from the fire under the vats nearby felt warm against his cold ankles.

"That Felts fella down in Wilkes, he caught himself another bootlegger."

"One less we have to worry about," Connor never failed to revel in what was his competition's demise and Jeb knew it.

"Yeah, old Jimmy's still was raided early this morning. Tommy told me they hauled off and dumped nearly 100 gallons of shine." Connor let out a low whistle at the prospect of losing that much liquor to Revenuers.

"Better keep this operation wrapped up tight Jeb," Connors eyes darkened in the glow of the flame. Jeb cleared his throat, "Of course I ain't talkin'. No sir, we don't need that kind of trouble up here."

It was the way in which Connor had warned the aging moonshiner, not so much his words, that sent a chill down Jeb's spine. Connor was known for a lot of things, but his temper and tactics were what made him practically legendary in this part of Appalachia.

"When is the car going to be ready?" Jeb asked, deciding it best to change subjects.

"Zane should be here any minute now."

The car could be heard idling in a small clearing close to six in the evening. It was a spot Jeb and his grandsons Tommy and William had made just off the main road. Thick mountain laurels and pine trees shielded the vehicle from notice, so well in fact, even Connor almost missed it.

Hopping out of the modified Roadster, Zane removed his hat and tossed it into the backseat, "Hey Jeb, your boys ready?' "Yes sir," Jeb motioned for his grandsons to hurry off the embankment.

"Did you get word they would be running tonight?" Zane asked as he lowered himself into the passenger seat. "Everythin' is on schedule," Connor reassured his partner and waved at Jeb, who stood with his hands in his pockets, as they backed out towards the road.

Nearly halfway towards town Zane once again voiced his concern, "Why can't this wait for a day or so until Thayer gets back?" Connor adjusted the radio, "Because, we need this haul tonight if we want to keep afloat."

Thayer Whitaker had left the county after Whitehead Grocery. Connor had told him it was so Thayer could keep a low profile, but Zane suspected Thayer was tending to some family business as Erick, his brother, was rumored to be in trouble. He had not been wrong.

Connor knew it would be a good week before Thayer returned. By then all the gang would have was fermenting corn, and not much else to show. The way Connor saw it, hijacking other runners was a necessary evil that saved him both time and money.

Stopping at the intersection of 18 and 21, he noted his friend's expression, "Did you bring the guns?"

"They're in the backseat." William reached down, lifted the sawed off shotgun and handed it to his brother, and then picked up a revolver, handing it between the seats to Zane.

Feeling a bit more secure Connor gave his final instructions, "Get out, follow us, but not too close. Once we're out of the car, you pull in. No shooting unless I say so, got it?"

Both boys gave a quick response and hurried out of the vehicle heading across the street to their pickup facing Smithey's. Connor turned in the direction of 21 North towards Virginia.

Close to two hours into their drive Zane tapped the dashboard, "There." Connors' eyes followed his friend's index finger towards the end of the back route that would take travelers towards Roanoke, Virginia.

Except, these travelers were not about to make it to their destination. Connor glanced up into the rear-view mirror making sure Tom and William were still following. They were.

"All right," Connor smiled, "Let's do this."

Without hesitation he steadily increased the Roadster's speed and flew down the highway at an astounding 100 miles per hour bumping into the bumper of the Ford coupe, jarring its passengers. Connor eased off slightly, just enough to give the driver time to decide if running was worth it.

Forcing the driver of the Ford to increase his speed Connor's next move proved they had made a bad decision. Thanks to Darrell the back of the Roadster was super light, the brakes more responsive than before, giving Connor the feeling the automobile was more of an extension of himself than its own machine.

Zane held tight to the top of the open window, aiming his revolver as Connor glided past the vehicle crossing the double yellow line on the Virginia highway.

"Pull over!" Zane shouted as he aimed the weapon at the driver's head. No response. The driver kept his eyes on the road and before Zane could blink, the car slowed down with Connor still racing straight ahead.

"Whoa!" Zane shouted as Connor applied the brakes pitching Zane inside, throwing his body up towards the windshield. With tires squalling and the smell of smoke from the burned rubber tires hanging in the air, Zane watched in what felt like slow motion as his partner backed the vehicle up and did a complete one hundred eighty-degree turn.

Just as Connor had planned, the rum runners had nowhere to go. Caught between Connor, Tom, and William in their Chevy pickup, these Virginia bootleggers had no idea what had just happened or who they had just crossed paths with. Connor opened the car door, having taken the revolver from Zane who reached into the backseat and picked up the remaining twenty-two rifle.

"Get out of your car! Now!" Connor could feel the steel in his left hand growing warmer with each passing second. Tom and William were holding guns between the pickup doors aiming straight into the backseat of the Ford.

The driver raised his hands calmly, locking eyes with Connor. The passenger reluctantly did the same.

With the revolver aimed at the driver's head Connor demanded, "Get your hands up!"

With great contempt, both men raised their hands and watched as Connor slowly approached, like a cat stalking its prey. Zane realized what Connor was doing, he was looking for any signs of these boys being police.

Despite there not being a badge in view on either man, Connor knew better than to assume they were not law enforcement.

"Get on your knees," Connors' eyes found Tom and William, their cue given to approach. Albeit reluctantly, the men did as they were told. Zane watched quietly, content to hold his twenty-two standing near the driver side door of the Roadster as William and Tom began searching the Ford.

"Stay down," Connor ordered as he watched the boys. "It's full," Tom called out. "How full?" Zane questioned, still skeptical that this was not somehow a set-up. "At least 50 gallons."

The passenger from the Ford exchanged a look with the driver that told Connor that was a lie.

"You sure about that?" Connor questioned Tom.

"It isn't 50 gallons," The passenger answered, mindful of the revolver aimed at his head.

"Then how much is it?" Zane asked, watching Connor closely for any reaction. Keeping his head down the passenger answered, "It's a hundred."

William, Tom, and Zane were all stunned as they stared at Connor whose expression aligned more with the likes of Napoleon than a bootlegger.

Connor tapped the passenger on the shoulder with the end of the revolver, "Who are you boys haulin' for?"

"We ain't going to tell you that," The driver spoke up, "They'd kill us if we talked."

"You're going to be *broke*," Connor said swinging the gun towards the driver, "So that's not much different than dyin' now is it?"

"Who are you?" The passenger asked without looking up. "You boys from around here, you probably already know exactly who I am. But tonight, I'm a ghost. It's best for everyone if you forget you saw us." Connor answered.

The driver clearly had his suspicions, but Connor did not really care. All that mattered in that moment was getting the liquor back to Devils Ridge.

"What do you wanna do?" Zane asked, the twenty-twos stock weighting heavy in his grasp.

"Leave us, take the haul," The driver insisted, "Please—we have families like—."

Connor cursed, looking back at Zane, "You believe them?" Zane knew good and well it did not matter what he believed; Connor would rather shoot these boys rather than have them telling everyone he was on Virginia soil stealing moonshine. Despite his feelings of uneasiness Zane answered, "Sure."

Connor looked towards the Ford motioning to Tom and William, "One of you drive the car, the other get in the truck. Let's go!"

"Keys?" Tom stared down at the two men on their knees in the middle of the dark road. The fumes from the Roadster floated by the Fords headlights giving both pale faced men an eerie ethereal quality. Connor aimed the revolver at the driver, "You heard the man."

Removing his keys from his pants pocket the driver tossed them towards Tom who caught them mid-air.

As the two bootleggers realized the mistake of not traveling in a convoy, as Connor often had, the Ford pulled away with the pickup and the Roadster in pursuit.

Connor watched from the rear-view mirror as the two men faded into the darkness, relishing the joy of having pulled off this latest heist. There was however, something about the darkness that clung to him and refused to let go—no matter how fast the car was moving.

CHAPTER 5

February 1931

Deputy Sheriff Walter Irwin put on his patrolman's jacket placing his hands inside its pockets protecting them from the bitter February air.

Small white clouds of his breath gathered before him as he stood mindful of travelers, at the intersection in front of Farmers Hardware.

Farmers had been established just two years earlier, in 1929, by Amos Wagoner. The windows displayed various home goods and gardening tools; a string of different cast iron skillets were currently on display. As Irwin began to head towards the courthouse steps, he heard someone calling out behind him.

Glancing up and back towards Smithey's store Irwin stepped away from the intersection, "May I help you?" He did not recognize the gentleman, but he could hear the urgency in his voice. "Officer," The man reached the sidewalk, half out of breath, "I need to make a report."

Irwin looked in the direction the man had come from, noticing a vehicle with a woman sitting in its passenger seat. Irwin gathered it must have been the man's wife upon seeing his left hand bearing a wedding band.

"Do you mind walkin' to the courthouse?" Irwin asked. Trying to catch his breath the man agreed, continuing to walk beside Irwin. Halfway up the steps he started relaying the cause of his distress, "We were traveling from Virginia; my wife has family up there."

Opening the courthouse doors both gentlemen stepped into the warmth of the building.

It took a few moments for Irwin's eyes to adjust to the light as he led the man into an office, two doors down on the right removing his patrolman's jacket. "So," the man paused as he sat down, "We are riding along and suddenly on the side of the road is a man, walking, and he's wearing robes."

"Robes?" Irwin took out a pen and a sheet of paper from inside a nearby desk drawer.

"Clergy robes," The gentleman clarified, "He had a collar, and it was raining, like it has all day. I couldn't very well leave someone out there on the road as cold as it has gotten the last few nights, especially not a man of God. Anyway, it started to sleet and rain," Wagoner paused, visibly upset.

Irwin sat patiently as Mr. Wagoner gathered his thoughts to continue. "I stopped the vehicle and asked if he needed a lift into town, or if there was someone, I might call for him when I got here—."

It was clear the man was shaken as he spoke, his voice becoming slightly more intense with each word. "He approached the car and before I knew what was happening, he pulled a gun on me and my wife attempting to steal our car!"

Clearing his throat, Irwin motioned to the hallway, "Would you care for a cup of water, or coffee?"

Wagoner acknowledged his voice placing his hand on his throat, "Yes," The man's voice was hoarse from either fear or an oncoming cold.

Before stepping into the hallway Irwin took up one of the mugs from atop a nearby file cabinet and filled it using one of the pitchers of cold water that the secretaries often left across the hallway from the Sheriff's Office.

Returning to the room, Irwin handed Mr. Wagoner the mug, "Forgive me for not asking earlier, but what is your name?' He inquired, sitting back down and picking up the pen.

"Roger, Roger Wagoner," The man answered, taking a long sip of his water. "It's a pleasure to meet you Mr. Wagoner, I'm deputy Walter Irwin." The men shook hands and Irwin jumped back to the report.

"Mr. Wagoner, where were you exactly when the incident took place?" "Just outside of Independence, maybe a few miles before the state line."

"Can you describe the would-be robber to me?" Irwin kept his eyes on the paper as he scribbled down his observations.

"Well, uh," Roger coughed, excused himself and then leaned back, "Six-one or so, green eyes, sandy colored hair, couldn't be more than a hundred eighty pounds."

"And how old do you suppose he was?" Irwin mindfully watched Roger Wagoner as he took another sip of water.

"Between twenty-five and thirty, definitely not older than thirty." "Did your wife see the gunman?" Irwin questioned.

"She stayed in the vehicle."

"What type of vehicle do you drive Mr. Wagoner?"

"A '29 Ford, a coupe style I guess you could say."

"And how long have you had that vehicle?"

"Since last July," Wagoner answered.

"Did any other vehicles pass you while this was happening?"

"No, not that I noticed. Like I said, it started to rain…"

"You said he *attempted* to steal your vehicle?"

"That's right."

"How did you get away?" Irwin, lifting his eyes from the paper, stared at Wagoner curiously. Leaning forward in his chair Roger shrugged, "You're probably not going to believe me, but that's all right because it baffled me too. He told me to get in my car and keep drivin'."

"What made you *think* he wanted to steal the vehicle?" Irwin hoped by rewording his inquiry it would garner more information.

"He had a gun," Wagoner iterated taking a sip of his water, "And he kept looking at the vehicle, inside of it, around it, as if he was searching for somethin'."

A knock on the door caused Irwin to look to his left, "Didn't hear you come in," Sheriff Dean Henson eyed the man sitting before Irwin, "Evenin', sir." "Evenin', Sheriff," Wagoner politely replied.

Dean Henson was a slender man with square shoulders, hazel eyes, a wide brow that sat upon a wrinkled expression caused by years of good humor and hard work. Most of the deputies liked Henson. He was forthright, and an upstanding lawman with several years of service under his belt.

"Everythin' in order?" The Sheriff inquired as he gave a slight look to insinuate that he preferred to conduct interviews himself.

"I was just givin' your deputy a report," Wagoner informed, "My wife and I were held at gunpoint outside of Independence this evenin'."

Henson glanced at Irwin, "Well we can't have that. Get that report to me as soon as possible, deputy Irwin."

"Yes, sir," Irwin consented watching as Henson proceeded down the hall, his footsteps faint against the worn wooden floors.

"Thank you, Mr. Wagoner. Rest assured we will investigate this. Is there a number we can reach you at if we have any further questions?"

"Yes," Wagoner took the pen and jotted down his home number and address, sliding it across the table to Irwin.

"If you need help identifying this man, please call, I am good with faces." "Appreciate that," Irwin stepped into the hallway with Wagoner and watched as he exited the courthouse.

CHAPTER 6

February 1931

L ifting the phone to her right ear, Rebecca Lincoln answered and was promptly put on hold by the operator. A moment later a familiar voice cut through the line, "Rebecca is that you?"

"It is, to what do we owe the pleasure of your call Judge Carico?"

"Well, I'm hardly a Judge these days my dear. I hope you're all doing well."

"Despite everything, we're getting by, and at least Frank kept his job." Rebecca did not mention the layoffs at the nearby factory, or that some families had been destitute. She did not speak about how others had mentioned traveling west, or wives confiding in her that their husbands had left their families to head into larger cities in hopes of finding employment. Still others however, had taken their lives, leaving their families with nothing.

The Stock Market Crash of 1929 had struck a lethal, if not fatal blow over much of the nation, but it had hit much of the farming community's way before the final broker stepped out of the New York Stock Exchange that October day. Farmers and families struggled to survive with the drastic decrease in crop prices, hardly able to put shoes on their children's feet for school.

Rebecca and other women from the local Baptist Church had pitched in when and however they could, but some people still refused to accept charity.

"There's always work for a G-Man as good as your husband," Carico commented, "Is he available?" "If you'll give me a moment Judge, I will let him know you're on the line. He is in the garage." Rebecca placed the phone down and quickly walked into the kitchen opening the side door peering into their two-car garage.

Her husband was tackling the engine of his Ford car. Standing at six foot three, Federal Bureau of Investigations agent Frank Lincoln was in his early forties and still had the shoulders of a college linebacker despite his inability to play the sport any longer. "Frank, it's James, he's on the phone for you."

Turning away from the vehicle she watched as he snatched up a rag from the nearby work table and wiped his hands before heading into the house. "What does he want?" Frank asked in a low voice before reaching the foyer. "I don't know, he just asked for you," Rebecca answered as she proceeded upstairs.

Frank's father, Eric Lincoln had been in the service with James Carico. The two were close friends and remained so throughout much of their lives. When Frank announced he wanted to join law enforcement at sixteen, James Carico did all he could to help the young man apply for and afford the academy the moment he was eighteen. As a result, James was still in contact with Frank, despite his father's passing three years earlier.

Picking up the receiver, Frank remained standing as his overalls were covered in grease, "James?" "Frank, how are you?" The former Judge of Virginia asked. "I'm doing all right, but I cannot say the same of my vehicle. I've been doing repairs all afternoon. What may I help you with?"

"Actually, I was hoping you would look into something." Glancing back at the stairs to ensure no one could hear, Frank switched the phone receiver from his right to his left ear, "I'm listening."

"Last month I arrived home just before dinner and parked my new Chevy Coupe outside like I always do. The next morning my wife and I woke up to find it missing. It has been brought to my attention that we've had a bit of trouble with car theft in this part of Virginia, to say the least across the line in North Carolina. "Now," James spoke as if debating a piece of legislation which was his way when he was serious. "Recently I was told a gentleman was robbed just about robbed a few days ago in Independence after visiting with family."

"Okay," Frank replied, sensing the Judge was about to cement his concern. "You boys track moonshiners, right?" Frank felt his pulse quicken a bit, "You know we do." Through the receiver Frank could hear a slight puff, the sound manifested the image of him smoking one of his signature cigars in Frank's mind.

"It is not lost on me Frank that the Volstead Act is often ignored, but even so, we cannot have citizens afraid to travel to and from North Carolina."

Staring at his shoes, his mind racing back to the last bust he and his team had conducted just six months prior. The still consisted of nearly five-hundred gallons of illicit whiskey, much of which the runners were not going to let go without a fight.

Agents had engaged with one of the bloodiest shootouts with the still hands up near the West Virginia line. Frank himself had not escaped unharmed. He had taken a bullet in his right shoulder and suffered a bad cut to his left jawline from a knife one of the boys had drawn.

When it was over and the dust had settled the agents had arrested close to twenty men, toppled the illicit shine, found close to five thousand dollars in the back of one of the men's trucks in a hidden floorboard compartment, and a crate of dynamite.

None of that included the guns and ammo that remained after the shoot out.

"To be clear James, I can't promise anything, all I can do is make some general inquiries. Was there a report?"

"I cannot say for certain; you may want to check with Grayson County in Virginia or Alleghany County, down in North Carolina. I have a contact in North Carolina. He's a highway patrol. Would you be willing to speak with him?"

"What's his name?"

"Rash, Holden Rash."

Lieutenant Holden Rash of the North Carolina State Highway Patrol, and Commander of Division II, stepped out of the Mecca Restaurant amid a bustle of afternoon residents. The restaurant, founded the year before in 1930, served the best fried chicken Holden had ever eaten. So much so he always took friends who visited the area there first.

Before he could open the patrol car door he heard his name called from up the street. "Hey Benny," Holden waved, "Going for dinner?" "Better eat while I can, caught a case on the other side." Benny Weaver was no rookie, he had worked for many years as a Highway Patrol.

"The front desk at the office asked me, if I saw you, to say there is a message at HQ. You should head over and pick it up before your shift ends." Holden nodded, thanked the veteran officer and then climbed into his car. Fifteen minutes later he was walking up the steps to the main office carrying his hat under his left arm.

As he reached the desk, he caught sight of Russell Hawks lingering near the front desk.

"I suppose you ran into Benny," Hawks asked as he handed Holden the message, "Came for you from someone called Lincoln." Wrinkling his forehead Holden opened the message and read it quickly, "The BOI?" "Call him back," Hawks instructed before heading into his office.

Proceeding to his desk Holden picked up the phone and dialed in the number, after three rings the operator connected the extension and a man answered. "Hello?"

"Yes, this is Lieutenant Holden Rash of the Highway Patrol in North Carolina. A message was left for me to contact someone at this number, Mr. Lincoln?" "That would be me. My name is agent Frank Lincoln, I am with the BOI."

"What is this concerning?" Holden leaned forward in his chair holding the phone tightly. "Earlier this afternoon former Judge James Carico of Virginia called my home. He said I should speak with you regarding some stolen vehicles, one of them being his. Something about moonshine."

Holden glanced towards his boss's office, "We've been tracking a few stolen vehicles and parts from other counties for a while. Over the last couple of years, we have seen an uptick in activity near Alleghany and the Virginia line."

"What can you tell me about a potential carjacking that took place near Alleghany around January?" Searching for a pen and some paper, Holden made a note, "Can I reach out to the Sheriff's office there and get back with you agent Lincoln?"

"Sure, you have my number." Despite the millions of questions Holden had for the agent he had no time to ask one before Frank Lincoln disconnected the call.

Lieutenant Holden Rash held the phone to his left ear waiting for the operator. A woman's voice finally answered after the fourth ring, "Operator, how may I direct your call?"

"Alleghany County, Courthouse."

"One moment please," She replied, shortly thereafter the line began to click.

"Alleghany County Sheriff's Office, how may I help you?" Another woman answered, this one sounding to be more in her mid-twenties. "May I speak with Walter Irwin?"

"I will check to see if he is back from patrol, please hold." Lifting his gaze to the nearby window Holden leaned back in his chair trying to wrap his head around what was going on.

"Deputy Irwin," The familiar voice of his old friend came through the line. "Walt, it's Holden, do you have a moment?" Irwin could be heard shuffling papers, "Go ahead."

"I received a phone call from Frank Lincoln, BOI, up near Arlington this afternoon. He has an interest in car theft and possible moonshiners in your neck of the woods."

There was a silence on the other end Holden could not ignore, "More specifically he mentioned a carjacking that took place, something about the Virginia, North Carolina line."

Sitting completely still Holden could sense his friend knew exactly what he was talking about, "Walt?"

"Yeah, I'm still here. We did have someone come in and file a report. I'll have to pull that information if you're looking for details. You said the BOI called you?"

"Apparently someone has friends in high places, and it appears Mr. Lincoln's friend is former Judge James Carico from Grayson County. I told the agent we had been seeing an increase in stolen vehicles the last couple of years."

"And Carico? Why would he call about these carjackings?" "As a matter of fact, the good Judge has been missing a car since January. According to the report he parked it in the front yard the night before and the next morning he and his wife discovered it missing."

Never one to miss something Irwin asked, "Does the report say what make or model?" "Master Chevy Coupe, new model. First upgrade since the late '20s."

"Let me get our report, hold on a moment."

Sitting the phone down Irwin walked over to the file cabinets beyond the small office door and pulled the third drawer on the second filing cabinet open.

The musty smell of paper and ink greeted the air as he leafed through to find the report filed by Mr. Wagoner.

"All right," Irwin lifted the phone picking up the conversation, "A Mr. Roger Wagoner filed a report stating that when he stopped along the road on his way back to Alleghany from visiting with family in Virginia with his wife, they were almost carjacked. According to Mr. Wagoner, the would-be car thief let him go. Apparently, the vehicle was not the one he believed it to have been."

"Wait, you said Mr. Wagoner told you he stopped the vehicle? Why?"

Irwin's answer was not one Holden had been expecting, "Mr. Wagoner said that they saw a man walking, in robes, and believed him to be a minister. They did not wish for him to be walking in the cold, so they stopped."

A bit perplexed Holden asked, "A *minister* tried to carjack them?" "Someone pretending to be a minister is more likely," Irwin replied, "Seems this person, whoever they are, operates a bit differently than most."

"Clever, you have to admit," Holden's voice was not without admiration. "Speaking of clever, I just came from a robbery over at Whitehead Grocery."

"And?" Holden asked.

"And these guys took some items that may be of interest to Mr. Lincoln."

"Like what?"

"Two thousand pounds of sugar, a few hundred dollars in the cash register and some other supplies."

Holden was completely silent.

"Bootleggers," Irwin continued, "Money, cars, and..."

"Sugar," Holden added without missing a beat.

"Like I said earlier, we've been watching vehicles get stolen, parts ending up all over the place, and have seen an increase in rum-runner arrests," Holden informed, "If you're willing, I would like to head up the mountain tomorrow and talk face to face. Maybe we can get some collaboration going on this."

"What about BOI Lincoln?" Irwin asked. "I'll get back with him, but not before I check a few more boxes. Is tomorrow good?" "Tomorrow is fine," Irwin hung up the phone while still staring down at Wagoner's file.

"Who was that?" Henson inquired as he walked through the office towards his desk. "Highway Patrol, they received word Judge Carico's coupe was stolen, shortly after Mr. Wagoner made his report," Irwin paused, considering what he was about to say next, "And the Whitehead Grocery robbery."

Henson lowered himself into his chair keeping his eyes on his deputy, "Judge Carico is a highly respected lawman and veteran. Whoever took his car certainly got the attention of some higher ups."

"Especially the BOI," Irwin added. Dean Henson placed his hands in front of him on the desk, the look on his deputy's face told him something more was going on. "Be straight with me Walter, what are you thinkin'?"

"Moonshiners, but a completely different breed from before. Whoever is behind the thefts and robberies I have a feelin' they're not workin' alone. And," Irwin added, "they're smart, so we are goin' to have to be smarter."

Henson nodded, "I agree. What did the Highway Patrol recommend?" "That we meet tomorrow to see where we go from here."

Henson rose walking towards the nearby file cabinets, "Report back once the meeting is over. In the meantime I will go back through reports from the last year, see if anything else stands out." "Thank you Sheriff," Irwin said as he headed out for his evening patrol.

CHAPTER 7

Deputy Sheriff Irwin walked into Smithey's, removing his hat. The two women at the front of the store gave acknowledging friendly nods and one said a good afternoon in passing.

Sitting down in the back of the diner Irwin removed his coat and leaned forward to look at one of the menus.

"What can I get for you, deputy?" The young waitress, not hardly sixteen, asked. "Coffee please, and a BLT if you still have it." "We do, and your coffee will be right out."

"Thank you," Irwin heard the door to the store open and within seconds saw Holden Rash.

Rash was forty-five, six-foot-two-inches tall with sandy brown hair and faded green eyes. There was not a better shot this side of Appalachia than Rash, nor anyone more trustworthy in Irwin's opinion. Rash could be confidential and discreet about obtaining information, but his contacts throughout law enforcement were also to his credit. "Irwin," He offered his hand to which Irwin shook firmly.

"Lieutenant, hope the drive wasn't too much trouble." Irwin knew Rash had traveled close to four hours from Raleigh, but it was a trip the highway patrolman often made since most of his family were still living in the area. "So long as it doesn't snow again," Rash glanced at the menu, "I appreciate you meeting me on such short notice."

Watching as the young waitress poured Irwin's coffee Rash ordered his own. As she moved out of earshot Irwin asked, "Were you able to check those boxes you mentioned?"

Rash poured creamer into his coffee, "Yes, as a matter of fact I was. Mr. Lincoln was appreciative of the information provided, but I contacted a few other departments that have an invested interest in these stolen vehicles."

"Has anyone been able to locate Judge Carico' car?" Irwin asked, sipping his coffee. "No," Holden shook his head, "Not yet, but now we're starting to see a pattern here."

"Let me guess," Irwin added, "You don't like what you're seeing."

Watching the waitress as she bought tickets to customers siting at the counter Holden frowned, "The grocery store being robbed of two thousand pounds of sugar in virtually minutes suggests that whoever stole it, was not working alone."

"I told Sheriff Henson the same thing after we spoke yesterday. It takes two people to lift that much sugar."

"Moreover," Holden elaborated, "It's the same case with these carjacking. Last year a man was robbed on Elkin Mountain. They said the thief held him at gunpoint, but someone was with him. Someone drove the man there to get the car and then followed him back up the mountain."

"A getaway driver," Irwin replied.

"They're stealing top notch vehicles, Fords, Chevy's, mostly coupes because of the room and the ability to modify them."

"Modify them how?" Irwin asked.

"Power up the engines to make sure more gas flows through for higher horsepower, and increase speed. Not to mention taking out the backseats sometimes or improving on the suspensions so they can haul more without drawing added attention, taking the drag off their bumpers."

"How much faster are we talking here Holden?"

"An easy hundred miles per hour, maybe more. Rumor has it these guys have stock races often on vacant farmland and old fairgrounds just to prove they are the best of the best."

"What's in it for the winner?" Irwin asked curiously.

"Money, and bragging rights." Holden answered.

"Because money plus faster cars equals more moonshine," Irwin said.

"More than enough to make a few legends in that illicit business," Holden agreed, "take those boys up in West Virginia last a while back."

Irwin clenched his hands as if trying to get a grip on the circumstances, "There is no way our vehicles can go that fast."

Taking a sip of his own coffee Rash looked up, "I also learned Carico's car isn't the only one missing. Herman Taylor reported his own vehicle stolen from Whitetop not long ago."

Irwin took a sip of his coffee, "What about this BOI agent you mentioned yesterday? How does he know Carico?" "Turns out Carico and Agent Lincoln's father were old war buddies, or so I was told by Carico. Lincoln doesn't talk much." Keeping his voice low Holden added, "However, there is some good news."

"What's that?" Irwin asked.

"By reaching out to those other agencies I mentioned, they have agreed to send some people your way. My understanding is that Agent Lincoln will also be coming to the county. Don't worry," Holden reassured his friend, "Whoever these guys are, they are on the BOI's radar now."

Feeling confident in their abilities to put a stop to the rash of thefts and robberies Irwin watched as their waitress approached with their orders, "In that case, lunch is on me Lieutenant."

The silence from the Sheriff's office had not gone unnoticed by Mrs. Gambill, or her assistant, since the Whitehead Grocery robbery a friend had informed her of a lunch Deputy Irwin had taken with a member of the State Highway Patrol.

The newspaper edition that had run the story of the Whitehead Grocery robbery had been snatched up within hours of its release. For the first time in the last year, since taking over the paper as Editor, Mrs. Gambill felt she could see the light at the end of the very long, dark tunnel.

"Jenny," Mrs. Gambill glanced up at her copy editor, "I'm going to step out for a moment, can you take any messages?" "Of course," Jenny answered as she stood working over the upcoming edition of the newspaper's front page.

Reaching over for her pen and notepad, Mrs. Gambill took her coat and headed through the empty courtroom towards the stairwell. Before she could step off the first landing, she glanced out the window, with its black paint trim, and spotted the familiar vehicle of Deputy Irwin parked in front of the Spartan Theater.

With her pen and pad shoved into her right coat pocket Mrs. Gambill quickly proceeded down the new concrete steps holding onto the railing as she glided into the street from the main entrance.

Irwin was engaged in a conversation with Mr. Hardin, a local businessman and store owner. Waiting as a mix of horses and buggies and automobiles bustled down Main Street, Mrs. Gambill crossed at the earliest opportunity.

Parting ways with Harding, Irwin greeted the Editor and removed his pocket watch as if checking the time, "Mrs. Gambill." To her, Irwin had said her name as more of a question than a greeting.

"Deputy Irwin," She replied, "Heading in for patrol?" "Should I be concerned that the press is taking note of my comings and goings?" Irwin inquired back to the patrol car with his left hand holding his watch and his right inside his pants pocket.

"The only reason I noticed at all was because a little birdie told me about your meeting with a certain Highway Patrol." Her gaze pointed in the direction of Smithey's, causing Irwin to partially look over his shoulder.

"And did this little birdie *happen* to be working at Smithey's?" Irwin questioned. Giving him a slight grin Mrs. Gambill answered quietly, "You gave me information about the robbery, and yet, somehow I can't help but wonder that there is more to this story, isn't there?" He noted how, like a journalist, she had avoided his question only to assert her own.

Irwin was slowly realizing he could not have things both ways. Either the press knew everything, or they knew nothing. Keeping quiet only made some journalists more ravines with questions. "For now, you will just have to trust that what I know, you will too in due time."

With a somewhat annoyed tone Mrs. Gambill gave him a look that was much like his wife's whenever she insisted something be done. "Deputy, I know there is a bigger story here. Do you know how I know?" Irwin remained silent, observing her as she spoke, trying to discern if there was any way to decide whether she was bluffing.

"The two thousand pounds of sugar stolen has led to a meeting with the State Police. That's nothing to sneeze at. There have been rumors in this county for years of hidden stills, moonshine makers, who refuse to stop running illicit liquor. Tell me you're not looking into moonshiners and I'll drop the questions."

Irwin took in a slow steady breath before answering, "Mrs. Gambill, I am looking into a rash of car thefts. The robbery at Whitehead may or may not be connected, and that's all I can say on the topic for now."

The newspaper journalist was intrigued, knowing he was giving her a half-truth, albeit willingly, yet she could not help but to ask, "You said carjackings, as in more than one?" Irwin glanced down at his pocket watch with a nod, as if he had just given her the time, all the while he had actually given her the answer to her question.

Sheriff Henson had been filled in after the meeting with Rash. Together he and Irwin decided to keep track of any further carjacking attempts and thefts in the county. Henson had gone through reports for the last two years only finding one that seemed to fit the MO of their current offenders.

It had been nearly a week since Irwin last spoke with Rash at Smithey's. He had hoped to hear something from the Highway Patrolman, or even Agent Lincoln. Yet, no call had come.

Standing in his living room Irwin listened to his wife and children in the nearby dining room as plates were being cleared. He stood near the window gazing out at his front yard.

"Walter, you hardly touched your dinner," Zora's voice pulled him back to reality. Her eyes followed his gaze out the window as if seeking what he was thinking in some image through the glass. Glancing down at her he noticed the slight frown lines on her forehead, lines he preferred she not have because of him.

"You're too quiet," She whispered, "Whenever you get this way I know something is happening." Walter wrapped his left arm around her shoulders and kissed her forehead gently, "Just thankful, that's all." Zora gave him a knowing grin, but since their days in college together she had been the only person who could read him like an open book.

"Besides it isn't anythin' that can't be fixed with that cake you made," He mused watching her expression relax. "Come on, desserts in the dining room." Zora said as she pulled away from him slowly. Irwin glanced back out the window and thought it best to relish in the peace while it lasted following her into the dining room.

CHAPTER 8

Spring 1931

The Whitehead Post Office sat empty after five in the evening. Just up the road was Connor's home, inside his family was having their supper. He leaned on his wife's promise to keep him a slice of her chocolate cake as worry began to cloud his mind with every minute that ticked by.

"Stop lookin' so worried," Erick Whitaker instructed as he peered through the rearview mirror of his Chevy pickup reaching for a cigarette in his shirt pocket.

Erick Whitaker was twenty-five, tall, with wide shoulders, sandy red hair, and eyes as green as pine tree bristles. His personality was just prickly and provocative to those who had the misfortune of crossing him.

Connor knew Whitaker's temper all too well having tussled with him over a still when they had first met. Although Connor had won that fight Erick had proven his stubbornness and his loyalty all in one moment.

"No sir," Erick had stated after their first disagreement over that still, "Ain't nobody ever been able to whoop me, and I ain't ever gonna say you did whoop me. But," He added, "you sure like to fight for your size."

Because of that fight Ridge made Whitaker one of the supervisors over Devils Ridge.

"Whenever someone tells me not to worry Erick, I worry," Connor replied, nervously checking the mirrors for himself.

"Look, he owes me."

"I want to know what you did to get in his good graces anyways? Don't see you doin' community service for free."

Erick spotted the lights and leaned his head back expelling cigarette smoke like a hot tea kettle does steam.

"Connor, have I ever not made you money?"

"What does this have to do with makin' money?"

"You'll see," Whitaker saw the headlights he had been waiting for, opened the driver side door and stepped out into the open. Connor lingered back a bit feeling the weight of his thirty-eight on his side.

The vehicle pulled up beside Erick's truck. The emblem on the front a warning to most in their profession, although as Erick had assured him, not in this case.

Connor wrapped his right hand around his gun and slid out of the truck slowly. Doing something Erick had not, Connor glanced back in the direction of where the car had traveled, then along the roadside for any signs of movement.

"Don't mind my friend here, he just stopped by to say hi," Erick motioned with his head towards Connor who preferred to remain out of sight. The man, a familiar face, gave him a quick glance but nothing more. "I got what you asked for," He said, opening the trunk of his vehicle.

Curiosity getting the better of him, Connor headed over and looked down into the back of the beat up Ford Model A. A black bag that appeared to contain nothing more than shoes lay there waiting to be picked up.

"You boys get caught with this; you forget my name. Understood?"

"What about the keys?" Erick asked.

Keys? Connor thought.

The man reached into his pocket and handed Erick a set of keys linked together on a copper colored ring. "Much obliged to you," Erick said as he picked up the contents inside the trunk and stepped back towards Connor. "Remember our deal," The man pointed to Erick, "Twenty-percent." "You got it," Erick grinned.

Connor watched cautiously as the man climbed back into his vehicle. He had a sudden urge to kill him right then and there, if only to stop whatever repercussions might come from the deal Erick had made. At the same time though Connor was relieved when the vehicle was out of sight and no one else was around.

Sliding back into the passenger seat of Erick's pickup Connor reached for the bag, "What is this?"

"You asked me what this had to do with money." Connor opened the bag carefully, his eyes adjusting to the fading light around them.

Inside was a tan colored suit...*No*, Connor thought, *a uniform.* Pulling out the shirt he noted the patches and then the items that lay underneath. The belt, the badge, the hat, and the gun holster. Turning his head towards Erick, Connor wondered just what information his still runner had to give up for such an exchange.

"Now all we got to do is get Darrell to find us a siren."

"Are you telling me you expect to make money as a cop?" Connor questioned.

"Not me, *you*," Erick replied.

"And the keys, what're they for?"

"They're a get out of jail card, and that's exactly what we're going to do. Just think," Erick explained, "If we get other shiners out who have been locked up, but for a price, we can make up that twenty percent easy. Not to mention they'll be in our debt."

Laughter took over the cab as Connor shook his head, admitting to himself, this would either get him killed, or help him and his boys make a killing.

Parking the beat up Ford pickup on the side of the road near some trees and just around a curve Connor could both hear and see motorists coming, but they would not see him until he was good and ready. His partner, Zane Shepherd sat with the passenger door open and a cigarette held loosely in his right hand.

"You really think this is going to work?" Zane asked, emerging halfway from the car and bracing himself on the open door. Connor adjusted his coat and then placed the gold badge on his belt buckle closing the driver door, "You have any better ideas?"

Taking a long drag on the cigarette Zane swore under his breath and stabbed out the butt with the heel of his boot. "Stay here," Connor instructed as he stepped away from the rear of the pickup and near the edge of the highway. Shaking his head Zane could only pray that his partner knew what he was doing.

It was not so much about how to get the vehicle Connor worried about, but whether it would be the right type of vehicle.

Model T's and A's were all right, but they were not the best for hauling illicit liquor, and they certainly were not fast enough. The car

Connor needed, or rather *wanted*, during this game of highway robbery was a Ford Deluxe Roadster.

The roadster was a much more sporty model with its shorter windshield, lower profile top, and four cylinder engine that would be a snap for Darrell to modify at the garage.

Most on the mountain did not own such a vehicle, but those coming from below it would no doubt have one in their garage. Sure enough, his keen sense of hearing had paid off as a light gray Roadster appeared. Smirking Connor could not help but to think that this was fate.

Careful he stepped out onto the paved road and held up his hand to signal the vehicle to stop. There were no other vehicles for the moment, making this the best and possibly the last opportunity he would have to take the car of his choice.

Looking back at Shepherd, Connor noticed the man had already climbed over to the driver side of the Chevy pickup they had arrived in.

Gradually Connor approached the halted Roadster and placed his hand firmly on his gun. The bright yellow badge that was hooked onto his Sam Brown belt was shined to perfection, gleaming in the late afternoon sunlight.

A middle-aged man rolled down his window, his wife in the passenger seat looked on with questioning eyes.

"Excuse me sir," Connor tipped the stolen uniform cap he had put on, "Are you heading to Alleghany?"

"We're actually passing through, on the way to Grayson County to see friends. Something the matter officer?" The man was in his mid-thirties, dark brown hair and unsuspecting hazel eyes that peered out from behind a pair of silver colored glasses with thick lenses.

"I don't want to startle you folks, but there have been a rash of robberies on this highway and we are just checking to see if anyone has come across anything suspicious." The wife turned her attention to the idle pickup on the side of the road, "Is that your vehicle officer?"

"Yes ma'am, my state car is being serviced today, so I had to use my truck." "Sorry to hear about the robberies," The man replied, giving his wife an annoyed glance, "We haven't seen anyone except you." "Good to know," Connor smiled politely and then drew his weapon. The sound of the hammer being pulled back caused both husband and wife to stiffen.

"Get out," Connor ordered in a calm voice as he quickly glanced up and down the highway knowing full well, they could be discovered at any moment. "Excuse me?" The wife asked in a staggered tone.

"I don't care to repeat myself," Connor stated, "Get out, or I shoot you both." The man stepped out first and then went around to escort his wife from the passenger seat.

Clearly distressed and confused, she clung to her husband's arm. Just as Connor was about to slide into the driver seat, she quickly grabbed her purse from the floorboard of the vehicle. He gave little time for her to get her arm away before pulling off in a rip-roar of squalling tires and unbridled speed. The force of which slammed the passenger door closed with a heavy thud.

Without wavering Zane put the pickup in drive and quickly followed suit. The two motorists had been left standing on the highway, their nerves, like their car, vanishing up the winding corridors of the mountain. Connor felt a rush of adrenaline and gave out a holler as he tapped the steering wheel with his hands eager to get back home.

Looking back, he saw Zane following a car length behind him so as not to draw attention. Surely the authorities would be notified, but by the time the news reached their little county Connor Ridge and his partner would be back to their dark corner of the mountain.

Grace Roupe listened as her friend Madison Smith told of her first week experience working with children at Laurel Springs school. It was a warm evening and the weather could not have been more perfect.

A full moon was forming in the sky as the sun was beginning to set. The hum of the car allowed Grace to let her mind wander for a moment, thinking how extraordinary it was to be able to travel in an automobile.

She had heard her grandmother speak of horses and carriages during Sunday dinners, even commenting every chance she got how worried she was when Grace was riding in a car. Grace, however, did not have this fear. All she could imagine was taking the coupe across the country and seeing the Pacific Ocean someday.

Both recounted their evening having listened to current jazz bands and discussed their favorite actors all while trying to escape the Depression in Madison's Model-A.

Grace had caught herself wondering what it might be like to even have a radio inside her car? She had seen an ad in a magazine at the general store advertising them. She knew they might be a great distraction, but she would have also welcomed one when things were quiet.

They had not stopped, not even once. Grace preferred to be home by dark. As a waitress in Independence, she had to be up early the next morning to make sure the kitchen was up and running smoothly.

Opening her eyes Grace spotted a set of headlights. It was not unusual for others to be out near eight in the evening, but what was strange was the rate in which the lights were approaching the coupe. "Madison?" Grace asked, noticing that Madison had caught sight of the lights too. "I see them. Maybe they want to pass."

"I don't think so," Grace had a bad feeling that had started in the pit of her stomach and was making its way down to her toes. "Maddie, something is wrong," Grace warned just as the car sped up closing in on the vehicle's bumper, hitting it with just enough force to cause Grace to swerve. Madison held tight to the steering wheel trying to keep the vehicle in the road.

"What does this guy want?" Grace asked out loud, her eyes staying on the road ahead as much as possible, she feared another, more forceful tap to the bumper could cause them to flip, or worse. "The mountain is just up ahead," Madison said, "If he hits us..." Grace frowned and looked over at Madison. She could tell her friend was uneasy as she gripped the seat belt and kept her eyes on the mirror. "Grace, we're going to be okay."

Try as she could to give her friend a reassuring sign Madison knew it would have done little to help ease Grace's nerves. Instead of slowing down and pulling over, Madison punched the gas and raced up the mountain. The duo rocked side to side as they made it up in near record time going a clear sixty miles an hour.

Once at the top Madison slowed to avoid any possible vehicles or riders who might merge into the road from nearby homes. Hoping that they had lost the other driver, Madison looked back in the rear-view. Her heart sank. The car had been on their tail the entire time, except now. The shrill whining echo of the police siren called out startling Grace and giving Madison even more reason to rush towards town.

"My God," Grace muttered, "What does he want? What's going on?" "I don't know," Madison said, "But I'm going to find out." "Maddie, you cannot stop this car!" Grace exclaimed.

"I will, just not here," Madison continued to drive. Once they were on Main Street, she pulled into a spot in front of old man Harding's Store across from the courthouse.

When the vehicle that had been following them pulled in a parking spot away, Madison wanted to get out, but kept her doors closed and her eyes trained on the courthouse for any signs of a deputy or the Sheriff. Grace just turned her head in time to see a man step out of his truck.

He was middle-age, maybe thirty, slightly six-foot-one or so, and appeared to be wearing a uniform. Madison kept her window rolled up, but the man could still be heard through the glass. "My apologies ladies, it seems we had a mix up back there."

Madison looked at him through the glass, his dark eyes with gold rims were like mirrors, "You could have killed someone you know that? Which county are you from?" The strange officer tipped his hat in apologies and looked back at the vehicle's bumper.

"Please, forgive me," The man replied, "Honestly believed you were someone else." He seemed to note the ages of the young women, "Rather late to be on the road isn't it ladies? Roads aren't safe this time of night."

Madison muttered under her breath, words completely unheard by the officer. There was just something about the man's overall demeanor that caused Grace to ask herself where his badge was? From experience she had seen the deputies in town wear them on their jackets or their belts making sure they were visible.

"It's fine officer," Madison replied as politely as the situation would afford her. Before the man walked away he laid something on the top of the car where Madison could easily reach up through the window and retrieve it.

Watching as his truck rumbled back down Main Street towards the First Baptist Church, Madison lowered the window and felt her fingers brush over a mixture of metal and paper.

"What is it?" Grace inquired as her friend sat back down behind the wheel. "It's—it's money," Madison could hardly believe the amount in her right hand as she rolled the window back up with her left. "You should report this," Grace said, "I have a feeling there was more to it than just a case of mistaken identity."

"Grace," Madison sighed out of relief, "He's gone, it's over, and I'm taking you home." Grace folded her arms, clearly unsatisfied with her friend's response.

CHAPTER 9

Walter Irwin sat in one of the barber chairs in his shop, his feet propped up on the foot stool as he skimmed the latest *Alleghany-Times News* left by a previous customer.

The paper had started to thin over the last year; the cost of replenishing their supplies, equipment, and staff was staggering due to the Depression.

Irwin glanced up as Talbert Smith, a local farmer and church deacon as he strolled in, "How are you Walt? Some weather we're havin' isn't it?" "It's hot that's for sure," Walter agreed and folded the paper tossing it onto a nearby stand, "How is the farm, and the kids?"

"The farm isn't doing like it used to. There isn't any stock in much else other than potatoes and corn these days, heck even then that's slim. The kids are well, Madison is teaching out at Laurel Springs. How 'bout yours?"

"They're all doin' fine, Zora's home today preparing for Easter Sunday. Does Madison enjoy working at the school?"

"You know Maddie, like her ma, loves kids that girl. And she loves to talk, so it goes hand in hand." Irwin smiled as he thought of his own kids. "I stopped in because the girls ran into some trouble comin' up the mountain yesterday evenin'."

"What kind of trouble?"

"Madison said Grace can vouch for her. A man practically ran them down before they reached town, he had a siren too. Madison thought at first he might be Virginia police, but said she didn't recognize him and he wasn't wearin' a badge that she could see either. He hit Madison's bumper."

"Hit it?" The lines on Irwin's brow deepened, "Are the girls all right?"

"Madison said Grace pulled up in front of the courthouse there at Hardin's," Talbert motioned down the street, "Said they exchanged words, the man paid Madison for the damage, apologized, and was gone."

Curious, Irwin leaned back in the barber chair, his hands firmly on the arm rests, "What made the girls think he was police?" Talbert sat forward, "They heard the siren all the way from Twin Oaks."

Puzzled, Irwin tapped the chair arm with his left hand lightly, "Appreciate the information Talbert, I'll make note and have the oncoming deputy tonight keep an eye out."

"Have you ever heard anything like that though? We heard about the couple near Elkin that had their car stolen at gunpoint."

Irwin knew precisely who Talbert was speaking of, "Yes, so did we. We contacted Jonesville Police, they got the case because it was closer to them than to us." Talbert placed his hands in his overall pockets, "Hope they catch 'em or you boys do one. Don't need that kinda trouble round here. We're a civil town, not like big cities."

Shortly after Talbert left, Irwin locked up the shop and walked across to the courthouse. First he took a quick look inside the Sheriff's office which was empty, noting Henson was most likely on patrol. However, the Clerk of Court was on duty and Irwin knew he would be there until closing when the next deputy came on duty.

"Randy?" Irwin leaned over the counter. The fans overhead hummed as they gave off a slight breeze. Randy Brewer lifted a few files and walked towards Irwin, "Deputy, what may I do for you?" "I need you to give a message to the oncoming deputy tonight. Would you mind?"

"Not at all," Randy sat down the files and grabbed a pen, "What's the message?" "Twin Oaks, patrol that area and report back to me, Irwin." "Report back to *you*, what about the Sheriff?" Randy asked, noting that this was not the usual protocol.

"It's important. Just give him the message please." Randy Brewer did not argue, he gave a nod and Irwin left the courthouse.

Deputy Charlie Shepherd had arrived with just two minutes to spare before his shift. Opening the doors to the courthouse he spotted Randy Brewer who was on his way out at half past six o' clock.

As if being hit by a jolt of lightning Randy jerked back towards the Clerk's office doors, "Deputy Shepherd, good you're here," He pushed open the doors disappearing if only for a moment leaving Charlie standing in the hallway a bit perplexed.

"You alright there Randy?"

"Oh, yes, but uh—," He locked the doors back and handed Charlie a piece of paper, "Deputy Irwin came by earlier, said to give you this. I don't know why he wants you to report to him, but figured..."

"I'll handle it, thanks," Charlie said as he continued towards the section of the courthouse that housed the jail. The two stalls were close together but the room was sizable enough for at least four prisoners if need be. The cells were empty at the moment, and Charlie knew that meant he would most likely be on patrol. Looking down he quickly read Irwin's note.

"Shepherd," Sheriff Henson was sitting in the nearby meeting room. "Evenin' Sheriff," Charlie greeted leaning on the door frame while tucking the note in his back pocket. "Need you to be on patrol this evening, we've had a few complaints on the roads leading in and out of the county. Thought you might head over towards Ashe—."

"Actually, Sheriff," Charlie interrupted, "I heard somethin' happened out near Twin Oaks, thought I'd nose around there for a bit, if that's all right." Henson put down his pen and stared at Charlie over his glasses, "What sort of somethin'?"

"If I find out I'll let you know," Charlie pushed away from the door frame and walked himself back out towards his patrol car. The county could only afford two, so it was his and the Sheriff's. When Irwin was on, it was his patrol car, when it was Charlie's turn it was his.

Settling in Charlie pulled out into the vacant street. The lights from the nearby theater reflected in his mirrors until he was out of view of Four Oaks, a local hotel near the courthouse.

Deciding there was no better a place to linger for a while Charlie reached the bottom of Twin Oaks near Sam's store and pulled in on the side of the hotel. The darkened lot was a refuge that only Shepherd and Irwin had known about. Music was playing inside the hotel, the vibration of banjos, fiddles, and the piano could be felt even in the parking lot.

An hour into patrol Charlie spotted a car making its way towards the hotel pulling in right up beside him on the lot.

Trying to keep a low profile Charlie drew his hat over his face and pretended to be resting in his vehicle. All the while he kept a trained eye on the driver.

Despite his best efforts Charlie could not decipher who the individual was. A combination of the lack of light and the lingering fog after a misty late afternoon rain, made visibility nearly impossible.

Without warning the tap on the passenger door caused Charlie to have to stir, but he kept his hat low, "Whatta ya want?" "Charlie, it's me, open the door." Charlie raised his hat to see the familiar reflection of Walter Irwin hoovering just behind the glass.

"Give me a minute," Charlie reached over and unlocked the door allowing his partner entry. Sliding into the passenger seat with his six-foot-three frame, Walter Irwin straightened his jacket and removed his hat, "Figured you'd be sittin' here."

Charlie grunted, "At least I have entertainment in the background." Irwin noted the sounds of the music, "I see you got my note." "Randy was eager to get it to me, that's for sure. What is this about anyway? Oh and by the way," Charlie added quickly, "Pretty sure I might be in hot water with Henson."

"I'll take the blame," Irwin replied, "After all I needed some help with this one." "This *one what?*" Charlie asked. Irwin went quiet for a moment, his gaze aimed at the lights from the nearby hotel and store. "How worried should I be here Walt?" Charlie questioned.

"Honestly, I don't know that we should be worried, just very concerned." Irwin answered without adding much else. Complete silence filled the vehicle for a good five minutes before Irwin shifted in his seat and looked over at his fellow deputy.

"Madison Talbert and a friend of hers were practically chased up the mountain the other night by someone who had a police siren. I know it wasn't you, and it wasn't me," Irwin explained before Charlie could swear his innocence on the topic.

"So who was it?" Charlie questioned.

"Beats me," Irwin answered, "That's why I wanted you here. Keep an eye out tonight, and let me know tomorrow if anythin' happens. I'll be in early just in case, and Charlie?" "Yeah?"

"Be careful."

"Got it," Charlie said, touching the holster of his thirty eight special. Irwin climbed out of the patrol car, closed the door, and proceeded to drive out of the Twin Oaks parking lot.

Sheriff Henson heard the singing which sounded more like hollering as it echoed up and down the empty pathway of Main Street into the courthouse foyer. It was close to two in the morning and he was about to head home after signing the deputies' time cards.

Squaring his stance Charlie Shepherd pushed a gentleman nearly half his size over to Dean Henson who was shaking his head, "Tell me you busted up a still this evenin' Charlie."

"No, but Seth here sure smells like one," Charlie acknowledged, the poor man cuffed, and dizzy could hardly stand still as Charlie paused. "Well you're not wrong," Henson said as he backed away from the smell of whiskey and cigar smoke. "Lock him up," Henson instructed, "and charge him."

"Just as soon as I get him in the cell, I'll get the ball rollin'."

"Oh, Charlie," Henson stopped him before the deputy could pass the interview room, "Was he the somethin' down near Twin Oaks?" Charlie shook his head, "No sir, not even close." He left Henson standing near the entryway with a curious expression upon his face.

While Henson was often looped in, Charlie wondered just how much his friend had told their boss about the Twin Oaks incident. In the end he decided to leave it for Walter.

"Sit down," Charlie said as he gave Seth Toliver a slight nudge towards the bed. The man sat there for a moment, wavering like a toddler trying to fight sleep, before finally falling over on the cot to rest.

CHAPTER 10

Spring 1931

"What are you talkin' about?" Jeb asked as he caught some of what Erick Whitaker was saying. "I'm talkin' about Seth Toliver, you know, Seth?" Erick half shouted knowing Jeb was sometimes hard of hearing when he had drank, as he had that evening.

Connor, Zane, Thayer, and a few others sat at a nearby table playing poker. Connor more or less was taking the boys for all they were worth. "How is that possible?" Zane slapped his cards down and took another shot of the white lightning they had left from the day's run. When Connor Ridge laughed, Jeb noticed he appeared more like a kid than a grown man with responsibilities, a family, friends to support, or a large moonshine operation to manage.

Thayer was trying hard not to laugh on the other side of the table, but Connors laugh was practically contagious. Jeb had been told once by his wife Lizabeth, that it was one of the reasons she had married that man.

Jeb turned his attention back towards Erick, "Seth Toliver ain't nothin' but trouble with a capital 't'. We ain't goin' nowhere near that, ya hear?" "You should ask him," Erick said, trying to keep his voice low.

It was too late though Connor was already standing in the doorway, his grin shifting into a serious smirk, "Ask me what?"

"Remember those keys we got?" Erick winked.

Connor nodded, "Sure. Why?"

"Well we could put them to good use tonight and get our friend his cut."

"How so?"

Now Zane and Thayer gathered in the same room listening quietly in the background while Jeb questioned why he even bothered talking to these boys. "Jeb seems bothered," Connor noticed, "Should I be?"

"It'll be easy," Erick insisted, "Like taking candy from a baby." "Heard that before," Zane snickered, "Remember Boone?" "Come on now," Thayer urged, "Let him talk."

"Seth Toliver got locked up according to Naomi, she said he had been drinking a little too much down at the Twin Oaks hotel and a deputy grabbed him up." Naomi Toliver was Seth's wife of nearly twenty-three years. Together they had four children, and one of their older boys was quickly following in their father's footsteps as a rum runner.

Jeb frowned, "Wait—what keys are you talkin' about?"

Connor shook his head, "Toliver's a big fish for that lawman, and he's going to be there for a while."

"Or not," Erick smirked, "Most officers leave by five in the mornin'. The Sheriff doesn't come back til eight and that gives us three hours to get in and get Toliver out. He'll owe us."

Connor looked at Jeb, "We have a friend who gave us a set of jail keys." "*The* jail keys?" Jeb exclaimed, "To our jail? How'd they swing that? How do you even know if they work?"

"No time like the present to find out," Erick answered, "And get a payday to top it off."

"Seth won't' just hand you money," Zane laughed, "He soon as leave you boys dead or get you locked up with him before he pays to get out." "Actually," Connor looked over his shoulder at his friend, "Seth owes me anyway, this will just be a better way to collect than if I go chasin' him down near the New River."

Jeb sighed, "You boys do what you want, I'll have no part of this." Lifting himself out of the rocking chair Jeb walked past Zane and Thayer heading out towards the yard. Connor put out his right hand palm facing upward and looked straight at Erick, "Hand 'em over."

It was five past five in the morning. Connor and Erick sat in his pickup towards the First Baptist Church, their eyes fixed on the courthouse.

At ten past Erick tapped Connors arm, "Last one out." The deputy was walking towards his personal vehicle, a Ford Model A, 1930 model truck with a faded green trim.

"All right," Connor acknowledged, "When he leaves, we move."

"We have to be quick," Erick said, "Deputy gets in earlier than the Sheriff, we don't need to run into him here."

Connor glanced over at Farmers Hardware and then back at the deputy as he pulled his pickup into the road and drove past them down Main Street completely unaware they had been sitting there watching.

"Let's go," Connor put the truck in drive, sliding his way up to the front of the courthouse and then parking, "Stay here," He instructed Erick who appeared confused.

"What for?"

"In case someone comes."

"What do you want me to do if that happens?" Erick questioned.

Connor sighed mostly out of impatience, "Drive off, circle back, and blow the horn, got it?"

"All right," Erick said as he watched Connor walk smoothly up the steps in the deputy uniform. Pushing open the main doors Connor was greeted with the scent of pine, paper, and ink. The building's wood floors seemed to roll and crackle with each step.

Carefully Connor glimpsed into each room before continuing towards the holding cells in the jail. The Clerk's Office was the last on the hall but the jail was to his right through a door and down a slight hallway.

From Connors recollection the cells could hold four people. The moment of truth arrived as he reached the door leading the cells. It was locked. Taking out the keys from his pants pocket Connor shoved the key given to Erick and him through the lock, turning it gradually. The lock gave with a click to Connors relief and astonishment.

Inside he could hear Seth Toliver singing off key and then humming to himself some tune Connor could not place. "Seth?" Toliver's eyes widened as he attempted to wake up, locking onto Connors. "Ridge? That you?"

"Seth, you want outta here?" Connor asked.

"You know I'd rather be in my bed than this thing," Seth pounded the cot, "Like sleepin' on a rock."

"You want out, you have to pay. Got it?" Seth glared at Connor, his dark brown eyes nearly as black as coals when he was angry. "Now why you gonna charge me for gettin' out? The law already gonna charge me—and Naomi..."

"Listen to me," Connor kept his voice low, "It's either you pay me or you pay the court and spend more time here. Which will it be?"

"How much we talkin'?" Seth asked, sounding slightly more coherent than when Connor had first walked in. "Let's say twenty percent of your haul this weekend and we're even."

"Even?" Seth glared, "That's robbery!"

"Way I see it Seth, it is the least you can do since I got you out of that pickle with McMillan a few years back. Saved your life, you even told me you owed me one."

"And you're cashin' in aren't ya?" Seth snarled, "You're a piece of work Ridge." "It's just businessman Seth, that's all. So, you want out or do you wanna stay here?"

Seth staggered carefully to his feet, "Nah, I'm out of here. Let's go." "You have to be quiet," Connor warned, "Or we will both end up in here." Seth followed as Connor closed the cell door and then closed and locked the door leading to the jail behind them. "Where's your car?" Seth questioned, his speech still slow. "Straight out the doors," Connor answered and led the way. Seth took hold of the railing down the steps and slid into Connor's pickup seat with Erick behind the wheel.

"Any trouble?" Erick asked. Connor closed the door once he was inside, "None at all. Drive."

"Say," Seth said looking over at Conner as they passed Four Oaks, "How'd you get in there anyway?" Erick laughed, "You just now askin' Seth?"

Connor reached into his pocket taking out a cigarette and pack of matches, "Just tell your friends Seth, if they get locked up, I'm the guy to call." Seth's laugh started out low and grew as he realized it was true what most said about Connor Ridge. He was full of surprises.

It had taken the span of three months to get all the agencies up to speed on what was happening. The robbery at Whitehead Grocery had also gained the interest of BOI agent Frank Lincoln. The man insisted upon collaborating and meeting with fellow agencies and departments to go over and investigate what each agency had learned.

Per Sheriff Henson's request, Irwin found himself in charge of coordinating the efforts between the state, local, and federal authorities. Each agency had quickly learned all they could about the individual or individuals behind the smuggled vehicle parts through Alleghany, Virginia, and even in parts of eastern Tennessee.

In need of privacy, preferably away from the center of town in general Irwin had been the one to suggest the Graystone Inn as their potential meeting spot. The Inn was secluded enough and far away from the small town spotlight that was already starting to shine on the incidents thanks to the newspaper.

Now, in the distance through a sparse line of pine trees Graystone Inn appeared at the end of the long narrow road. Slowly to his right Irwin began to catch a glimpse of the hazy blue covered mountains below.

It was a view Irwin had taken in on a couple of occasions during his trips to speak with the Inn's owner, Hugh Chatham. Sheriff Henson was driving as the skies began to cast over threatening the possibility of rain.

As the Inn came into full view Irwin spotted Holden Rash standing near the side entrance smoking a cigarette. Once parked both men stepped out of the patrol vehicle greeting the Highway Patrolman, "Morning Holden," Henson said offering his hand.

Rash put out his cigarette and shook the Sheriff's hand, and then Irwin's. "Sheriff, Deputy. The boys are waiting inside for coffee, have either of you eaten?"

"Not yet, we came straight out." Henson answered as he glanced up somewhat suspect at the graying sky.

"Well, let's get started" Rash led the way through the foyer passed the offices and check-in counter into a large spacious sitting room.

A number of staff hurried about their duties, the promise of summer had its way of increasing travelers, especially to the top of the mountain. "Morning," Irwin said politely to one of the young women carrying a tray of coffee and pastries.

"Good morning, Sheriff, Deputy" She smiled warmly at both men accompanied by Rash while balancing a large tray. Irwin observed how much larger the tray was to the woman carrying it and offered his assistance.

Rash held the door open to the meeting room, so Irwin and Henson could step inside. Sitting at the large oak table with high back chairs covered in a dark green velvet padding, were three individuals Irwin did not recognize.

Once he had aided with the lowering of the tray the young woman began to commence serving the guests with hot cups of coffee. The two lawmen settled into their chairs facing away from the door, with Holden Rash across from them.

"Would any of your gentlemen care for breakfast? We have an excellent cook." "Please," One of the men on Irwin's right answered, "Eggs, scrambled, a couple slices of bacon and toast." The young woman made note of the request and took the other orders quickly before leaving them to their business.

"Well, good morning," Holden started the meeting, his voice carrying through the room, "and welcome to Alleghany County. I trust you gentlemen enjoyed your stay last evening?"

"It's a beautiful county, no doubt." The man across from Irwin answered.

Holden cleared his throat, "Sheriff, Deputy Irwin, this is Caption Russell Hawks from the Raleigh Highway State Patrol office. He will oversee assembling any additional manpower when and if needed. These other gentlemen here are Adam Lewis, with the Motor Vehicle Bureau of Investigations and David Whitman from Greensboro with the Automobile Underwriters Bureau."

After exchanging acknowledgments, Irwin's attention quickly turned towards the man sitting at the opposite end of the table. The stranger in his dark blue suit and matching tie had remained silent throughout much of the exchanges, and Irwin noticed, had not touched his coffee. The strangers hands remained clasped firmly on top of the wooden table with his copper colored eyes focused squarely on Holden.

Without waiting for anyone to comment Irwin asked, "I am going to assume that you are not part of the Highway Patrol nor the Insurance agencies represented?" "And you'd assume correctly Deputy Irwin," The stranger shifted his gaze in Irwin's direction. "Agent Lincoln. I have heard a lot about you the last few months. Lieutenant Rash spared no details as to how you were helping to organize this operation."

"He's one of the best deputies I have," Henson spoke up, "No one is more qualified to handle this task than Deputy Irwin." "Pleasure to meet you too," Irwin said, lifting his coffee.

Lewis craned his head in Lincoln's direction, "Are you from Raleigh?"

"Actually I'm federal, BOI, better known as the Bureau of Investigations."

Lewis sat back in his chair as Whitman began to speak. "We thought we might also rope in another county, possibly more, seeing as to how extensive this investigation is about to become."

Irwin leaned forward, "How many counties?"

"Yadkin, Surry, to be more exact," Captain Hawks informed as the steam from his mug curled before him, "Seems this individual has been busy all over the upper northwestern part of the state and into Tennessee."

"And Virginia," Adam Lewis added before anyone else could speak. Henson took in a slow breath, fixing the palms of his hands onto the chair arms and keeping his focus on Lewis and Whitman. "Why don't you boys tell us what you know so we can see if we're all on the same page here."

"For starters, there is no denying corruption in this part of our great state. It's hardly something we can ignore and pretend is not there." "What do you mean *corruption*?" asked Henson cautiously.

"What they are saying sir, is that there are reports of some law enforcement individuals looking the other way when it comes to car thefts, robberies, and bootlegging because of certain... incentives," Everyone at the table could sense Lewis' hesitation while he made such a statement. Henson frowned, "Not in *my* department."

"No, certainly not," Lewis held up his hands in mock surrender, an obvious tint of red creeping up his neck for having possibly offended the Sheriff. Leaning forward Irwin felt the need to ask, "Do Yadkin or Surry County officials know you're all here?"

"No, not yet," Hawks answered, "But they will by the end of the meeting. Enough from us. Tell us what you know Sheriff," Hawks motioned to Henson.

Glancing at Irwin, Henson stayed silent as his deputy provided the necessary information, "Back in January a man was held up by someone who he claimed appeared to be searching for something either inside or around his vehicle. He was held at gunpoint. Thankfully the carjacker did not take the vehicle, but the would-be victim did come in and file a report about the incident."

Irwin paused before continuing, the next part having gained their full attention, "Another incident occurred with two young women traveling back to the county from Virginia. Again, thankfully no one was hurt but they reported the man had a police siren. Before that I learned of Judge Carico's stolen Coupe from Lieutenant Rash. However, the event that really caught our attention was the robbery at Whitehead Grocery."

"What was stolen?" Lewis asked curiously, his pen poised to take note of what Irwin was about to report. Looking at Rash, the deputy continued, "I'm not sure you boys are going to believe me if I tell you." "Try us," Whitman insisted. Looking over the rim of his glasses. "Two thousand pounds of sugar, and cash from the register," Irwin explained.

The room was so quiet after that statement that the opening of the door by the young woman bringing their breakfast made Lewis jerk slightly in his seat. "Two thousand pounds?" Hawks repeated the number as if he had misunderstood.

"More than likely for making moonshine," Rash spoke up.

Lincoln lifted his fork, "It's not uncommon." All eyes turned to the agent as he lifted a piece of toast from a nearby plate, "In some cases stores, and owners, can be bought in order to carry access to high quantities of supplies needed to make white lightening, like sugar. The only obstacle for your run-of-the-mill bootlegger is which ones will take the payoffs versus which ones will not. And since money is scarce, jobs even more so," Lincoln added, "It's not hard to believe most would take the hit and the money."

"You're not suggesting—," began Henson but was cut off. Frank Lincoln spoke, shrugging, "Happens all the time. In fact," He informed, "In some cases a lot closer to your mountain home than you might believe."

"Tell us more about this potential carjacking," Hawks pressed motioning to Irwin with his free left hand. "The gentleman who filed the report said the gunman was dressed as a minister which is why he had stopped in the first place."

Whitman reached down, pushed his chair back and lifted a suitcase onto his lap. Moments later he had several files sitting before Irwin and Henson.

"About six months ago the bureau began to search for connections to the stolen vehicles in this area. I learned from Agent Lincoln and Lieutenant Rash, former Judge Carico of Independence, Virginia, that his vehicle was stolen. There have been other incidents, like the one you described, that have also taken place on Elkin mountain. Reports were filed in Yadkin because most motorists were from that area."

Rash could see Irwin's wheels turning as he looked over one file after another, scanning them quietly. "Any ideas as to who you think it might be?" Hawks questioned. Irwin took a bite of his eggs, and after a few seconds answered, "I think we can certainly narrow it down given Mr. Whitman's information, and if all else fails," the deputy added, "The gentleman who filed a report with us, Mr. Wagoner, did say he was good with remembering faces."

CHAPTER 11

Spring 1931

Jeb Dalton sat with his grandsons Tommy and William in the front of their Ford Model A pickup parked just a few feet from the entry of the construction company.

Days earlier Connor had managed to get a good look around the facility thanks to one of the workers he knew. "Be sure he says his name is Ben and that I mentioned you," Connor instructed before having left Jeb the evening before at the site of the still.

"This guy isn't going to show," William said as he squinted his eyes trying to peer through the soiled windshield. "It's still early," Jeb replied leaning over the steering wheel, "be patient."

"Where is Connor anyway?" Tommy questioned, "Haven't seen him since we took all that moonshine over near Galax."

"Connor has his own work to do, don't worry 'bout him." During the winter months Connor would often help neighbors with their pine trees or shoe their horses.

Once, Jeb had overheard Zane Shepherd refer to his friend as a jack-of-all-trades. It was a title that after having gotten to know Connor, Jeb knew fit him rather well for someone so young.

Aside from bootlegging Connor Ridge could make his own weapons from scrap metal, fix cars with the right tools, and he often found ways to help farmers uproot stumps.

By no means was Connor book smart like some, but he had proven to be smarter than law enforcement having dodged them for close to two years.

Following Connor had proven to be somewhat of a delicate balance between adventure and danger at times. Despite their close encounters with the law, Jeb could not ignore how much Connor had helped him and his family.

Jeb was also indebted to Connor for helping to bring his grandsons into the business providing them with an income. Not to mention Jeb had made more money working with Connor than he ever had bootlegging alone.

"Look sharp," Jeb spotted a young man wearing a pair of light blue overalls approaching the vehicle. William rolled down the passenger side window while Tommy kept a firm grasp on the revolver between him and his brother on the seat.

"Evening," The man nodded, "you boy's friends of Connors?"

"Who's askin'?" Jeb replied.

"My name's Ben, I showed him around the other day. Connor told me some of you might stop by."

The words Jeb had been waiting to hear had been spoken, "I told the boys you would show." The man motioned with his right hand, "If you go down this street and turn off onto the gravel path on the right there, I think we can all get this loaded without any difficulty, but we have to be quick."

Starting the truck Jeb watched as the young man proceeded to walk ahead of them towards the back of the building. "I have a bad feelin' about this," Tommy muttered.

"It's not the time nor the place to be getting all yeller Tommy, we get in and we get out," His grandfather stated. "What's here that Connor needs us to get anyway?" William asked, noting the concern on his brother's face.

"He didn't say," Jeb replied, "But we're 'bout to find out." The truck proceeded up the gravel path and when the road leveled off Jeb pressed on the break and parked the truck. Ben appeared carrying a large oblong shaped box in his arms, "There's more than a few dozen in the warehouse." "Get out," Jeb instructed looking at his grandsons, "The sooner we get this loaded the sooner we can leave."

Reluctantly Tommy slid out of the passenger door following his brother. William, who was five feet ten inches, had never been afraid of much. Always long headed, their father feared he might end up in jail before he turned twenty-one, but so far, William had been good at keeping his head down.

After the fourth crate was loaded Tommy paused to wipe the sweat off his forehead, his light blond hair matted to his skull. All three boys were perspiring by the time the final crate was on the pickup bed "Thanks," Ben said as he waved to Jeb, "Tell Connor we're even."

"Even?" Tommy asked without realizing he had said anything out loud. William shot his brother a warning glance, "Get in the truck." "Let's go," Jeb shouted from the cab. "Comin'," William shoved the gate on the back of the pickup closed as Tommy climbed back into the truck.

Once William was beside him and the passenger door was securely closed Jeb turned on the engine and proceeded back out into the road.

They would not be taking their traditional way back to Alleghany, instead they would be taking a longer route to get them back to Cherry Lane. The sun was sitting just as they crossed the bridge on 21. A light orange gleamed over the shimmering water of the New River as they passed over it.

"Grandpa, what did that man mean when he said he and Conner were even?" Tommy asked, his curiosity getting the best of him. "Connor did him a solid a few years ago, this was his way of thankin' him." Tommy wished he could have been satisfied with the answer, but found it lacking.

Once they arrived at the county line Jeb slowed the truck and pulled over onto a side road he knew well. Without explanation he opened the driver's door, climbed out walking around to the truck bed.

"What's he doing?" William asked, "Those crates are so heavy they aren't going anywhere." "Beats me," Tommy replied as he watched his grandfather examining the haul.

"It can't be more liquor," William opened his door, stepping out, the cold air sending a chill down Tommy's spine. Following his brother Tommy got out too. When he reached William, he noticed the look of disbelief on his and their grandfather's face.

"What is it?" Tommy asked as he glanced down at one of the crates his grandfather had partially opened. It was clear that inside were several cylindrical tubes, compact, and wrapped in a yellowish colored tube with a black stripe at the top.

Like much of any job they did with Connor Ridge, Tommy could already tell there would be more questions than answers.

Sitting in the middle section of the First Baptist Church located on Main Street beside her husband Robert, Mrs. Gambill glanced up at the minister as he spoke.

The cool evening air slid down the aisle as the door opened allowing George Edwards and his wife Renee to take their seats a few pews back.

Robert momentarily turned to acknowledge his neighbor, and then focused his attention back on the sermon at hand. Mrs. Gambill had, like most of the congregation, admired the recently built structure. The church itself had been organized in 1884 and the Gambill's had been attending since its founding. After the sermon reached its conclusion and hymns were sung to close the evening, Mrs. Gambill collected her hat and coat.

"Let me help you," Robert insisted as he took her coat in his hands gently wrapping it around her shoulders. "Robert," George Edwards approached, offering his hand, "How is everyone?"

"Doing well," Robert answered, glancing at his wife.

"How are you George?" Mrs. Gambill asked in return. George and her husband had worked together a few years on various farms helping with everything from tobacco to pine trees. The two were old friends who had gone to school together, and the families knew each other well.

"To be honest," George answered, "it has been a rather busy day." It was the way in which he made this statement that perked Mrs. Gambill's interest, "Good busy or bad busy?"

Robert glanced at her out of the corner of his right eye, but she paid her husband no mind. "We were robbed earlier," George confessed.

"Robbed?" Robert Gambill kept his voice low while carrying a concerned look upon his face. His dark brown eyes had a way of drawing people in. At times Mrs. Gambill wondered if her husband had missed his calling as a journalist, his ease with people and quiet tone often smoothed over any hesitation they may have previously had. It was just one of the many reasons she loved him.

"My car, the Ford my boy left behind when he went to Tennessee last year, was stolen. Thankfully Renee had the truck in town. Renee heard some dynamite was taken near Independence too. Scary times we are livin' in. What would someone want with dynamite around here? I mean unless you were blastin' rock to build…"

"There's a construction company in Independence," Mrs. Gambill interrupted, "Do you think they took it from there?" "I can't say for sure Mrs. Gambill, all I can speak to is what happened to me."

"Of course," Robert said almost apologetically. Ignoring the urge to keep quiet Mrs. Gambill pressed on with one more question. "Mr. Edwards, can you tell me who told you about the dynamite?"

"Sure can, that'd be Samuel Walker at Twin Oaks." Robert knew the look on his wife's face all too well and as they headed out of the church, down the steps, he stayed close at her side. They bid their farewells to a few friends and then got into their car that was parked along the street.

Closing her door Robert made his way around to the driver's side, his six-foot-frame casting a long shadow on the hood. Once settled in behind the wheel he kept his eyes on the church doors. "What?" Mrs. Gambill inquired, noting her husband's silence.

"You're going to go talk to Sam, aren't you?" He asked. "Tomorrow mornin', yes." "You know I love you," Robert said turning towards her, "And you also know I cannot keep you from whatever makes you happy. Whether that's me, our home, or…"

"The *newspaper*," Mrs. Gambill finished his sentence. A habit she was never able to break, nor did she wish to. Just as she could complete his sentences, Robert Gambill completed her. He was the only man who truly understood her desire to write, her need to be involved in her community, and her drive.

"Yes, or the *paper*," Robert confessed, "But all I ask is that you be careful. This sounds more like somethin' the Sheriff's office should handle and a lot less like what a journalist should be doin'." "An Editor," She corrected with a crooked smile.

"Just promise me you will be careful, or at least take an officer with you?" Just as she started to protest, Mrs. Gambill glanced towards the courthouse. "I believe I just might."

CHAPTER 12

J enny Wyatt proceeded towards the office of Editor and Chief. Jenny, twenty-one, with fair blond hair and light green eyes was known for her soft-spoken demeanor and dedication to her work.

The oldest of six children, Jenny worked to assist her mother in the care of her younger siblings, of whom there were five. Jenny's father had passed three years prior, forcing her to find a steady income and assist with household duties. The paper made this possible as Mrs. Gambill understood the circumstances.

Knocking softly on the door before entering Jenny awaited her employer's voice. After a few moments, and with no response, Jenny opened the door to peer inside. Indeed, Mrs. Gambill was not there.

Closing the door Jenny proceeded towards her own office to find Mrs. Gambill staring at the layout of the paper on her table.

"I went by your office after arriving, but you were not there," Jenny explained apologetically, "Is everythin' alright?" "I'm not sure," Mrs. Gambill motioned to the layout, "What else do we have?"

"There's a story about John Dillinger again, but—."

Without missing a beat Jenny recalled having heard about a race that was to take place in Wilkes County and recounted it to Mrs. Gambill.

"A friend told my mother and I there were well over a hundred and fifty people at those races sometimes. Could you imagine? That field must have been flooded with cars."

Mrs. Gambill stood with her arms folded, her eyes fixed on her copy editor, "Where exactly is this race to happen?" "Well, my mother's friend said Friday," Jenny confessed with a shrug, "Boys, you know how they are. They like their fast cars and their drink." A bit surprised, Mrs. Gambill smiled.

Catching the look on her employer's face Jenny turned a beet red, "Heavens, I don't drink ma'am," Jenny's eyes displayed the same horror that laced her tone, "It's just what people tell me." "Do you know anyone in particular who might go to such a race?" Mrs. Gambill questioned.

"No, but I heard some of the older school boys have gone before." Arching her left eyebrow, Mrs. Gambill unfolded her arms and proceeded towards the door, "I have a story of my own to follow up on and won't be back until after lunch. Take calls, and whatever you do, don't send anything in until I've reviewed it before press."

"Yes ma'am," Jenny sat behind her table and began work on the next section of the front-page layout.

Less than six minutes later Mrs. Gambill was walking across Main Street towards the local barber shop where she knew she would find Deputy Irwin. It was his day off as Deputy which meant he was more than likely at his regular post as the town barber.

The doorbell above the shop's entrance alerted her presence. The shop smelled of rubbing alcohol, cigarettes and cologne, but much to Mrs. Gambill's relief the shop itself was empty.

Walter Irwin rounded the corner of the back room wearing a white barber jacket and dark trousers, his glasses perched on the edge of his nose as he held a copy of the latest Times issue in his right hand, scissors in the other. "Mrs. Gambill?"

"Deputy," She gave him a polite smile, "I apologize for any intrusion. Can you spare a moment?" Walter Irwin sat down in the nearest barber chair and motioned for her to sit across from him but she seemed too distracted by her thoughts to notice.

"How may I help?" Irwin inquired as he placed the half-folded newspaper on the sink.

"My husband and I attended service at the First Baptist Church the other evenin'. We were approached by a friend, George Edwards," She let the name sit for a moment before continuing, "He told us he was robbed. His vehicle was stolen out near 93 and later his wife learned from Sam down at Twin Oaks grocery of a dynamite heist in Independence."

Walter Irwin sat down the scissors, seeming careful not to let his expression give her much insight into what he was really thinking.

"I spoke with Sam, but I really believe it would be worth someone's time to speak to the company that had the dynamite stolen."

Clearing his throat Walter Irwin folded his arms, "I'd be interested in talkin' to them too. How much dynamite?" "Sam didn't know, he just heard it was a good bit of bang for anyone's buck."

"Somethin' tells me there is more to this story," Mrs. Gambill replied, "But I suspect I don't have to tell you that."

Mulling over the information she had given him, Irwin stood up with his hands in his pockets, "What's the name of the company?" "Cassell's Construction," Mrs. Gambill answered as she watched him place the closed sign in the front window.

"Does this have anything to do with your car theft ring?" Irwin opted not to reply, but answered instead, "I suppose you would like to speak to the construction business yourself, for the paper?" Mrs.

Gambill, who was peering out the glass window onto Main Street nodded, "I would like to, yes."

"It's really out of our jurisdiction Mrs. Gambill, I cannot go in any formal capacity with the Sheriff's Office—."

"I know," She interrupted him, "Think of it as research." Walter Irwin grabbed his coat off the nearby hanger and felt for his keys.

"I'll ask all the questions." She assured him.

"Fine, but first I need to make a quick phone call," Irwin replied, heading back into his office.

Having left Mrs. Gambill out in the waiting area of the barber shop Walter Irwin lifted the phone on his desk and dialed the extension needed to speak with Holden Rash of the State Highway Patrol. The moment he heard the click Irwin spoke, "Afternoon, this is Deputy Irwin in Alleghany for Lieutenant Rash." "One moment please," The young woman on the other line directed. Holden answered a split second after the second click, "Holden—."

"Rash it's me," Irwin had closed the door to his office and was careful to keep his voice down.

"I was actually going to call you tomorrow," Holden offered, "Any progress?"

"Well, a few things have been brought to my attention and I am on my way out to verify them. If they pan out, and they are connected I will be calling back."

"What sort of things?" Holden asked curiously.

"Another vehicle theft, rumors of stock races below the mountain, and then there is the dynamite."

"*Dynamite?*"

"As I said, I'll be callin' back if this turns out to be connected." Irwin was holding his breath, half listening as Holden shuffled some papers and looked towards the door for any signs Mrs. Gambill may have been listening.

"Okay Walt," There was a clear concern in his friends' tone, "I'll fill Lincoln and the others in, just be careful." Irwin placed the receiver on its hanger, picked up his hat and headed out of the shop.

Mrs. Gambill followed and when they were both in the vehicle Irwin placed the key in the ignition giving it a twist. Moments later they were headed down US-21 North towards Independence.

Mrs. Gambill took out her pen and pad and started to scratch down some notes, questions Irwin surmised from what little he could glimpse. "How do you imagine someone steals dynamite without being caught in the act?" She asked. Irwin shook his head, "Not by themselves I'll assure you of that."

"There is more than one person involved in your little car theft case isn't there?" She questioned. "Off the record?" Irwin made the turn onto the bridge overlooking the New River. "Of course," Mrs. Gambill answered, watching him as she often did for any signs that he might be concealing more than he thought she should know. Irwin shrugged, "It's possible."

"*Possible* isn't really an answer, Deputy."

"It's the only answer I have, for now," Irwin admitted.

"So more than one person," She paused emphasizing her next word "*possibly*, which means you believe there was more than one person that held up Whitehead Grocery too."

"I never said that," Irwin replied without glancing in her direction. Mrs. Gambill folded her gloved hands in her lap, "Reports said the carjacking on the mountain involved two men, didn't they?" She was snooping around for any information she could get and Irwin knew it. His frown caused his forehead to wrinkle, "Maybe."

"Three men?" Mrs. Gambill continued. "Still off the record?" Irwin asked. The Editor nodded, "Of course."

"Yes, there were two."

"You must have someone in mind who could be behind this," She replied. Irwin remained silent and once again his inaction spoke a little louder than Mrs. Gambill's questions.

The construction company came into view a few minutes later, the warehouse parking lot full of vehicles and a work hand or two standing outside on their break.

Once parked Irwin got out of the vehicle, "Afternoon," He called to the workers. "Sir," One of them, a young man in his early twenties, greeted. "Can you point us in the direction of your main office?" Mrs. Gambill asked, "Or a manager?"

"Pete's in the main building here," The young man motioned behind him towards a set of metal doors. "Pete have a last name?" Irwin asked.

"Caudill," The young man said, looking Irwin over. "Thank you," Mrs. Gambill smiled politely, allowing Irwin to walk a few steps ahead of her. He opened the door only to have the smell of rock and water greet them. The heavy earthy scent would no doubt cling to his jacket for the next few days, a prospect he knew his wife would dislike.

Mrs. Gambill coughed for a moment and then took slow breaths until they saw a man who looked to be the manager. "Excuse me, are you Pete Caudill?" Mrs. Gambill asked. The man was in his mid-forties, five feet seven inches with a thinning hairline and light green eyes. In his right hand was a clipboard and in his left a pair of glasses.

"I am, how may I help you?"

"We understand that some dynamite was stolen the other night. What can you tell us about that accusation?" Mrs. Gambill stated. The manager drew in a sharp breath, "I have already addressed this issue with local law enforcement, are you with the insurance or—." "No sir," Irwin spoke up, "We're with law enforcement." Mrs. Gambill gave him a slight look of surprise when Pete's attention was on him.

"I see," The manager seemed weary from all the attention the theft had brought to his doorstep,"Well, as you heard, we did have dynamite stolen the other night. Of course the company would like to have it back…" "Of course," Mrs. Gambill said apologetically.

"What we cannot figure out," Pete put his glasses back on and reached for a handkerchief to blot the sweat from his brow, "Who would need that much dynamite and for what?"

Irwin gave Mrs. Gambill a look prompting her to ask the obvious. "How much dynamite was taken Mr. Caudill?" "The others didn't tell you?" He asked. "They were a bit distracted," Mrs. Gambill forged on with the deception.

Stepping a little closer to the two of them Pete managed in a low voice, "Four crates, possibly around a hundred pounds." Irwin kept his expression as neutral as possible, all the while wondering what someone would need with that kind of fire power outside of a quarry.

"The owners nor I could imagine what exactly these people would want with that amount of explosives. Most of the blastin' we're helpin' with these days takes place at quarries."

"Like the one near Laurel Springs?" Irwin asked. "Yes," Pete answered, his voice breaking a bit, a nervousness settling into his tone.

"Do you have any suspects? Employees maybe who felt wronged in some way?" Mrs. Gambill implored. The manager shook his head, "No, no one that we could think of."

"Anyone been caught snoopin' around the place?" Irwin asked.

Suddenly the manager had a look of revelation upon his face, "As a matter of fact, yes. A young man. He seemed very interested in the factory, but that was over a month ago."

"Can you describe this individual?" Irwin inquired just to see if he could get the same description as the one given him by Mr. Wagoner the evening he and his wife were nearly carjacked.

"Six foot or a little taller, unusual eyes, maybe in his late twenties to early thirties," Pete answered. "When you say unusual eyes, what do you mean exactly?" Mrs. Gambill asked.

"They were dark brown I think, but had a tint of yellow around the outer iris."

Irwin stepped back, looked around the facility and then recalled something he knew connected the two cases. The very act of *looking itself.*

The thief had looked at Mr. Wagoner's vehicle as if he were searching for something. Now, months later, he turned up again, this time across state lines looking for something at the construction company. *Dynamite.*

After a few more questions Mrs. Gambill followed Irwin back out to the parking lot, her heels clicking on the pavement as she tried to keep up.

Clearly, Pete Caudill's answers had the lawman thinking. Sliding into the passenger seat of the truck Mrs. Gambill turned towards Irwin as he cut the engine on.

"Somethin' he said got to you, what was it?" She asked. "Did you get all of your questions answered?" Irwin inquired, wishing to change the subject.

"Deputy, I saw that look when he mentioned the description. It's someone you know isn't it?" Irwin backed the truck out of the parking lot and without saying another word drove towards the county line.

Deep down he knew certain pieces of these very different cases were starting to come together. The picture was becoming more and more clear with each passing case, each report, with each found vehicle part, and each physical description of the thief himself.

"I'll tell you this," Irwin said as they approached Twin Oaks, "it isn't a coincidence when you get the same description at the construction company as you do when receiving a stolen car report."

Mrs. Gambill, who had been riding in complete silence for the better part of ten minutes, remained so as the deputy gave his admission. "And that's still off the record," Irwin added quickly before she could find her voice to ask otherwise.

"Have a seat Martin," Sheriff River Hayes of the Jonesville Police Department ordered. His booming voice echoed off the concrete walls almost as loudly as the doors to the jail cells around the corner when they were slammed shut.

Standing at just over five-foot-eleven and a hundred and eighty pounds with a chip on his shoulder to match, Hayes was fit to be tied. "Someone get that phone!" He crossed the room to retrieve a file from his secretary's desk only to remember there was no one in the office except for him. His secretary had taken the day off due to her mother being ill, and two of his men were out on patrol.

Looking over his shoulder Hayes pointed directly at the gentleman he had just arrested, "Don't move Martin." The man shrugged, his half-unbuttoned shirt and ruined sports coat falling from his left shoulder.

"Sheriff Hayes," He answered the phone, holding it to his left ear so he could turn his head to keep an eye on his detainee.

"Good morning Sheriff, honestly I was expecting a secretary…"
"Yeah well we're stretched a bit thin today. Who is this?"

"Frank Lincoln," The man replied.

"And what may I do for you Mr. Lincoln?" Hayes watched as Martin leaned forward, his head between his knees. Deep down Hayes groaned knowing answering phone calls was about to be the least of his worries.

"I'm with the Federal Bureau of Investigations," Lincoln explained, "We're currently working with your neighbors in Alleghany." Hayes kept his eyes on Martin, "I see, and what does that have to do with my county Mr. Lincoln?"

"Actually, there is a good chance what we are investigating has crept into Yadkin County. At least we suspect someone there is helping the individuals here to get away with stealing cars and hacking their parts."

Hayes rubbed his eyes, "And who might I ask, do you suspect?"
"Well that's the problem, we can't really pin down the person, or persons, involved. That's why we need your help."

"Sure, hold on a moment, will you?" Hayes put the phone down, grabbed a trash can from beside the bench Martin had been sitting on and placed it under his head. Before the man could look up, he vomited straight into the can.

Taking a step back Hayes shook his head, "When are you boys ever going to learn that all that 'shine does is make you sick as dogs? You're as green as the grass in June—."

Martin lunged his body forward again heaving into the trash can, making it enough for Hayes to turn back to the phone. "Sorry 'bout that Mr. Lincoln, as I said we're a bit short handed today."

"It's *agent* Lincoln. We would like to meet with you, Sheriff Hayes. Would you be available tomorrow?"

"*We?*" Hayes inquired.

"Deputy Walter Irwin from Alleghany, a member of the State Highway Patrol, and myself," Lincoln clarified, "Say lunch time?"

"One o' clock usually for me," Hayes answered, "Meet me at the office here and we will head over to Nu-Way Cafe for lunch." Lincoln had not had time to agree before the Sheriff clicked off.

Walter Irwin sat in his patrol car watching the horizon as the sun began to ascend over the hills peppered with pine trees. A burnt orange cast a streak through gray clouds that were starting to clear a path for the sun.

Irwin had spent the better part of the morning on the skirts of Cherry Lane Township. At intervals he had watched as children walked in groups of four or five to school. Some had teasingly thrown small powder like balls of the newly fallen snow at one another, while others tightly grasped their books.

The direction of the sun nearly blinding him Irwin turned on the engine of the vehicle heading towards the main road from the gravel path where he had been sitting. Part of him hoped he might have a bit of luck, find the individual or individuals behind the carjackings just by going off the descriptions of Wagoner and the construction company manager.

The static of the newly placed car radio came to life, "Walter," The radio crackled, "There is a disturbance on 18 North..." In his side mirror Irwin spotted a pickup turning up the road towards Cherry Lane and a thought occurred to him. *A hundred pounds of dynamite could easily level an entire mountain. Moreover, it could level the competition—or,* Irwin thought, *law enforcement.*

Jeb had done as instructed, delivering the dynamite to Connor without question. The boys at the still were working extra hard to make sure the mash for the next batch turned out just right.

"Nathan over in Whitehead said he would cooper some more barrels if we need 'em," Matthew Jones informed, his left jaw bulging with a pinch of his chewing tobacco. Jeb knew of the man Jones was referring to but said nothing because his mind was on other things, yet the young man noticed.

Matthew Jones was six feet three inches before he had ever left school. He was also quick on his feet, having outrun many a revenuer in the ten years he had worked on stills. A few years prior, prohibition had forced Jones to pick up his family and move further east into North Carolina from Tennessee.

"Is it Connor?" Jones asked.

"Nah," Jeb waved him off."

"You see the paper?" Jones inquired as he took out his can of tobacco and offered some to Jeb knowing it was the only way to get him talking. Taking a bit of the tobacco between his index finger and thumb on his right-hand, Jeb watched as his grandson Tommy carried water from the waterfall run-off nearby so it might be heated in one of the barrels.

"That paper is becomin' a regular pain. First the story about the robbery, then I hear the lady runnin' it has been askin' questions down at Twin Oaks store. Somethin' about stolen cars, hijackin's, and now dynamite."

Jeb scoffed, although just as concerned as Matthew, "Sam Walker don't to know nothin' about our dealin's, got that?" Jones took a step back from Jeb, "Listen, I am only warnin' you before things get worse. Either we shut that newspaper up, or we're lookin' at more than just havin' to set up shop elsewhere." Jeb calmly chewed on the tobacco, "Not up to me."

Connor seemed to take form out of the early evening shadows, Zane following close behind. The two men glanced towards the still operation in progress, then back at Jeb. "You boys get the supplies?" Jeb asked, wondering if Connor had any real need of so much dynamite. "We did," Connor said, staring inquiringly at Matthew Jones.

"Any word on those barrels?" Zane questioned.

Matthew nodded, "Nathan will do 'em, but he wants a few pints of the liquor when it's ready."

"He'll have 'em," Connor assured his still hand.

Zane noted the look of concern on Jeb's face as the aged moonshiner motioned for Connor to follow him. Stepping away Connor tracked after the man whom he considered to be more like family than a member of his gang.

"All right what's troublin' you," Connor leaned against a maple tree, a mixture of pine needles, leaves, and rock crunching under his and Jeb's boots. The two men shifted the stances against the slightly slanted embankment to remain balanced.

"Matthew brought something to my attention, and I wanted to run it by you," Jeb explained, "The newspaper—." Connor raised his hands, "I have it under control Jeb." "I know, but hear me out," Jeb insisted.

Out of respect Connor folded his arms remaining silent which was Jeb's cue to start talking. "What if we offered the lady reporter somethin'? Maybe money or maybe—."

"No," Connor shook his head dismissing the idea, "I'll handle her when the time comes." "It's already time Connor," Jeb kept his voice low, but his eyes were as sharp as blades as he spoke, "What did you need with dynamite?"

"What'd you think I need it for?" Connor questioned, his tone matter-of-matter. "We ain't in no killin' business Connor, but we do need to pay this lady off, or at least keep her on our side and point the laws attention some-where's else"

"What do you know about her?" Connor questioned.

Jeb shrugged, "Nothin', Matthew seems to know who she's been talkin' to though."

"Who?" Connor asked.

"Sam Walker."

"What she askin'?" Connor responded as he stared back towards Matthew who was helping Tommy keep the fire lit that was boiling the water.

"Matthew says she's talkin' about the carjackin's and the dynamite. Connor, what if she's talkin' to the cops too?" It was the expression of pure disquiet upon Jeb's face that gave Connor pause before he turned back to Jeb. "Sam Walker is who we deal with, not the newspaper lady, and I know exactly how we can do that."

Although Jeb had not liked the thoughts of scaring the newspaper Editor, he hated the thoughts of roughing up Sam Walker. The store and hotel owner had let his guests come and go without calling the authorities regardless of liquor on his premises. Most knew Sam to turn a blind-eye, even to the gambling machines having kept one out of view on certain days of the week for customers.

Connor dipped a tin cup into one of the vats and took a slight swig of the ready made moonshine. The expression on his face told Jeb all he needed to know, "Nearly two-hundred proof."

"More like a thousand proof," Connor coughed, the cooler evening air stinging his face and throat as he pulled in a single breath reminding him of the similar effect peppermint often rendered.

"Tastes like fire ants," Nathan Caldwell, the cooper, announced as he climbed the hill to Connors' right. "Silk and fire ants," Connor corrected, "Where's our barrels?" "Where's my moonshine?" Nathan retorted with a smile. Jeb was familiar with how Connor was towards Nathan. He often treated him like a little brother. The two shook hands and Connor offered him the tin cup, "Grab you a few jars. I have to go talk to Zane."

"What you goin' have him do?" Jeb inquired. "Never you mind Jeb," Connor patted the aging rum maker on his shoulder with the sneakiest of grins forming across his lips.

Connor took out a cigarette, lit it, and handed it to Matthew Jones, "Hold this." Matthew arched his blonde eyebrows skyward, "What for?"

"You'll see." Connor motioned for both men to follow him towards the Chevy Coupe Darrell had modified and repainted. Popping the trunk Connor reached in and pulled out a cylinder tube in a dusty yellow colored wrapping.

Zane instinctively took a step back from the car, his countenance the only communication needed in that moment. "What for the love of—?" Matthew started but stopped as he realized he was still holding the burning cigarette and knocked some of the ash to the ground.

"You two listen to me," Connor leaned on the open hood while flipping the stick of dynamite in his hands as if it were a baton. "We're listenin'," Zane assured his friend, albeit his eyes not lingering far from the stick of dynamite.

"You're goin' to use this when you visit Walker."

"How? To blow up the store?" Zane inquired, his tone one of disbelief. Connors crooked grin made Zane's skin crawl, "Not yet.

Think of it as a motivational tool." Connor tossed the stick to Zane who reached out and caught it before it could hit the ground.

"It's not glycerin Zane," Matthew muttered, "It can't go off unless it's lit."

"Speakin' of," Connor motioned for Matthew to hand him back his cigarette that was by then nearly halfway burnt.

From the still Jeb witnessed the tossing of the stick to Zane, his heart catching momentarily in his throat as he realized the damage that could be done but also the undoing of them all if it were in fact used.

"Someone's up to no good," Nathan whispered, having also witnessed the discussion below. Jeb agreed knowing full well the measure of wrath Connor Ridge may be willing to unleash when it came to his plans, his still runners, and their livelihoods.

CHAPTER 13

Irwin had picked up Bureau of Investigations agent Frank Lincoln and Lieutenant Holden Rash at the courthouse before heading out to see Sheriff Hayes.

Having arrived in front of the police department, Agent Lincoln glanced back at Holden over his left shoulder, "How well do you two know the Sheriff?"

"Not well to be honest, I can't speak for Walt but…"

Irwin adjusted his glasses, "River Hayes has been in law enforcement for quite a while. He is well known and respected." Lincoln heard the pause in Irwin's tone, "Why do I hear a '*but*' coming?"

"Between us," Irwin added, "It has been said that some law enforcement members here are friendly with the moonshiners."

"As in paid off," Lincoln said rather than asking to which Irwin remained silent on the matter, a sign Holden knew to be an answer all its own. "I suppose my next question is deputy; do you suspect him of being on the payroll?"

"No," Irwin shook his head, "And if he were it would be a surprise to me." "How so?" Lincoln asked, sensing there was more to the deputy's profile of the Yadkin County Sheriff.

"I was told years ago by former Sheriff McMillan that River Hayes was ten years old when his father was shot in a drunken brawl one night in Wilkes County. No one was ever held responsible though."

"Why not?" Holden inquired from the backseat.

"Because no one came forward as a witness," Irwin answered simply. Without further inquiry Frank Lincoln put on his hat and opened his car door, "Then let's get started."

Holden climbed out of the backseat of the patrol car and followed both men up the steps to the entrance of the Yadkin County Police department.

Standing in the foyer of the police station the thick heavy scent of cigarettes and coffee clung to the air. Behind a small wooden desk sat a petite woman in her mid-thirties, "Afternoon, may I help you?"

"Sheriff Hayes," Lincoln flashed his badge.

"You must be the BOI agent that called him yesterday," The woman rose to her feet and politely excused herself as she disappeared into the hallway. "Sheriff, agent Lincoln is here to see you." Pausing briefly she then placed the phone back on its cradle, "He'll be right with you, if you would, please have a seat." She motioned to the bench against the far wall, but not even a moment later two deputies burst through the entrance hanging onto what appeared to be an unconscious man.

"Heavens," the secretary gasped, "What happened to him?" "A casualty of a fight downtown Mildred," one of the men replied, "Call the doc. Are there any cells open?"

"Cells two and four," Mildred replied, shaking her head in astonishment. Lincoln watched as the deputies turned the corner to the holding cells. "Must have been some punch," Holden was sitting with his legs stretched out and his feet crossed.

Irwin noted the time on his pocket watch and removed his own hat but remained standing as he watched the woman place another call to the local doctor.

Five minutes later Sheriff River Hayes was standing before them, "Gentlemen." "Sheriff Hayes," Lincoln introduced himself, followed by Irwin and Rash.

"Apologies if I was a bit blunt when you phoned Mr. Lincoln yesterday," Hayes apologized in his gravelly voice. "Well you did warn me that you had your hands full." Lincoln replied. Smirking River Hayes nodded, "You got that right. Arrested a guy for drunken disorderly that morning, he was heaving his guts out by the time you called. Just lucky he didn't get any on my shoes. What's this all about anyway?"

Irwin cleared his throat, "We have reason to believe that there is a man who has managed to find his way into our counties via vehicle theft, robbery, and possibly worse."

River Hayes eyed Irwin questioningly, "And by worse I am going to assume you mean rum runnin'?"

Lincoln acquiesced, "Afraid so."

Sheriff Hayes placed his hands on his gun belt, "Well, let's go have lunch and see if I can't help you boys make an arrest." Lincoln was first to follow Hayes with Irwin hanging back near Holden for a moment.

"What?" Holden noted Irwin's expression.

"Remember that dynamite I mentioned?"

Rash frowned, "Tell me it wasn't a lot of dynamite."

"At least a hundred pounds," Irwin kept his voice low as they proceeded out the door.

Holden Rash stopped walking, "Are you sure?"

"Yes, and the same description of the individual was given by the manager at the construction company as the one provided by Mr. Wagoner from his report earlier this year."

Rash kept walking, "Then we're definitely getting closer."

"And that means this person, or people involved could be looking to hurt someone," Irwin cautioned, "Namely law enforcement. What if they were to use that dynamite on us?" Holden stopped walking again, "Then we need to make sure that doesn't happen."

Sam Walker held the store door open for Mrs. Cornett, a local seamstress, as she carried a single bag of groceries out to her vehicle. Opening the passenger door for her he watched as she sat down the bag of dry goods.

Once satisfied with their placement she proceeded to the driver side, "Have a good evening Sam, thanks again," She smiled. Sam waved as she pulled off, waiting a few moments before heading back inside to begin his evening routine.

It had been a few hours since he had stepped outside in the warmth of the sun. A cool wind washed over the mountain side as he lifted his eyes upwards. There was not a single cloud in the sky, yet Sam felt a heaviness he was unable to place. The feeling lingered a moment more before he turned to head back to close up for the day.

First he would wipe down the counters, organize the cans on the shelves customers had browsed, and then finally he would sweep the floors.

While he was close to the storage room he stepped inside taking hold of the broom and dustpan bringing both out into the store.

Walking over to the counter he made sure the broom was propped up before hearing a few vehicles pulling into the lot.

A quick glance at the clock near the cash register informed him he could spare some last minute customers the trouble of driving into town.

The screen door gave its usual greeting, a slight squeak among its hinges, signaling to Sam someone had entered. "Evenin'—," He started to greet in his usual customary tone before crumpling to the floor. The store owner did not get the chance to say anything else.

Zane Shepherd held firmly to the end of his Winchester rifle. The weapon was good for injuring, but Zane had found it more useful to render people unconscious.

Erick Whitaker and Tommy Dalton stared down at the incoherent store owner. "Get him in a chair, tie him up, and put him in the stock room." Zane ordered for Tommy to look. The young man moved faster than Erick and proceeded to remove the rope he had been instructed to bring from his back pocket.

"I don't suppose I need to tell you how this will go over if he ends up dead?" Erick asked as he removed the toothpick he had been chewing on since the drive over.

"Do as you're told," Zane replied, "Just help Tommy get him in that chair." Tommy finished tying Sam up and together with Erick they placed him in the chair carrying him into the store room. Erick watched as Zane closed the store's main door, locked it, and drew down the shades to indicate it was closed.

"Zane?" Tommy called out from the storage room.

"What is it?"

"You've gotta see this..." Tommy's disbelief could be heard in his words as the last one trailed off.

"Well I'll be..." Erick said as he peered into the stockroom where Tommy was standing just behind Sam, "Is that what I think it is?"

"Looks like it to me," Tommy grinned, "What about you Zane?" Connors' right hand man and friend folded his arms, leaned on the doorway, and smirked, "I say we're in business."

"Come on," Tommy said to Erick, "Help me move this..."

"Move it where?" Erick asked, trying not to laugh, "Best we can do is hope Zane can bust into it."

"I can't bust into that here," Zane exclaimed.

"What about—," Erick started.

"How heavy could it be?" Tommy interrupted, "Take two of us at least, that's it. We have the truck..."

"That's right, we have the truck, not a coupe or a roadster Tommy. Use your head for somethin' besides a hat rack boy," Erick said, shaking his head.

"How much do you think is in there?" Zane questioned looking at his partners. Tommy scratched his head, "Solid twenty, maybe a little more."

"Know they come 'round every Monday and unload it..." Erick answered, pausing as he realized what day it was. "That's a good four days worth of cash sittin' in that machine," Tommy's grin widened into a smile.

"Connor would..." Erick let the words speak for themselves.

"He would take it," Tommy replied, "Or find a way."

"All right," Zane relented, "But we have to be quick and we have to be prepared. We get caught—it's over."

"Got it," Tommy said, "Come on Erick, I'll get this side." The two men lifted the slot machine gradually off the table when Zane got the idea to toss the white covering cloth over it.

Peering out from behind the closed blinds of the store Zane made sure no cars were coming or going from the nearby hotel or up the mountain into Sparta.

When he felt confident enough to move Zane opened the door and motioned for the two to follow, "Come on." Walking slightly ahead of them he then opened the door to the passenger seat of the truck.

As they gave him puzzled stares, Zane explained "It's the only way to hide it from the open until we're finished here." "All right," Erick acknowledged. It took a good five minutes to get the machine into position on the seat, and covered well enough so passers by would believe it to be something other than what it truly was.

Tommy made it back inside the store first, then Erick as Zane heard a car coming from the mountain and ducked back inside just as it drove past. Letting out a long breath Zane turned his attention back to the stockroom. "Get your masks on," He ordered, "And let's wake up sleepin' beauty."

"There's only a few people around here that can work on cars like that, or with that much expertise," Sheriff River Hayes explained, picking up his tuna sandwich with his left hand, "Darrell Joines is one of 'em."

Irwin held onto his warm coffee mug with both hands as he half-listened and half-worried over what he and Mrs. Gambill had learned the day before.

"Darrell is the go-to guy around here for vehicles, even telling Roger over at the Chevy dealership that he is hoping to build a new garage." Irwin glanced at Lincoln, apparently both thinking the same thing.

"You have an address?" Lincoln questioned as he pulled out a pen and pad from his inside jacket pocket. Hayes swallowed, "Sure do, down on River Lane. It's a good five or six miles out from town."

"You like him for these car thefts?" Hayes questioned looking at Irwin. "Maybe for helpin' to scrap the cars," Irwin admitted, "Not sure what we're dealing with until we have a run at him."

"Shame," Holden spoke up as he stabbed the piece of pie he ordered with his fork, "Looks like a man with those skills could get by repairin' cars, especially 'round here."

"Lots of folks here, like up in Irwin's county," Hayes motioned upward with a nod of his head, "fell on hard times with their crops. Corn ain't worth much, and tobacco ain't much better. Folks do what they can to survive," taking a sip of his coffee he paused then added, "be it lawful or otherwise."

Switching gears Agent Lincoln spoke, "Deputy Irwin here tells me you are a loyal lawman Sheriff Hayes." Lincoln hoped Irwin was right in his assumptions as far as Hayes' character. Glancing over at Irwin, Hayes asked, "Does he?"

"It's no secret that some lawmen around here take bribes from bootleggers," Holden informed. Sheriff Hayes' steely expression drilled across the table into the Lieutenant.

"You think I would risk my career in the department for a few extra dollars Lieutenant Rash?"

Holden shrugged, "I don't know. Would you?"

Hayes scoffed, "No, and neither would the men who work for my department. First I catch wind of it, they're out."

"Good to know," Lincoln said, "We meant no offense. We're all on the same team here. We just have to be sure things are kept between department heads and a few select men. Think you can manage that Sheriff Hayes?"

Hayes took another bite of his sandwich and after a few seconds agreed, "I think I can help you with that."

Exiting the diner they thanked Sheriff Hayes for his time, and lunch, all three men walked back to the patrol car and climbed inside.

Irwin turned on the car as he noticed Lincoln in the passenger's seat focused on the courthouse. "Tell me you were thinkin' what I was thinkin' back there," Irwin said. The Federal agent locked eyes with Irwin, "I'm up for it if you are."

"Up for what?" Holden asked clearly, having missed out on something. "We're going to pay Darrell Joines a visit," Irwin informed, "Except he isn't going to know we're law enforcement."

Holden smiled as he caught on, "And which one of us is going to pay him this visit?" "I nominate Irwin," Lincoln said, "You're not local, Darrell wouldn't recognize you for sure." Irwin shook his head, "He wouldn't recognize you either, or Holden to be fair."

"One look at how I walk, talk, and dress and Joines will know I'm not a Southern boy," Lincoln explained, "Holden here is clearly a cop from head to toe."

"He has a point," Holden rubbed his head and leaned back, his eyes darting between the two lawmen in the front seat.

"What do you say, Deputy?" Lincoln questioned.

"Where do we get a car?" Irwin replied.

"Nearest car lot," Lincoln motioned down the street at a Ford sign.

Holden cleared his throat, "Do you even know which parts you would be looking for in order for us to consider making an arrest?"

"I memorized a brief list that Lewis and Whitman gave me when they arrived," Irwin explained, "If we can find one of those parts, we'll have probable cause to search the garage," After a second Lincoln added confidently, "Maybe we'll even have our car thief too."

Sam Walker slowly opened his eyes. The pounding in his head was so loud he thought his eardrums might burst. As powerful as the light was, he forced himself to focus on the silhouettes of the two figures looming in the doorway of the storage room.

The last thing Sam could recall was reaching for the broom propped against the store counter. He had been anxious to clear away the dust and gravel tracked in by customers and lock up for the evening. That was before he completely blacked out.

"You alright there Sam," One of the figures approached, his blurry outline slowly coming into focus, "You bumped your head pretty good." Sam tried to raise his arms and failed. His hands had been strapped down on one of the wooden chairs he was sitting in.

"What do you want?" Sam finally managed despite feeling as if his mouth was full of cotton. "You see this?" The man held up what at first appeared to be a stick.

Sam squinted reading the lettering embossed in black down the seam of the tightly wrapped yellowish cylinder. It took only a second for him to realize what this man was holding.

"We need to have an understandin' here Sam," The figure, who was still out of focus replied. "You keep your mouth shut 'round that reporter lady, or we're gonna have a very explosive problem."

A jolt of panic raked through Sam as he sat strapped to that chair, his head aching, and his vision compromised.

"Do we have an understandin' Sam?" The assailant twirled the stick in his hand as he patiently waited for the store owner to find his tongue.

Sam pushed through his fear offering a quick nod. When he did not speak the man crouched down in front of the chair, "I can't hear you." Sam noticed the sheer height of the man before him and his distinctive gray colored eyes. "Yes," Sam managed without looking away.

"Good, in exchange I think we can work somethin' out, don't you?" The man stood straight up, his partner kept his face towards the lot outside, watching for any potential customers or hotel guests wanting to stumble in.

"Now, I need you to be straight with me, think you can do that?"

"Who are you?" Sam asked curiously, finding the man slightly familiar.

"Don't worry bout who I am, worry more bout what I can do to you," the assailants gray eyes glanced around the room "And your business if you don't cooperate."

Taking a deep breath Sam fell silent as his captor asked another pointed question, "The reporter, *who* is she talkin' to?"

"Talkin' to?" Sam repeated, confused.

"Is she talkin' to the cops?" The captor inquired.

"I don't know—I wouldn't think—," Sam heard a loud snap that moved him to silence.

The stranger looming near him had popped the stick of dynamite hard against the door frame, "Wrong answer! Who is she talkin' Sam?"

"No one—I don't know—!" Tilting his head, the man Sam likened to the weapon he was holding, dynamite, adjusting his jacket, looking at the other men in the room.

"What do you think? Think he's a lyin'?" The man looked Sam over from his spot near the door and shrugged, "Maybe, maybe not."

"Wanna take a go?" Dynamite inquired of his partners.

Sam shuttered to imagine what that meant so he started talking, "Look all I know she's the editor of the paper. She's a nice lady, just doin' her job. Please, I don't know that she's talkin' to anyone about anythin'—."

Grinning Dynamite wielded the stick of the explosive towards Sam Walker's nose, "You're going to find out for us. Understood?"

"Understood," Sam answered, feeling the word catch in his throat as the realization of what could happen finally sank in.

"In exchange you can keep your nice little life, but we're takin' that slot machine and if you make one wrong move me and the boys here will have a good time watchin' everythin' you own burn to the ground. Clear?"

"Crystal," Sam managed his heart racing almost as fast as his mind. The man to his left pulled out a long bladed knife which caused Sam to jerk to his right.

"Hold still," The man ordered.

Sam clenched his jaws together so tight his back teeth ached before he realized the man was cutting his left hand free of the ropes. "Have a good evenin' Sam," He muttered as they all walked away leaving him in the stockroom still halfway tied to the chair.

The dealership had been more than obliging with agent Lincoln. Irwin had traded his uniform for a regular set of clothes purchased at a nearby store while the vehicle was being prepared across the street at the dealership. He hoped that his black patrolman's shoes would not give him away to the unsuspecting mechanic they were about to visit.

Having insured the borrowed vehicle through the Federal Bureau of Investigations Irwin found himself seated behind the wheel of the brand new Lincoln Model K heading towards River Lane and the home of Darrell Joines.

Halfway to the address of Darrell's garage provided by Sheriff Hayes, Irwin pulled over and pretended to be looking at his tires. Kneeling, he spent a few seconds checking each one until reaching the passenger's side to throw a few tacks on the pavement.

Climbing back into the vehicle Irwin started the car and proceeded over the tacks hoping one of them, maybe two, stuck. Lincoln had assured him that if any damage was incurred the Bureau would cover it.

The sign at the driveway alerted passersby that there was indeed a garage for vehicle repairs. Irwin felt the car becoming sluggish in its movements, thankful the tacks had done their job. Turning down the driveway Irwin descended, seeing a house to the right with a newly built back porch and a very old, very small garage off to his left.

A man wearing a set of faded blue coveralls carrying a rather rusted part from a car emerged with a cigarette hanging from the corner of his mouth. Irwin estimated him to be no older than thirty, maybe in his late twenties, with sandy blonde hair and a face worn by a hard life, or just as easily from drinking plenty of hard liquor.

Opening his door Irwin got out with both feet planted firmly on the worn dirt driveway, "Afternoon." The man put the part down and pulled the cigarette from his mouth, "Can I help you?" "Maybe," Irwin tapped the hood of his car, "I stopped up the road a few minutes ago. I've been havin' trouble drivin'. I think the tire is low, but don't know which one."

Grunting, the man walked all around the car slowly, eyeing each wheel and then knelt at the one on the passenger's side, "Yep, you're gonna have a flat alright."

"Well what seems to be the cause?" Irwin asked approaching, watching as Joines felt the wheel all the way round, "Not sure, but you're leaking air." Rising to his feet, Joines informed, "Repair will be a dollar."

As though it were nothing, Irwin shrugged, "Just as long as I get back on the road."

"Wait here," Joines went back inside the garage to no doubt retrieve the tools of the trade needed to repair the flat tire.

When he resurfaced he was carrying a jack and a pump along with some other instruments Irwin was not familiar with. "Never seen you 'round here before," Darrell commented as he jacked the front of the car up, "Where you from?"

"Asheville," Irwin lied albeit convincingly.

"Explains the car," Darrell said as he worked to free the wheel.

"How so?" Irwin replied.

"This a Lincoln K model right? V-12 engine?"

"That's right," Irwin acknowledged.

"Fast car, I'm guessin' you travel for work?"

"I do," Irwin lied again.

"Ever race?" Darrell inquired. "No money in that if you lose, am I right?" Irwin chuckled, trying to be as friendly as possible. "Keep tellin' guys round here the same thing," Darrell agreed laughing. Irwin was struck by how skilled the mechanic was removing the wheel in under a minute and locating the source of the leak quickly.

"There it is, looks like a piece of glass got in your wheel," Darrell held up the short but very sharp piece of coppery glass, its color heightened partially by the late afternoon sunlight.

"Huh," Irwin took the piece from Darrell, noting it must have come from a jar. The tracks had not worked, but by divine intervention it seemed he still ended up at the garage, or maybe it was simpler than that.

Irwin knew that sometimes people like Joines would place things in the roadway a few miles back to drum up business. He also realized that the simplest answer was always often the correct one.

"At least you found it."

"Gotta be careful on back roads," Darrell cautioned as he worked effortlessly patching up the tire before securing it back into place.

While he did this Irwin strolled a bit through the lot, taking stock of the yard and some of the parts. His memory was suddenly jarred with the realization that there was one part standing out above the rest.

The fender of what appeared to be a Master Chevy Coupe. Irwin might have shrugged it off if it had not been for the shine on the fender, sitting there gleaming in the sun. Holding his breath Irwin recalled the description of the coupe stolen from Judge Carico's home back in January from Holden's report. Moreover there was another car in the garage, one that appeared to be undergoing serious remodel to its backseat. All seats were out and the hood was wide open suggesting engine modifications too.

"All right sir," Darrell announced as he cleaned his hands on a rag from his back pocket, "As I said, that'll be a dollar." Irwin took out his wallet, acting as if nothing had happened, and handed Joines his fee, "Thank you."

"No problem tell your friends Darrell Joines is the best there is on vehicles round here." Irwin fought the urge to tell Joines he might be good on cars, but not at hiding his crimes that could land him in cuffs.

"Will do, have a good afternoon." As he slowly backed out of the lot Irwin watched as Joines went back into his garage. After reaching the main road the deputy knew that what he had just discovered would connect the dots to the case they had all been working on for so long.

Lieutenant Holden Rash adjusted his gun holster as the Lincoln Model K finally appeared on the dusty road. Breathing a sigh of relief Rash looked over at Lincoln who had taken a position near the front of the patrol car and was smoking a cigarette.

Irwin pulled over a few feet from the patrol car and climbed out. Holden noticed his friend appeared as though he had just struck gold. "Gentlemen, I believe we can say without much doubt that Darrell Joines is in fact doing as Mr. Lewis suspects."

"What'd you see?" Holden asked.

"There is a new fender laid up just outside Mr. Joines' shop. It isn't rusted, yet, and if memory serves it comes right off a Master Chevy Coupe." Surprised Holden asked, "Are you sure?" Irwin answered confidently, "Yes. But that's not all." Lincoln let his cigarette hang at his side in his right hand, "Do tell."

"He's modifying a car in his garage now, looks like the backseats are out and the engine is being worked on." Holden ran a hand through his hair, "He's the one soupin' them up, makin' them faster." "He sure knew all about the Lincoln Model K right off, asked if I ever raced."

Lincoln frowned, "Did the tacks work or did you have to improvise?"

"No, they didn't work, but a piece of broken glass still cut the tire." Holding it up for the two of them to see Lincoln examined it closely.

"My guess is Joines throws fragments of bottles up on the nearby road to get business. However, it suited me just fine because I got a closer look."

Holden let out a low whistle, "We'd better call Lewis and get back to Alleghany. We've got a lot of work to do between now and tomorrow morning." Neither Lincoln nor Irwin argued. "Dealership first, then we call Lewis," Lincoln instructed, sliding back behind the wheel of the patrol car giving Irwin the right of way back into the road.

CHAPTER 14

Mrs. Gambill had written about the stolen dynamite but shortly after finishing the article, she had decided against turning the column in for publication.

Earlier, while taking lunch, she learned Irwin would be in much later having overheard Deputy DeBord speaking with Henson outside the Clerk's Office.

It was a little after four in the afternoon now, and Jenny had already gone for the day. The paper was all but put to bed.

The rest of the copy editing would have to be completed tomorrow before the deadline.

Removing her jacket from the nearby hanger Mrs. Gambill picked up her purse and keys before closing the door, locking it behind her.

On the street she could hear the steady hum of a few cars going by the courthouse before opening the door. Before she could touch it Sheriff Henson pushed it open from behind her. "Oh, Sheriff—," He had clearly startled her, "Thank you."

"You're welcome," Henson said, "Walk you to your vehicle Mrs. Gambill, or is Robert comin' to pick you up?"

"No, I'm drivin'," She said, "Although, it took me some gettin' used to."

Henson proceeded to follow her across the street in front of lights of the Spartan Theater., "Don't see many women drivin' cars to be honest."

"Robert showed me," Mrs. Gambill explained, "or as he would say *he hung in there*." Henson laughed softly, "That sounds like Rob. Be safe gettin' home."

"Thank you, I will," Mrs. Gambill got into the driver's seat and closed the door. She watched the Sheriff go back up the courthouse steps wondering silently to herself, *does he know his deputy has been talking to the paper?*

After a few minutes she decided to push the thought from her mind. It was time to go home, but first she had to make a stop at Twin Oaks Store.

Minutes later she was standing in the lot watching as a couple of other women came out carrying some grocery items.

Sam Walker had been kind enough to hold the door for them and was still standing in the doorway when Mrs. Gambill reached it. "Afternoon Sam," She greeted, "I need a loaf of bread if you have any." "We have a few more loafs," He stepped aside, allowing her entry.

The store smelled of gum and candle wax as she glided through to the shelves holding loaves of bread. "New supply of candy?" Mrs. Gambill asked curiously, eyeing the counter. "Tootsie Roll Pops," Sam answered, his tone seeming somehow different.

Mrs. Gambill picked up the loaf of bread from the middle shelf before heading to pay for it. "I'll take one of those new pops too, nothing like trying something new." "That'll be once cent," Sam rang her up and placed the items in a small paper bag.

"Sam, is everything all right?" Mrs. Gambill asked before turning to leave.

"Everything is just fine Mrs. Gambill," Sam's eyes betrayed his words. She had been asking questions long enough to know who might be hiding a story, "I'm sorry Sam, forgive me," She said in a concerned tone, "But I don't believe you're being honest with me."

"Mrs. Gambill, it's best you go home before it gets too dark." "What's the matter?" She pressed, having a sinking feeling as she noticed his inability to look squarely at her, "What happened?"

Clenching his jaw Sam placed his hands on the counter in front of him and stared at the door as if he were expecting someone. "I had a couple of visitors the other night, not friendly one's if you catch my meaning." Mrs. Gambill stepped back towards the counter with her full attention on the owner.

"They were askin' 'bout you ma'am—," He continued. "Me?" Mrs. Gambill frowned, "What on Earth for?"

"They know you've been here, and know I told you about the construction site."

Tilting her head to the right Mrs. Gambill lowered her bag onto the counter, "Sam, what did they want exactly?"

"For me to find out who else you may have told," Sam admitted in a low voice. "No one," Mrs. Gambill lied, deciding this was her best course of action.

"They suspect you may've been talkin' to the cops," Sam continued, his eyes occasionally drifting to the door, "Have you?" Shaking her head Mrs. Gambill took hold of her bag again, "The fact these individuals believe hearsay in a small town doesn't astonish me Sam, but they shouldn't. You know law enforcement don't mingle with reporters."

Sam turned his head to the right hearing the clock strike five in the evening. This simple motion made his bruised temple visible to Mrs.

Gambill for the first time since she had walked through the door. "And if you have any more trouble you should call Deputy Irwin, he'll see to it no one comes back to bother you," The newspaper editor informed.

Unable to shake the undesired feeling of the panic Sam must have endured from the visitors he mentioned, Mrs. Gambill proceeded to leave. The store owner walked a few steps behind her, watching as she got into her car safely driving away.

Looking in her rear view mirror periodically on her drive home, it was then Mrs. Gambill realized she would have to tell Irwin.

Erick, Tommy, Zane and Jeb all stood near the stills on Devils Ridge. The mash was almost finished fermenting in one of the larger vats but the smaller ones were filled with fresh moonshine.

Jeb was preparing a Mason jar to sample some of the product that had already been run through the barrels. "That'll burn you quicker than the sun Jeb," Erick stated, careful never to drink straight moonshine right out of the pipe.

"Did that once and couldn't taste anything for a week," he warned as Zane sat in a crouching position examining the slot machine they had taken from Sam Walker's store.

Footsteps gave all four men reason to pause and reach for their weapons. Erick however, drew his aiming it just slightly at the ground. A moment later a low familiar whistle echoed over the ridge making it possible for them to relax. "It's Connor," Zane said as he rose to his feet walking towards the sound. Connor emerged from the shadow of trees, "I didn't expect all of you to be here."

"Change of plans," Zane said as Connor's eyes fell on the slot machine.

"What in the name of—?" Connor looked to Jeb, but the old man had no explanation.

"Hear me out," Erick said as he stepped forward, "It has money in it."

"I'm sure it does," Connor snickered, "How you fixin' on gettin' it out?"

"That's what I'm workin' on," Zane replied.

Shaking his head Connor looked at Tommy, "Which one of them talked you into bringing it with you?"

"Actually Tommy found it," Erick answered.

In disbelief Connor stepped back with his hands firmly on his hips and stared down at his boots, "All right, where was it?"

"At Twin Oaks General Store, in the stockroom," Zane explained.

"And Sam Walker?" Connor questioned knowing full well why he had sent them to Sam's in the first place.

"He's agreed that he'll let us know if he finds out who the newspaper editor has been talkin' to. He got the message loud and clear that we'd come back," Zane stated, "He won't be an issue." "Better not be," Connor warned. Zane took in a deep breath while staring down at the slot machine, "We can use the crowbar, which may or may not work, or..."

Connor interrupted, "Or blow it open."

"We'll be heard for miles," Jeb said, "And there is moonshine here—."

"I am aware of the moonshine Jeb," Connor retorted. Tommy cleared his throat, "Gunpowder." "What?" Connor asked. "Pour a little gunpowder in the key hole and light it. It'll blow it open but not with the same force as a stick of dynamite. Right?"

Connor grinned, "Go get some and lets find out. Erick, Zane, take this thing further back, keep it away from the stills. Jeb went back to filling up a mason jar with the finished product, it was still slightly steaming from the pipes but nevertheless test worthy. "How'd it turn out?" Connor inquired as he walked over.

"Let's have a look," Jeb closed the lid on the jar and shook it. Connor kept his eyes on the jar watching as the large bubbles formed and then quickly dissolved, "Hundred proof."

"Hundred proof," Jeb agreed, opening the jar back up to take a quick swig before handing it to Connor. "Probably best I don't," Connor said, "Someone has to supervise this slot machine operation." Jeb chuckled in agreement, his lazy eye rolling.

"All right," Tommy called, "Here we go." Connor motioned for Jeb to stay where he was as he headed up the slight embankment towards the second clearing where they often kept their shovels, axes, and other sparse tools for repairing the still when needed.

Zane lit the gunpowder on the ground watching it snake up to the slot machine before giving a slight puff before only slightly jarring the machine. Tommy cautiously walked over, bent down, and jerked the lock upwards.

"Did it open?" Erick asked, watching Zane as he stepped in to help Tommy.

With a good firm yank Zane broke the door open, "See," He said looking up at Tommy, "A little elbow grease goes a long way." Tommy rolled his eyes, "How much is in it?"

As he looked inside Zane took out a fist full of nickels, "Enough to buy us all a good meal and then some." Jeb gave an excited holler from behind the still, Connor figured the moonshine was getting to him.

"Count it out, you boys take your cut. I have to head to Darrell's first thing," Connor turned heading for the trail leading off the ridge.

"What for?" Zane asked, following him down the embankment.

"If this works out, you'll see," Connor assured his friend, "Keep an eye on things here and meet me in town tomorrow afternoon." Despite his hesitation Zane spoke up, "Answer me this first?"

"What?" Connor slowed his pace before turning around.

"Does this involve another robbery? If so, I think it's wise we stay out of town for a while..." "It isn't a robbery," Connor said keeping his voice low, "But it's big."

"How big?"

"Big enough to make up for lost time and get the haul movin'." Nodding Zane looked back at the boys listening to them dividing up the slot machine coins, but when he turned back to Connor his friend was already gone.

CHAPTER 15

"You're very quiet this morning," Robert Gambill commented as he watched his wife stare out of their kitchen window towards the driveway.

"Everything all right?"

"Fine," She lied. The evening prior she had a horrible feeling in the pit of her stomach, one that she could not shake no matter what she did.

Maybe it would be that way she thought, *until I tell Irwin about Sam and the incident at Twin Oaks.*

Someone had to know who was behind the threats to Sam. The store owner certainly did not deserve such treatment from anyone, least of all criminals, in her opinion.

"Big day?" Robert pressed, trying to get her to talk. Fearing she might give too much away Mrs. Gambill forced an easy smile, "We print tomorrow if all the articles are finished, which Jenny promises they are."

"Do you want me to meet you for lunch?"

"No, no," Mrs. Gambill said quietly as she took a sip of her coffee while Robert arched his right eyebrow suspiciously.

"Do you have an interview?"

"Mmm hmm."

"Mind if I ask with whom?"

"I've been sworn to secrecy, but I promise to tell you all about it if it becomes news." She reassured him.

"This isn't about that dynamite is it?"

"Robert," She said his name with a hint of playful annoyance in her tone and a sign it best for him to relent, at least for the moment.

The old pickup wound its way down the familiar dirt path into the lot behind Darrell Joines' garage. Staring out of the driver side window he could make out Darrell's figure moving back and forth through a small slit in the door that was partially open.

Stepping onto the gravel Connor closed the vehicle door and walked at a leisurely pace towards the garage.

When he reached the door, he opened it wide enough to gain Darrell's attention. "About time you came round," Darrell took a drag on the cigarette he was holding in his left hand, "Harold's comin' by later to take names for the race, needs the money if you're in."

Reaching into his blue jeans Connor took out a roll of money and tossed it towards his friend. The action of catching the cash caused Darrell to lose his cigarette, having to crush it under his left boot, "How much is this?"

"You'll have to count it to find out, but I reckon," Connor took out his own cigarette, "it's enough to get us in."

Darrell cursed under his breath, "You must've carjacked a gold mine?"

"More like part of a slot machine," Connor commented."

Darrell began to count the money, it came to a clear fifty dollars, "That's the buy in all right. What's this bout a slot machine?"

"Some nonsense the boys got into over at Sam Walkers." Darrell knew all about the issue with the newspaper, but had been curious as to how Connor planned to play that one.

"Sat Mr. Walker straight, for now," Connor continued as he stepped further inside the garage eyeing the car Darrell was working on.

"This here the car you mentioned on the phone?" The current '31 Model Ford-A was as smooth in appearance as it was on a race track. Darrell had sharpened up the dark red trim applying all new slick black runners.

"This A-bone roadster will get you exactly where you need to go, and she handles like a dream. Gears are as smooth as butter when changin' them."

Connor patted the car's hood, "Where'd you find it?"

"I know a guy," Darrell said keeping his voice low, "He helped me out on this one and I owe him."

"And you what, painted this one hopin' no one would be the wiser?" Connor inquired. "I'm good at improvisin', you said so yourself," Darrell shot back jokingly.

"Suppose you and your friend want a cut of the winnin's?"

"You know I don't care, I get enough from the runs y'all do, but my friend—yeah, like I said he wants to get paid for jackin' this beauty."

Connor folded his arms, "How much do you reckon will tide him over?" "For this, probably a hundred." Without hesitation Connor handed Darrell a hundred dollar bill, "Consider him paid." Darrell's jaw gaped open, "Connor you serious? I can get him down to fifty..." "If you do, take the other half for your troubles," Connor insisted.

Darrell stuffed the money in his overalls before picking up a wrench. "Say," Connor asked, "How much are these boys racing for, did they say?"

"They said four hundred," Darrell replied. Connor smiled like a possum who had just found an entire cooked chicken he could eat all to himself.

"I know I don't have to tell you this, but I will anyway," Darrell added, "Be careful. Don't get cocky. If the cops show up, get outta there as fast as you can."

Connor lit the cigarette he pulled out of his pocket and nodded, "Shouldn't be a problem in the Model A right?"

Darrell chuckled, "Right."

Zane Shepherd paid for his cup of coffee at the counter of Smithey's store then headed out onto Main Street. Before he could take two steps towards his truck, he noticed the stare of his friend and partner who was parked in front of Farmer's Hardware.

Careful of the few cars that were making their way down the main section of road, Zane stepped out to cross the street. After seeing the passenger side door was still locked Zane lightly tapped on the glass of the window with his left index finger.

Inside the cab Connor had a certain expression on his face. It was the expression that said he was about to commence an undertaking, and everyone in his crew had best be behind him.

"Things go well with Darrell?"

"Actually better than I thought," Connor replied.

"So what's going on? You said it isn't a robbery—is it another raid?" The raids often involved stealing from other bootleggers, an endeavor, while lucrative, was way more deadly than running the shine oneself.

"No, not a raid. We have an opportunity," Connor lit a cigarette, holding it between his index and middle finger while gripping the steering wheel with his free hand. Feeling uneasy, Zane shifted in the seat, "All right, I'm listening."

Connor watched as the smoke from the cigarette curled into the air, "It's a race." The words hung between them, simmering like the slow burn of the cigarette.

"A race, as in a stock race? That's why you went to see Darrell?" Zane asked.

"If we play our cards right, we'll win," Connor took another drag, "I did some askin' and found out who the guys we raided were. Unfortunately for them, I also know they're going to be at that race."

Clearing his throat Zane shook his head, "Connor I really don't think—," The protest was drowned out by Connors sharp sideways stare.

"I have a plan," Connor said in his matter-of-fact way, "And it's a good one." Zane relented, allowing his partner to continue. Deep down Shepherd knew whatever, and whoever these men were Connor was about to run them out of business, and probably for good.

"To recoup their losses from the raid we did, they entered the stock race. The buy-in was fifty, and the post is close to four hundred dollars. The race is Friday night in Wilkesboro. I plan to be there. Darrell got us a smooth Ford Model A he is working on, top speed will be well over sixty."

"What do you need from me?" Zane inquired curiously. "Fuel, lots of it." "I know this probably isn't worth mention' Connor but some of those boys over in Virginia have long arms and even higher reaches inside law enforcement. Lots of them have the lawmen bought off."

Nodding his head Connor exhaled a ring of smoke from his lips, "Listen, we're gonna kill two birds with one stone. Before we head to the race, we're droppin' off our latest haul to Tanner Mullins. Understood?"

Connor made all of it sound effortless, as he almost always did. Despite this Zane decided to ask, even if it was not in his best interest, "What if you don't win?"

"That isn't an option," Connor gave him a stern look, "It's off to the races Zane, either you're in or you're out. If you're out, say so."

Holding up his hands in mock surrender Zane caved, "All right," Connor could still hear the reluctance in his friends' tone, "I'll talk to Jeb, see if he can come up with the needed fuel. What time is the race?"

"Eight," Connor answered.

"OK, I'll see you Friday at five, should give us enough time to drop the haul and head to the race."

Climbing out of the vehicle, Zane closed the door, worried for the first time in a long time not just about hauling moonshine into Wilkes County, but of the possibility they could both get locked up, or worse—lose their lives.

The hallways of the courthouse were bustling with various individuals. Some were there to pay taxes, some were there for court and others were there looking to speak with the Sheriff. As he made his way towards the Sheriff's office Irwin caught sight of Deputy James DeBord. James, or Jim as he preferred, was thirty-eight and a high school History teacher during the day.

However, while Charlie and Irwin went on patrol, James was more of the Sheriff's right hand man. The deputy made it his mission to ensure all detainees were booked properly, all cases were filed, and the records remained organized for any court hearings, trials, or depositions.

"Deputy Irwin," James approached, holding a piece of paper, "Were you responsible for a Mr. Seth Toliver the other night?" Irwin shook his head, "Not me, I think that was Charlie. You should have the report."

James stared down at the paper in his hand, "I do, but now I'm curious as to why Mr. Toliver is gone from the cells and why Charlie did not sign his release form?"

Irwin knew Charlie to be very thorough, "Leave it with me and I'll talk to Charlie," Irwin offered. "The Clerk's Office never booked a hearing date either. Mr. Toliver was drunk in public, caused a scene, and was brought in on a disorderly charge."

Holding out his hand Irwin waited for James to do the right thing. After a few seconds of self debate DeBord just as he was asked, "I want this cleared up by mornin'." "I'll handle it," Irwin assured him as he walked back towards the meeting room to his files.

Knocking on Henson's door Irwin could hear him shuffling about in the office.

"Sheriff?"

"Come in," Henson announced.

"Good mornin' Sir."

"Mornin'," Henson acknowledged, "How did it go?" He questioned referring to the evening before while motioning for Irwin to close the door.

"We have probable cause to search Darrell Joines' property there. He's the man Sheriff Hayes pointed us to and who we believe may be helpin' these individuals to get away with car theft."

"Well at least that's some good news," Henson admitted, "Although not so good for their victims. What does agent Lincoln think?" "We both feel it's time for a warrant," Irwin said, "And it looks like we will be needin' more man power on this."

"How much more?" Henson questioned.

"I'll defer to agent Lincoln on that matter," Irwin said, "But most likely ten or so."

"I take it Lieutenant Holden is still here too?" Henson questioned. "He's at Four Oaks," Irwin informed, "As is Lincoln, Lewis, and Whitman." "Go see Judge Doughton upstairs, he's in his chambers this morning preparin' for a few hearin's. He'll sign this," Henson put his pen to the paper giving his go ahead on the matter before handing it to his deputy.

Exiting the Sheriff's Office Irwin stepped out into the hallway and headed towards the stairs when he noticed Holden and agent Lincoln standing near the meeting room across the hall with Adam Lewis from and David Whitman from the Underwriters' Bureau. The men were speaking in hushed tones but Irwin surmised they were going back and forth about what needed to be done and who was going to do it.

"Good, you're already here," Lincoln said motioning for Irwin to follow him into the meeting room. Closing the door Irwin saw Caption William Hawks sitting at the table with two cups of coffee in front of him.

"Mornin'," Irwin greeted. Captain Hawks handed him one of the coffee cups, "Mornin' Deputy." without Lewis said without looking up at Irwin or the others.

The nearby telephone rang only once before Holden scooped it up, "It's Hayes," He motioned to Lincoln who took the phone.

Holden left Lincoln with the receiver and settled in across from Lewis, "Have a seat, we'll fill you in." He motioned to Irwin. Taking a sip of the black coffee Irwin did not bother, he knew he would need to leave shortly if he were to catch Doughton in his office.

Standing at the opposite end of the table where Lewis and Whitman were sitting he listened as Holden started talking.

"We have plenty of manpower on this. Where are we on the warrant?" "Need Doughton to sign off," Irwin said, holding up the piece of paper Henson had given him. "We've lined up Whitman, as well as a Sergeant and Corporal from the Raleigh office who will be arriving shortly, to head to Joines'."

"May I ask the names of the Sergeant and Corporal?" Irwin inquired. "Morris and Upchurch." Before he could respond the door opened and Deputy DeBord stuck his head in.

Jim's hand rested on the butt of his weapon, his eyes searching the room until he found Irwin.

"Deputy Irwin, the editor from the newspaper is asking if she can speak with you?" Holden raised his eyebrows in inquisitiveness, an issue Irwin knew he may have to address sooner rather than later.

"Can it wait?" Irwin asked. "She said it's important," DeBord answered. Shrugging, Irwin looked at Lincoln, "I need to get this signed off on so we'll be all set anyway." Lincoln nodded, still holding the phone to his ear, listening to Hayes. From the way he was talking it seemed Hayes had also received approval to go after Darrell Joines and his garage. Irwin stepped away from the table following DeBord into the hallway.

Mrs. Gambill was standing near the stairs holding tight to the end of the iron railing. The look on his face told her he was not pleased with the action she had just taken. However, she had not known any other way to speak with him.

"What can I do for you Mrs. Gambill?" Irwin asked as he watched James DeBord head out the front doors to his car, leaving his shift in the wake of his shadow.

"Actually," Mrs. Gambill answered, careful to keep her voice low, "it's what you can do for Sam Walker down at Twin Oaks. He was threatened." Irwin could tell by the look of concern on her face something much bigger was going on.

"Threatened *how?*"

"I think there was more Sam wasn't telling me but—."

"Like there is more to what you're not saying?" Irwin questioned cutting her off. Mrs. Gambill folded her arms and shook her head, "Someone has to watch out for Sam, after all I got him in trouble." "And how is what happened to Sam your fault exactly?" Irwin asked.

"I told you about the dynamite," She whispered, "Among other details. Now, whoever hurt him told him to find out if I was talking to the police—."

Gazing up the staircase momentarily Irwin realized his fear might very well be a reality. These individuals were dangerous, so much so they had indirectly just threatened the Editor of the *Alleghany Times-News*.

"All right," Irwin exhaled, "I'll give Sam a call later to check up on him. Can Robert pick you up this evening? You should not go home alone," Before she could protest, Irwin raised his hands, "It isn't safe Mrs. Gambill and I am very sure Robert would prefer you ride with him than be harmed along the way."

Mrs. Gambill turned and proceeded up the stairs only taking three or four steps before realizing Irwin was following her, "Where are you going?"

"Don't worry, before this is over, you'll have your front page," Irwin said as he went around her and headed upstairs to the courtroom.

CHAPTER 16

Charlie turned his boy up and threw him over his shoulder. The toddler giggled along with his siblings who were watching their dad. His days off were far and few, but Charlie took pleasure in early morning breakfast and good coffee while his wife prepared to take them off to school.

"All right, say goodbye to daddy!" His wife called as she started to usher them towards the front door. "Bye daddy!" The three of them called out. "Charlie," His wife stared at him, their youngest still dangling from his shoulder.

Smiling Charlie lowered his son to the carpet, "Go on, get to school." "Bye daddy!"

"You're almost as bad as the children," His wife said teasingly as she kissed his cheek just as the telephone rang.

"I got it," Charlie said watching them as they filed into his brother-in-laws car through the screen door.

"Shepherd," Charlie answered.

"It's Walt," Irwin replied, "You busy?"

"Does having a decent cup of coffee count? What's goin' on?" Charlie inquired, "Tell me you're not duckin' out of your shift." "I'm not takin' off," Irwin answered, "I'm callin' to ask you a question." "Ask away," Charlie said, picking up a homemade biscuit and taking a bite.

"Seth Toliver, what happened to him the other night?" Irwin questioned. "Toliver? I don't know, I thought they sat bail and he went home. Why?"

"DeBord said no one had signed his release slip and no hearing was scheduled at the Clerk's Office." Taking a sip of his coffee Charlie swallowed before answering, "That can't be right." "Well I'm starin' at the slip," Irwin replied.

"I'm sure you are, but I didn't let him out."

"Well someone did," Irwin insisted.

"How's that possible?"

Taking in a deep breath the deputy could be heard leaning back in a chair, "I don't know yet."

"You know I'm tellin' the truth," Charlie stated firmly.

"You don't have to convince me."

Deciding it best to change the subject and quill his curiosity, Charlie asked, "By the way, how did Yadkin go yesterday?"

"We have a warrant and we're headin' back tomorrow to raid a garage."

"Need any help?"

"Always," Irwin replied.

"Does that mean I can come along?"

"If you're coming, we leave before dawn."

"I'll be there," Charlie answered without hesitation, "And I'll handle DeBord after."

It had felt like hours since he had taken a single breath. Holding steady to his weapon Deputy Sheriff Walter Irwin cautiously rounded the corner of the garage swiftly taking an inventory of its inhabitants.

Satisfied that no one was in the garage Irwin looked over his shoulder at the two men who had followed him and motioned towards the house.

Quietly Corporal Upchurch and Sergeant Morris climbed the slight embankment approaching the stairs to the newly built back porch of Darrell Joines' residence.

At the front entrance stood Yadkin County Deputy Mitchell Boyd who had been dispatched by Hayes to help execute the search warrant and seizure of any evidence that might help bring a close to the car thefts if not the bootlegging. At the bottom of the steps stood Charlie Shepherd, his own weapon in hand.

Irwin managed a few quick breaths before banging on the backdoor of Joines' home. The force was so quick and so loud that it roused the neighbor's dogs who commenced barking.

"Darrell Joines!" Irwin shouted, "This is the police, open the door!" There was some movement from inside prompting Irwin to raise his weapon. He motioned to Charlie to warn the others in the front with a quick glance to his right. Charlie whistled signaling Sergeant Morris to be on alert.

Once more Irwin slammed his left fist into the wooden trim of the screen door, the force sounding something next to thunder rumbling over the valley the house sat in.

Dogs stirred in the distance barking, howling, and rousing their owners who called for them to be quiet.

"You have five seconds to open this door Joines or I'm coming through with my friends out here. We know you're in there!"

"Hands!" Morris shouted from the front of the house. Irwin looked at Charlie and patted his shoulder, "Stay here." Rounding the side of the home Irwin kept his weapon ready as he caught sight of Darrell Joines wearing his coveralls and carrying a cigarette in his right hand.

"Put out the smoke," Irwin instructed as he kept his weapon square on Joines' right kneecap. Looking at the direction the weapon was pointed, Darrell Joines took a final pull on the cigarette before tossing it to the porch, crushing it under the toe of his boot.

"Might I ask what you fellas are doin' on my property?" "We have a search warrant," Irwin reached for the papers in his back pocket and held them up, "And we're going to search every square inch of this house and your garage Mr. Joines."

"For what?" Darrell scoffed at the thought he could be hiding anything of value. "Oh, I dunno," Irwin answered as he walked up the steps removing his handcuffs from his belt, "Maybe a bumper belonging to a Master Chevy Coupe."

Staring straight at Darrell Joines, Irwin sensed the man was starting to realize the two of them had met before. "You—you're a cop?" Darrell staggered.

David Whitman, who had put his weapon in his holster leaned on the railing at the bottom of the steps, "Take it you two have met?" "Had a flat tire," Irwin explained, "Mr. Joines here fixed me right up." Darrell refused to speak another word.

"Turn around and put your hands behind your back," Irwin instructed. The cuffs went on and Darrell was led slowly back into his house. Once Irwin was satisfied Joines was not going anywhere he proceeded to assist with the hunt for parts linking him to the thefts of several vehicles.

"Irwin!" Sergeant Morris called out from the garage. "What you got?" Irwin asked as he walked down the embankment, Charlie following.

"You were right," David Whitman said as he motioned to a Roadster that was sitting beside a beat-up Model T.

"See this engine?" Whitman said, "It doesn't belong to this car. It never has."

"What car does it belong to?" Charlie questioned curiously.

"Let me venture a guess, it belongs to a Chevy?" Irwin said as he eyed the piece of machinery.

Smiling Whitman nodded, "That's my thinking. We will get it lifted and take a look at the numbers on it to be sure though."

"Deputy," A familiar voice called from just up the driveway causing Irwin and the others to turn their heads. It was Sheriff Hayes.

"Sheriff," Irwin left Morris and Whitman to the rest of their searching while he discussed what they had found since serving the warrant with Hayes.

"I just dropped in to speak with Joines, he's clammed up." "I expected he might," Irwin admitted. "You seem convinced he's involved," Hayes observed, "What have you found?"

"Enough so far. Mr. David Whitman there," Irwin pointed to the Detective, "Is with the Automobile Underwriters Bureau, he's handling the search for parts." "Want to take a run at Joines together?"

Hayes offered, "See if we can figure out who else might be involved?"

"I think we should do exactly that," Irwin replied as he led the way back up to the house.

The Elkin City jail parking lot came into view as the patrol vehicles rolled closer to the entrance one by one. In the passenger seat of Irwin's car was Deputy Boyd.

Darrell Joines occupied the back, sitting just in the line of sight of Irwin's rear view mirror.

The following vehicle transported David Whitman, Corporal Upchurch, and Sergeant Morris. Charlie Shepherd had left after Darrell was hauled into the car in cuffs. Irwin had insisted he head back before dark and start his evening patrol.

"I'll get out, let them know we're here," Boyd got out but paused looking back at Joines. The warning glance informed the mechanic it would not be wise to try anything.

Irwin noted the man's calm demeanor as he stared through the rear view mirror. "What?" Joines took notice, the sound of his voice was slightly strained.

"Why'd you do it?" Irwin asked.

"That's all you want to know. Why'd I do it?" Joines snickered as he watched Boyd talk to an officer beyond his window. "No, it's not," Irwin answered as he looked over his shoulder. A knock-on the driver window interrupted his impromptu discussion with the mechanic.

It was Morris motioning of him to get out. Irwin opened the door and stepped onto the concrete rounding the car with Morris at his side.

"Everything all right?" He asked before Irwin opened Joines' door. Irwin nodded, opened the door, motioning for Joines to exit the patrol car. Moments later the detainee was seated in a small room with two wooden chairs in front of him.

The process had taken all of thirty minutes between paperwork and fingerprinting. Rubbing his eyes Irwin decided to take one final go at Joines. Looking down the hallway he noted Boyd and Walker were talking, probably going over what had been found at the garage thus far.

Opening the door to the room Irwin sat down across from Joines, adjusting his tie. "Don't you have any better place to be?" Joines scoffed.

"Actually, yes," Irwin replied, noting it was nearly four in the afternoon and the drive back to Alleghany was going to take at least another hour. "Well don't let me keep you," Joines replied.

Leaning forward, Irwin placed his hands firmly in front of him interlacing his fingers, "Darrell, I'm going to be straight with you. You are looking at some serious time. At least fifteen years unless you let us help you."

Darrell raised his eyebrows, "You can't help me."

"Oh, but I can," Irwin offered, "I can see to it the Prosecution goes easy if you tell me who you were working with?"

Frowning, Darrell shook his head, "I ain't tellin' you nothin'."

"Darrell, if you don't give us somethin' the next guy that is brought in here in connection with these vehicle thefts just might. Do you know what that means?"

Darrell was silent, his eyes fixed on Irwin as he spoke. "It means they will get the deal I'm offering, and not you. You'll get more time, not less."

"You can't promise me—," Darrell started but stopped.

"Look, I know you have a family. A mother, a father, siblings. They count on you," Hoping that by the mere mention of his family Darrell might offer up some information.

Irwin drove home his point by remarking, "If you were my boy I'd tell you to talk, and to tell the truth."

Closing his eyes Darrell's left leg started to jump up and down rapidly. After a few moments of what appeared to be a copious mental debate Darrell looked towards the door and then back at Irwin, "All right."

Taking out his notepad and pen from his pocket Irwin waited as Darrell seemed to be trying to gather the strength to say the name.

"He's dangerous deputy," Darrell cautioned, his tone conflicted, "My family has to be safe." "Of course," Irwin replied even though he himself was uncertain as to what he may be dealing with.

Having read the papers from New York, Chicago and other major cities in the last few years, Irwin knew good and well that bootleggers often intertwined themselves with some unsavory characters. Most were of the deadly variety.

"Connor," Darrell managed after a few seconds, sweat forming on his forehead, "His name is Connor Ridge. He's from Alleghany." Irwin wrote the name down on a nearby notepad with a quick stroke of his pen.

Irwin slid into the passenger seat of the patrol car with Charlie positioned in the back sitting off to his left, "How'd it go with DeBord?" Charlie shrugged, "I didn't know what to tell him. I didn't let the guy out, not without a court date—."

Irwin straightened his jacket watching for the others to exit the jail's front office.

"Anyone seen Seth since that night?" Irwin asked.

"Beats me," Charlie replied, "Why?"

"Somethin' isn't right Charlie," Irwin stated. "Don't you think I don't know that Walt? Look, who's to say DeBord didn't let him out and wants someone to take the heat? You know he doesn't care for either of us." "He has his moments," Irwin admitted, "But he's solid. James is by the book." "Unless he's *on their* books," Charlie retorted.

The statement caused Irwin to turn his head, "You sure about that assumption?" Charlie shrugged again, "Do you have any better ideas as to how Seth Toliver got out of a county jail cell?"

Before Irwin could respond the driver side door opened and Whitman sat down behind the wheel. A few seconds later UpChurch slid into the back seat with Charlie. "Ready?" Whitman asked. Irwin nodded hoping his friend was wrong, while also fearing Charlie's assumption may be right.

CHAPTER 17

Irwin had remained quiet for much of the drive back to Alleghany with Charlie, Upchurch, and Whitman. Arriving at the courthouse just as the lights were starting to come on inside. After saying goodnight to the men Irwin made it to the entrance and bounded up the stairs.

Passing through the courtroom, the smell of floor polish drifted in the air, Irwin spotted the light on towards the back. Mrs. Gambill could be heard rustling papers, walking from table to table getting the latest issue of the *Times* in order. Knocking on the door frame Irwin glanced at the clock on the far wall, "My apologies."

With her hands full of various printing items Mrs. Gambill turned towards him, "No need, I'm still putting this together." "Are you about finished?" Irwin asked. "Nearly, a few more minutes and it'll be ready for submission. Where have you been?"

"Long story," Irwin answered, "Do you have a ride home this evenin'?" He asked. "I drove in this morning with no issues, and I plan to return the same."

"Mrs. Gambill," The look he gave was one of concern, "Whenever you leave, let me know. I have to check in downstairs."

"It isn't necessary for you to follow me home," She said before he could step back into the hallway. "We've been over this," Irwin replied, "I'll be downstairs." Shaking her head, Mrs. Gambill continued her work.

Once on the main floor Irwin saw Rash standing in the doorway of the Sheriff's Office. Dean could be heard saying something about the Elkin Sheriff's office, but Irwin decided to search for something first.

"Boyd called," Whitman announced as Irwin entered the interview room. He was sitting at the far end of the table, coffee in hand, with papers strewn before him.

When William Hawks had asked if the information would be safe and untouched by other staff, Henson had made it a point to inform the Captain of the State Highway Patrol there was never more than one officer on duty each shift, with the exception of James DeBord.

Irwin proceeded towards the filing cabinets hoping to satisfy his curiosity, "What did he want?"

"He said you talked to Joines after he was processed, without a lawyer." "He never asked for a lawyer," Irwin answered, not bothering to look at Whitman who continued his line of questioning. "I think the question on everyone's mind now is what *did* Joines tell you?"

Unable to find what he was looking for in case files, Irwin ignored Whitman's inquiry, instead heading down the hall to the Clerk of Courts Office where Randy Brewer was preparing to close up, "Randy, let me borrow your phone for a moment?"

The Clerk sighed as if he had little say in the matter, "It's all yours, please lock the doors when you leave."

Lifting the telephone to his ear Irwin listened for the dial tone after the operator clicked off. It took all of a few seconds before Sam Walker picked up, "Walker residence."

"Sam, this is Deputy Irwin at the Sheriff's Office. How are you?"
"Uh—I'm fine sir, what can I do for you?"

"Someone told me you had a good bruise on your head, you all right?"

"Yes—," He stuttered slightly at first, "I'm fine."

"How'd it happen?"

"Oh—clumsy is all. Went to grab the broom and fell. Tripped hitting the countertop."

"Listen Sam," Irwin cleared his throat, "I know what happened." The line went silent.

"I'm sorry those boys thought it was a good idea to threaten you. Can you tell me about them?"

"I don't know—."

"Sam, it's me," Irwin pressed, "I'm going to get these boys, but I need your help."

After a few seconds of silence Sam spoke up, "There were three of 'em. Rough lookin' boys. I don't remember anythin' except wakin' up tied to a chair in my storeroom. When I woke up this guy was holdin' a—." Sam's hesitation was obvious as he struggled to inform the deputy what it is he believed he had seen.

"A stick of dynamite?" Irwin asked.

"How'd you know?" Sam questioned.

"It's my job to know."

Sam cleared his throat, "I didn't call y'all because they said—they threatened—."

"I already know that too," Irwin assured him, "Sam?" The storekeeper remained silent but Irwin knew he was listening, "Did they take anything?" Sam could be heard taking in a sharp breath, "They did." "What did they take?" Irwin asked, uncertain he would like the answer.

"The slot machine," Sam admitted, the frustration clear in his voice. Irwin looked out one of the nearby windows, "They didn't take anything else?" "No, but that alone had a good amount of money in it deputy. I can't replace all that was in there this month..."

"Sam," Irwin kept his voice calm, hoping to ease the store owner's worries, "We'll handle it. They won't threaten you again. You got that?"

"You didn't have to call..." Sam sounded relieved, and at the same time indebted.

"Felt like I should. Do you want to press charges?" Irwin questioned. "If you catch 'em I just might."

"Be careful Sam, and don't hesitate to call us, you hear?"

"I hear you," Sam hung up, ending the call. Irwin waited for the operator, a young woman whose voice was all too familiar.

"Susan?"

"Yes, Deputy?" She asked.

"This conversation is to remain between the three of us, am I clear?" "Yes sir," She answered. "Thank you," Placing the phone on its hook, Irwin headed back into the interview room where Whitman was still sitting with his coffee.

Going back to the cabinets a second time Irwin hoped he had just overlooked the file. After several minutes of being unable to find a name to match the one Joines had provided, Irwin leaned on the cabinets with his arms folded. "So," Whitman asked without looking up from his work, "What did Joines say?"

"I need to talk to Rash before I can get into it." "Well here I am," Rash appeared in the doorway, "Mr. Whitman would you mind giving me and Deputy Irwin a moment?"

Whitman obliged, leaving his papers, but taking his coffee. "Guess Whitman told you Boyd called, said you spoke with Joines, but he isn't saying what he told you. Even Upchurch and Morris said you were quiet during the ride back. What's goin' on?"

"He gave me a name," Irwin handed Rash the notepad he had used to write down the information. "Gotta hand it to him, this is an interesting name." "I came in here to see if we might have a file already, we don't," Irwin took back the notepad and removed his glasses, "We'll have to pull records tomorrow…"

"Any chance the newspaper journalist can help?" Rash asked. It was the tone of his voice that caused Irwin to pause.

"What are you talkin' about?"

"For starters she called you out of the meetin' yesterday. What have you told her?"

"About this? Nothin'."

Rash sat down in a nearby chair as if preparing for a long conversation.

Taking a seat across from Rash, Irwin explained "The dynamite situation I mentioned, Mrs. Gambill was the one who told me about it. She overheard the construction company was robbed while attending an evening church service. Then she came to me yesterday and informed me there was an assault. Someone was threatening."

"Who?" Rash inquired. "A local store owner here, and he was assaulted by people who showed him a stick of dynamite."

Rash's expression shifted from serious to panicked, "So now civilians and businesses are possible targets?"

Irwin took in a slow deep breath, "These guys suspect Mrs. Gambill is feeding us information, which she has. Part of me thinks she is, and the other part tells me this guy isn't someone who goes after women."

"I hope you're right," Rash replied, "I'll see you in the morning, get some rest, and let's see what else we can get out of Joines before somthin' does happen."

Agreeing, Irwin left the interview room to see Whitman holding his coffee and talking quietly with Mrs. Gambill.

"Ready?" Irwin asked. "Ready," Mrs. Gambill shook Whitman's hand politely and bid him a good night.

"See you tomorrow," Irwin said, putting on his coat and following Mrs. Gambill out of the courthouse.

As the door closed behind them the editor spoke, "The other day when we went to Grayson County, I forgot to make mention of something."

"What's that?" Irwin asked.

"Jenny was telling me about a race that is happening in Wilkesboro tomorrow evening. It's well known, or at least it is to some of the young people. They race for money, she said."

"I'll look into tomorrow," Irwin promised as they headed down the steps. Reaching the sidewalk a familiar black Chevy pickup pulled up alongside her car.

Robert Gambill rolled down his window waving at them. Irwin felt a sense of relief knowing she would get home without incident. "Have a good evening Mrs. Gambill, you too Robert," Irwin said walking towards his own vehicle parked near Farmers. Robert exited his truck to talk with his wife, "You too deputy Irwin," Robert called back.

Sheriff Dean Henson listened as the men at the table conveyed all that had taken place in the last twenty-four-hours. "We have a name," Irwin announced.

Bureau of Investigations agent Frank Lincoln sat to Irwin's left, his eyes fixed on the Deputy, "That'right?" "After his arrest, Mr. Joines wanted to ensure the safety of his family and secure a deal."

"What kind of deal?" Lincoln asked. "A lesser sentence in exchange for certain information leading to an arrest of the person or persons behind these crimes."

In all his years as BOI Frank Lincoln had known few to turn on their bosses, those who did usually did not survive. Nevertheless he accepted the terms, "If what Mr. Joines has given you is any good, then I say we work that out. What's the name?"

"Connor Ridge," Irwin answered. Whitman, Lewis, and Lincoln all fell silent. "Sounds like an alias, something you would give someone in Joines' situation to protect yourself." Whitman responded. "Can't be real," Lewis muttered, "These rum runners are notorious for also changin' or usin' false names to dupe law enforcement. We've seen it before."

"It's real," Rash took a piece of paper from the table and slid it towards Lewis. The motor vehicle investigator frowned, surprise in his tone, "I'll be."

"This man, this Connor Ridge, he wants to be known. He isn't hidin' behind an alias," Irwin said looking at Henson, "Darrell was clearly afraid of him and that leads me to believe, he's worth being afraid of." "Why's that?" Henson asked.

Clearing his throat Irwin answered, "Because there is one more thing y'all should know." All eyes fell on Irwin, including Lincoln's.

"In the course of my investigation, it was brought to my attention by an informant that 100 pounds of dynamite was stolen over in Grayson County."

Sheriff Henson leaned forward, "And you suspect it has somethin' to do with all this?"

"Unfortunately I do," Irwin answered, "Shortly after learnin' of the dynamite theft, I was also informed of Samuel Walker's unfortunate run-in with a few boys who appear to be workin' with Ridge. Sam got a clear look at one of the cylinders. They threatened him, and his business."

Frank Lincoln adjusted his cuffs, "Did you speak to anyone where it was stolen?" "Yes, and the foreman wanted it kept quiet so as not to cause a panic." "I should say so," Lewis replied, unable to hide the shock in his voice.

Rash spoke up, "It's time to arrest those responsible for all of this. What's next?"

"Another agent has been assigned to this case as well," Lincoln announced, "I expect him tomorrow."

"I'm going to reach out to a contact I have in Elkin, he left a message saying he might have some information related to the car thefts," Rash informed. "Good," Henson stared at Irwin, "Now that we have a name, let's see how fast we can catch up."

"There is one other matter," Irwin said, stopping everyone before they could even stand up from their chairs. "What's that?" Holden asked.

"We need to reach out to the Wilkesboro Sheriff's Office." "Why?" Henson inquired.

"Because maybe, just maybe, our boys are heading to a race there," Irwin stated. The look on Henson's face turned quizzical, "A race?" "Stock cars," Holden informed, "It's how these boys learn how to modify coupes, trucks, and other vehicles." "And how they learn how to outrun the law," Lincoln added. "Who's the Sheriff in Wilkes?" Lewis asked. "Killsworth," Henson answered, "Sawyer Killsworth."

At forty-eight Sawyer Killsworth had seen a bit of everything, but the bootleggers in his county were about to get the better of his expertise.

From the jail cell hallway Killsworth could hear his deputy Curt Mullis telling the secretary about a recent exploit, "They jacked that car up so far it can go a clear one hundred mile-an-hour," Curt related recalling their most recent bust over in Boomer.

"I think you're exaggeratin' a bit Curt, or pullin' my leg," His secretary Wilma Parlier replied. Wilma was well into her seventies but sharper than most of his men.

"Afraid he isn't," Killsworth replied as he passed her desk heading towards his office, "You boys took it for a test drive didn't you?" Deputy Curt Mullis shrugged, "Have to know what we're up against right Sheriff?"

Killsworth had to admit, if age had not been a factor he would have tested out the coupe too, but as he started to close his office door the telephone on his desk rang.

Forgetting the door he reached down and lifted the receiver to his ear "Sheriff Killsworth."

"Good afternoon Sheriff, I'm deputy Walter Irwin from Alleghany." Killsworth glanced up at the map of North Carolina that hung just left of his desk, "What can I do for you deputy?"

"We received information that there is goin' to be a stock car race in your county this evenin'." "That's not unusual," Killsworth replied, "Just busted one up last weekend, I appreciate the heads up though."

"Wait," Walter said hoping the Wilkes County Sheriff would stay on the line, "We're working with the BOI here—,"

"BOI?" Killsworth cleared his throat, "What's goin' up there?" "The reason I'm callin' Sheriff is because one of the men who we believe is involved in countless car thefts, robberies, and possibly moonshine runnin' may be at that race. His name is Connor Ridge, we arrested his mechanic yesterday in Elkin—."

"I heard about this," Killsworth stopped Irwin, "You raided a garage early yesterday morning and hauled the suspect to the Elkin City Jail right?"

"That's right," Irwin confirmed.

"Any idea where this race might be held, Deputy?"

"I'm sorry, I don't. However," Irwin added, "I wanted to ask if you would coordinate with Sheriff Hayes over in Yadkin?"

Killsworth heard the sense of urgency in Irwin's tone, "What's the description?" Irwin provided the details given to him by Wagoner, the construction manager, and the father of Madison Smith, "Six-one, maybe taller, green eyes, sandy colored hair, approximately one hundred eighty pounds."

"Got it," Killsworth said, turning to see Wilma standing in the doorway of his office. He tore off the paper he had taken the information down on and handed it to her. Wilma took it, read it quickly, and nodded promptly returning to her desk, "Actually deputy, I might just know someone who can help pinpoint where that race may happen. We'll let you boys know if we catch 'em."

"And Sheriff," Irwin caught him before he could hang up.

"Yes?" "He may or may not have dynamite on him so tell your men to be careful." Killsworth acknowledged the advice and placed the receiver on the hanger.

Peering out of his office door Killsworth looked towards his secretary's desk, "Wilma?"

"Yes, Sheriff?"

"Get me Hayes over in Yadkin, we need to talk."

Watching as the mountain road curved before them Connor Ridge pulled out a cigarette, cracked the window less than an inch and lit it. "I got a bad feelin' about this," Zane said trying to break the silence.

"I told you to say out if you wanted out," Connor reminded his partner, "You said you were in, so here we are. Besides," He added, "This will be over before you know it."

"You know that paper mentioned some stolen supplies from Grayson?" Zane inquired, wondering if Connor had done much else other than smoke, drink, and continue to plot ways to run moonshine right under the noses of law enforcement.

Connor would have been upset by the article except the editor had left out the part about the dynamite, which told him his gut had been right all along about Sam Walker. She was feeding news back to the Sheriff's Office from the store owner. Their handling of Walker had kept her quiet, for now.

Holding his cigarette between his index and middle fingers Connor nodded, "Sure did." "We could've gotten caught." "Could've, but didn't." "The rest of the fellas didn't like it, not Jeb and certainly not Darrell."

"Darrell knows to lay low, and Jeb and the boys are handlin' the business on Devils Ridge. The cops don't know who we are so there's no need to be gettin' all worried. After all I paid a king's ransom for those who do know to keep their mouths shut."

"Well they better is all I got to say," Zane replied.

As they reached the bottom of Wilkesboro mountain the two men fell silent again.

Connor finished his cigarette as Zane turned onto an unpaved road as directed following what appeared to be a fork. "Which way?"

"Left," Connor motioned. Moments later, believing that they were possibly led on a wild goose chase for this race, Zane spotted several vehicles parked near an empty field and several people leaning on hoods or the old jagged fence posts nearby.

"See," Connor grinned, "I was right." As he parked the car Zane got out, feeling more at ease having found the place, and threw Connor the keys, "She's all yours."

"Connor Ridge?" A woman's voice called from a few feet away. Connor turned to see Clara Faw, his wife's half-cousin.

"Well Clara aren't you a sight for sore eyes," Connor threw his arm around her shoulders, "Where's Ernie?"

"Gettin' ready to race, are you racing too?"

"You know I am," Connor smirked, "Have mouths to feed."

Rolling her eyes in playful doubt that Connor truly cared about feeding his kids Clara asked, "How is my cousin?"

"She's fine, probably upset with me, but otherwise…"

Clara laughed, "You're a rounder, I tried to warn her." Connor motioned to Zane, "This is my friend Zane Shepherd."

"How do you do," Clara offered her tiny slender hand with her megawatt smile.

In another life Clara Faw could have been a movie star with her bubbly personality. Her auburn colored hair, high cheekbones, and ivory skin often reminded Connor of Katherine Hepburn.

"Let's get started," Someone shouted from near the main gate to the field. "That's my cue," Ridge said, stepping towards the car, "Tell Ernie I said good luck."

"He doesn't need luck," Clara winked, "He's got me."

Connor made the turn, barely skirting the wooden fence that lined the eastern portion of the field. A few cars lagged, one was stuck in the mud and already a half round behind. Connor could feel Ernie's eyes boring a hole through the back of his skull as he rode a little too close for comfort on his bumper.

Zane watched from behind the fences with a cigarette in his mouth leaning on a nearby truck bed. Feeling the rush of gasoline through the engine Connor raced ahead of the only vehicle that stood between a clear victory and a major loss. *Losing*, he thought, *is something other people do.*

Tonight, Connor knew that if he did not meet his objective, there would be consequences and setbacks. Both of which he could not afford, nor would his crew approve.

Making the sharp left turn Connor practically catapulted himself past the red Chevy roadster, its custom paint job awash with mud, without so much as even glancing at his opponent.

The roadster took a swipe to the right causing Connors back tires to fling mud onto its windshield, only further blinding the driver.

Regaining control of his back end Connor straightened his wheel, pushed on the accelerator and switched gears again before seeing a blur of white signaling him to stop.

With his heart pounding so loud he could hear the sound of his own blood rushing through his ears Connor took a second before emerging from the car. Behind him were all the other drivers, their engines idling and some smoking.

"What's your name son?" An older man whom Connor surmised to be in his late seventies asked as he approached from the fences. He had been the one heralding the white flag at the finish, and was still clenched in his left hand.

"Connor Ridge."

"Well Mr. Ridge," The gentleman offered his hand, "You just won yourself $400.00." Connor shook the man's hand and grinned, "No congratulations necessary."

Before the judge could respond there was a flurry of activity from the eastern side of the field. Connor spotted Zane running towards the vehicle waving his hat, "Get in the car! Get in the car now!" Zane shouted as Connor took the $400 from the judges hand and rocketed back inside the car landing square in the driver's seat of the Ford Model-A.

Sirens were blaring just as Connor jumped out of the field and onto the dirt path leading back towards the main road. Despite so many cars swirling around them Connor kept his cool, remaining several steps ahead of the others.

Zane kept himself low in the seat knowing full well that cops in Wilkes did not care to shoot first and ask questions later. "Come on girl," Connor urged the vehicle as he opened all cylinders pushing a brisk 80 mph on a dirt path that abruptly transitioned into the two lane road opposite the farm and jarring Zane in the passenger seat.

Sirens wailed behind him yet the torn up field from the race had seen a few of the patrol cars get bogged down. The two that were still in pursuit by the time Connor hit the gravel two lane were several feet behind them.

Before Connor had the chance to lean into an oncoming curve the back wheels of the Ford Model-A skipped on the pavement, the scent of burning rubber reviving his adrenaline.

"Connor, they're too many of them!" Zane exclaimed, glancing through the side mirror seeing that now four patrol cars were in pursuit, "They're gonna to catch up, we're bout out of gas anyway!"

Laser focused on the road ahead, having driven it many times over the years Connor clenched his jaw and removed his revolver, "It's loaded, just hang onto it!"

"Hang on to—?"

Although he was momentarily concerned, Connor knew he could lose the lawmen, all he needed to do was make the next turn.

Zane was not given the time to worry about what to do with the weapon. Connor turned a sharp left onto a steep gravel road that led straight up onto a hill. The Model-A fishtailed halfway up leaving a cloud of gray dust behind them.

As if by sheer will Connor Ridge did a complete 180 degree turn that swung the car behind several large oak trees and completely out of view of the highway below.

The fading evening light and sitting sun made it difficult for the patrol cars to find anyone who was not burning their lights. Connor had instinctively cut him off and had the brake lights on the Model-A cut prior to the race as a precaution. Darrell had warned against it, but now Connor was glad the mechanic had listened to him.

They waited for a few moments and soon the sirens blared past the road below unaware of the onlookers from on top the embankment.

A few minutes later Connor and Zane watched as the patrol cars returned without having arrested another stock driver. Their sirens a blaring angry reminder of their loss as they retreated back to the field from whence they had come.

Having heard nothing from his partner in several minutes Connor looked over at a very pale, very relieved Zane Shepherd. "Y'all right Zane?"

"I think so," He replied. Connor noted he was still holding tight to the gun grip.

"Can I have my gun back now?"

Zane looked down at the loaded weapon, "Sure. Tell me you still have the cigarettes?"

Connor smirked, "And the $400.00," He confirmed as he removed the money from his pocket handing Zane a few crisp twenty dollar bills. "That's the least you owe me," Zane sat back in the Model-A shaking his head, laughing quietly at the fact that Connor Ridge had once again out ran the law.

CHAPTER 18

Sheriff Killsworth had implored his men to learn as much as they could about the impending stock race that Deputy Irwin had mentioned during their phone conversation.

Having built up a good rapport with a gentleman at a local dealership Mullis had asked quietly about the stock race. Although the salesman himself had no knowledge of the race, he quickly learned of someone who did. That led them to Horton's field just a few miles outside of North Wilkesboro.

Slowly and carefully the deputies had executed their plan to surround the field, taking off the moment the race was over. However, a number of patrol cars found themselves in otherwise less than fortunate circumstances.

The field, muddy from an earlier rain, had been torn up by the vehicles who had raced giving them no traction and causing some of the officers to immediately get stuck.

Unable to go any further the officers watched as a few random coupes disappeared having made their way out of the field and onto a back road, hidden just past a treeline.

Mullis had been in the patrol car that was able to chase one of the remaining coupes. Sadly, the vehicle had managed to disappear from view just around a curve.

The deputy pressed on in pursuit but there was not a single sign of a coupe ever having been on the road.

Now he stood in the middle of the Yadkin County Sheriff's Department with two individuals in his charge. Both had been runners and both had nearly escaped arrest.

A moment later Mullis caught sight of the man he believed to be Sheriff River Hayes who eyed the numerous Wilkes County deputies standing near the door.

"Sheriff Hayes?"

"That's me," River acknowledged, "Y'all a long way from your neck of the woods."

"I'm deputy Curt Mullis," The youngest of the deputies stepped forward offering his hand to which Hayes took hesitantly, "All right."

"These here are two of the individuals from the stock races earlier up in Wilkes County. We chased them across your county line. Sheriff Killsworth said he was workin' with you—."

"Yeah, that's right," Hayes nodded looking at the two individuals sitting on the bench having recognized them right off.

"Stock racin' uh?"

Mullis nodded then Hayes motioned for him and the detainees to follow him "Come on then, let's get 'em settled in. Margie?"

The woman behind the desk turned her head towards the Sheriff, "Call Mrs. Faw's mother, tell her she's here." "Of course Sheriff," Margie lifted the phone slowly to her ear as she watched the men disappear into the hallway leading to the jail.

From his spot in the farthest cell Darrell Joines could hear the two new detainees being brought in and placed in an adjoining cell. Darrell listened as the main doors opened and locked shut from his spot against the cold brick wall.

"Well this is a fine mess you gottin' us into Ernie Faw!" The woman was sharp, her voice like knives to Darrell's ears almost making him feel sorry for the man in the cell adjacent to his own.

"Hush up Clara! They ain't got nothin' to hold us for." Clearly the gentleman did not understand the gravity of the situation, the woman stayed seated on the bench, her arms folded from what Joines could tell as he peeked around the corner of his cell.

"Racin' that's what they're holdin' us for, and it *is* illegal," She fired back.

The man whom Darrell believed to be her husband slammed his fist onto the bars causing them to rattle and vibrate throughout the block. "I said shut up woman!"

"I ain't your *woman*, I'm your *wife*," Clara retorted, "And if you are gonna to be mad at someone, be mad at yourself!" "Excuse me for tryin' to get money. You know work has been lousy, and the bills, the kids—!"

Joines could hear the locks on the main doors starting to turn and watched as Hayes stepped back into the hallway, "Mrs. Faw?" "Yes," The woman's tone was changed, she was much more quiet, even polite sounding. "Your mother is here, and you're free to go."

"Free to go?" She seemed uncertain of the Sheriff's statement.

"Yes ma'am," Hayes opened her cell door and ushered her out of the block.

"What about me?" Ernie shouted.

"I'll be back to talk to you Mr. Faw," Hayes answered. It was a good fifteen minutes before Hayes did resurface from behind the main door.

Ernie was fit to be tied in his cell, his hands hanging out over the bars and Darrell able to hear him talking to himself about how stupid the whole thing had been. That he should have never tried it in the first place.

"All right Mr. Faw," Hayes pulled up one of the iron folding chairs from a nearby wall, "You're gonna to be charged with illegal racin' and evadin' the police, you're lookin' at anywhere between six months to two years in jail."

Faw could be heard letting out a sickening groan, "Come on Sheriff, you know my pa, you know it'll kill him if I end up in jail. I didn't mean anyone any harm, honest, I was just tryin' to feed my family." The statement prompted Hayes to ask, "How much was it?"

The question caught Faw's tongue, and he fell silent. "Come on Ernie, I know you boys ain't out there chasin' your tails for nothin'."

Ernest groaned mostly out of the thought of having lost the reward, "Four hundred dollars."

Hayes let out a low whistle, "Who did win?"

"I don't know," Faw lied. It was clear he was lying and Hayes knew it, as did Darrell who sat quietly in his cell hoping the Sheriff would not make mention of him.

"If you can confirm for us someone was at this race tonight, I might just reconsider lettin' you walk out of here Ernie."

"You mean you'd drop the charges?" Ernie asked, seeming a bit skeptical. "Just this once and only because I haven't ever caught you in any trouble like this before." It was too good an offer to pass up and Darrell knew someone like Ernie would take it.

"Come on Ernie, you got a wife and kids at home. Clara is actually waiting in the parking lot with her mom now. She knows you'll do the right thing."

"She know about this deal?" Ernie asked. "I told her I was going to have a word with you and see what we could do. Now, what do you say?" Ernie must have nodded because Hayes started to talk about Connor Ridge.

"He's my wife's cousin's husband," Ernie said, trying to keep the words from running in together.

"Was he there this evenin'?" Hayes asked.

"Yeah he was there."

"Did he win that money?"

Ernie snickered, "He smoked that coupe I had. Never saw him comin'. Connor's a lot of things but mostly he's just fast."

"What else is he doin' with a car like that?"

"What you mean?" Ernie asked, folding his arms.

"You know what I'm askin'. Is he runnin' stuff through my county?" Ernie was silent, "I don't know nothin' about Connor Ridge's business Sheriff, honest. I hadn't even seen him in months till tonight. Whatever he's doin', ain't none of my business."

Hayes leaned back in the metal chair causing it to squeak. After a long silence it appeared the lawman was satisfied, "What does he look like?"

"Connor?"

"No, the car," Hayes replied sarcastically.

"All right, all right," Ernie raised his his hands running his left hand through his hair, "Connor's six foot one or so, dark hair, green eyes. Clara said they used to tease him about his eyes."

Curious, the Sheriff asked, "How so?"

"They look like they're part fire, part emeralds. The edges of his eyes, they're gold lookin', or reddish in the right light. Always reminded her of a snake she said, like he was waitin' to strike any soul that dared cross him."

River Hayes was on his feet and his keys were rattling, "Ernie I'm gonna need your word that you don't reach out to Connor and tell him about this discussion. If he runs, we'll know who tipped him off and you'll be right back in here with additional charges of aidin' and abidin', understood?"

Raising his right hand as if swearing an oath, Ernie Faw answered, "I won't say nothin' to no one."

Darrell kept out of sight as Hayes walked Faw down the hallway and into the main office area.

With each passing hour he was becoming more and more afraid of what Connor would do once he learned who had betrayed him.

In addition he now feared Ernie's deal would also be laid at his doorstep, and Connor would suspect him of more than just name dropping. However, in order to get himself out of this mess, Darrell knew there would be plenty of risks and he was just going to have to take them one at a time.

It was nearly three in the morning when Connor pulled up the driveway to his home. Climbing out of the vehicle he wondered if the latest batch of moonshine would be ready for their next haul

They had a trip to make and money awaiting them in Richmond. Walking up the wooden porch steps Connor took out his keys but tried the door just in case Lizabeth had been left unlocked.

Sure, enough the screen door gave way with its usual low squeak. Connor realized the door had altered his wife, and the lights came on in the nearby kitchen. Standing there holding his keys as the front door opened he caught sight of Lizabeth whose look was a mixture of relief and worry.

Her dark blue eyes always seemed to stare right through his soul, even so, she was the most beautiful woman he had ever seen and never cared for another.

"Lizabeth," He said, "I know it's late."

"Where have you been Connor? For all I knew they finally caught up with you." Her body language told him he was not coming inside unless he had a good enough reason why she should let him. By all rights, he knew she had every reason to be upset. Lizabeth Richardson Ridge was thirty years old and worked as a seamstress.

Between them they had four small children, all of whom were keenly aware of their father's absence.

"I had a job to do and I did it," Connor said as he reached into his back pocket showing her the bills tied up in a band. "I got back as soon as I could, I never meant to worry you."

His wife stared at the money and twisted her mouth to the right side of her face. "Money will not replace you Connor. I kept thinkin' somethin' had happened—." He placed the bills back in his pocket while moving towards her wrapping her in his arms, "You know I avoid trouble when I can, or out run it. Money may not replace me, but it will replace those shoes you've been wearin'."

Lizabeth looked up at her husband, "How much did you get paid for this *job*?"

Connor shrugged, "A few hundred."

"And will you be leavin' again?" Lizabeth asked, although part of her already knew the answer to this question.

"You know I have to," Connor admitted knowing his wife could smell the difference between the truth and a lie quicker than a bloodhound could find a dead body.

Proof being when she had confronted him in the middle of town over her suspicions of his bootlegging. Thankfully, he had managed to convince her it was for the family, rendering her silent but it had not stopped her from worrying.

"I don't know why I put up with you," She stated a smile forming slowly across her lips. Connor handed her the money and squeezed her hand gently, "Someday it will be more than this, because you deserve more Lizabeth."

She did not let his hand go, instead she held on and refused to let him just walk away.

"Connor Ridge you will not spend a single night at one of your friends' homes. Get in here," She tugged on his hand softly. Connor followed her inside and closed the door, happy that at least for now, for the time being, he would be able to enjoy being home for now.

Della Henson swung her 1930 Chevy into a vacant parking spot just outside of Farmer's Hardware. Her turquoise dress was paired with a matching set of turquoise low heels, a stark contrast to the grayish street.

Towering in the distance was the courthouse. Reaching into the backseat Della took out a bag and headed towards the courthouse steps.

She noted movement in front of a window where the newspaper office was located. She had heard the publication had been taken over by a woman, but had yet to meet her.

A gentleman exiting the courthouse held the door open allowing her to proceed through the foyer where and into the hallway leading to her husband's office.

"Afternoon Mrs. Henson," The young woman smiled as she exited the building. "Afternoon," She called without looking back.

Her husband's office door was open, and she could hear him speaking to someone. Knocking softly she stepped around the corner, "Excuse me, Dean," She smiled warmly, the bag clutched tightly in her hands. "Della, what are you doing here?" Henson stood up and walked around his desk to greet his wife, "Is everything all right?"

"Yes, yes, everything is fine."

"It's two in the afternoon Della, you should be home." He was scolding her like he usually did, but she knew it was only a sign that he cared.

"I left the youngins in good hands for a few moments while I ran this over," She handed him the bag. "I know you've been workin' hard recently, so I brought you lunch."

The man sitting across from her husband was nicely dressed, but not in any uniform.

"Pardon me," Sheriff Henson placed the bag on a nearby cabinet with one hand and motioned to the gentleman who had Della full attention with the other. "Lieutenant Holden Rash, this is my wife, Della Henson. Della, this is Lieutenant Rash with the Highway Patrol."

Della shook Rash's hand, "It is a pleasure to meet you Lieutenant Rash." "You as well ma'am," Rash answered. "What brings you to Alleghany County?"

"A case ma'am," Rash replied. Della gave him a look that stated she knew there was more to the story, "Well I hope my husband and his deputies have been helpful."

"They have," Rash assured her.

"Are you gonna be here long?"

"Maybe a few more days, but we're not certain—"

"Then I must insist you have dinner after church on Sunday with us." Sheriff Henson shook his head, "Now Della he might not be here on—."

"I would love a home cooked meal Mrs. Henson." Rash answered interrupting. "Sunday after church it is."

"Thank you for lunch Della, I'll be home in a little while." "Try not to be too late Dean, the children would like to see you." Nodding Sheriff Henson excused himself and followed his wife, "Let me walk you back to the car." Rash heard him say.

Gathering his jacket and papers Rash went out of the office to find Whitman, Morris, and Upchurch still seated at the table in the interview room going over leads and vehicle information.

Before speaking with the Sheriff, Rash had spoken with a colleague out of Yadkin County, Highway Patrol. Sergeant Wyatt, a well-respected officer and friend of Holden's, wanted to meet and would arrive in Alleghany shortly. Rash also believed that taking Whitman, Morris, and Upchurch would be beneficial.

"You guys ready?" Rash asked. Out of the three Upchurch was the only one who glanced up from his papers, "We'll meet you outside." Rash left the interview room door open and headed out to make a quick phone call.

CHAPTER 19

After having had a long few days, David Whitman, Sergeant Morris and Corporeal Upchurch accompanied by Holden Rash sat in the Four Oaks Hotel lobby.

Wyatt arrived a little after three and had agreed, per Holden's information, to coordinate the search for stolen vehicles and their parts in nearby Yadkin County.

Lodging had been arranged for Wyatt by Sheriff Henson at the Four Oaks Hotel located on Main Street. As Wyatt approached the men at the table he spotted Rash and joked, "Could've stayed at the Graystone."

"If only the state would pay for that luxury," Rash retorted with a smirk.

"Where's the BOI agent staying?" Wyatt inquired as he admired the Four Oaks lobby.

Rash shrugged, "Here at Four Oaks I think." The hotel lobby was a pale robin's egg blue with hardwood floors and white trim around the check-in counter.

"Are you Mr. Wyatt?" The woman at the counter inquired. "I am," Wyatt stepped forward to collect his room key then placed it in his pocket and sat back down with the rest of the men at the nearby lobby table.

"Cigarette?" Wyatt asked, holding a pack of Lucky Strikes. Rash and Upchurch declined, but Whitman and Morris took one. As Wyatt lit the cigarette Rash began explaining the details of the case they were working.

Exhaling the vapor Wyatt cleared his throat, "Well a few things make more sense now. We've been getting those reports of carjackings on the mountain, just couldn't ever catch anyone in the act. If we did, not sure we wouldn't have thought they were one of us."

The sun was slowly starting to fade from the windows they were sitting near. Rash noticed the looks of confusion on the others' faces at Wyatts statement.

"What do you mean you would have thought they were one of us?" Rash asked.

"The way it was reported these boys dress like cops."

"It's on record?" Rash asked.

Nodding Wyatt continued, "Sometime last summer. A couple had their new roadster stolen on the mountain. The husband claimed the man who robbed them was a law enforcement officer, but there was some other guy drivin' an old beat up pickup truck. At which point a few of the boys at Yadkin Pee Dee thought they were jokin'. They told us the uniform was spot on. Hat, shoes, belt, weapon, all of it looked like the standard uniform."

Rash leaned on the table, "We have reports of him dressing as a minister, but also, a couple of young women were pulled over by who they believed to be a cop. Even their vehicle had a siren, but they never saw a badge."

Wyatt frowned, "Really?"

"Really," Rash stated seriously, "But if he has an actual officer's uniform—." Before Wyatt could add anything to the conversation Rash walked out of the hotel heading towards the courthouse. "Where's he goin'?" Wyatt inquired looking at Whitman who replied between puffs on his smoke, "I suppose he's headin' to the courthouse."

Samuel Walker heard the telephone up front ringing as he emerged from the stock room. Weaving his way around some of the stray produce boxes he reached it somewhere between the third and fourth ring.

"Twin Oaks General Store, Walker speaking," He answered.

"Turns out we were right uh Sam?" The voice was not familiar. "I'm sorry, who is this?" Sam questioned. "My boys must've hit you harder than they said," The man's voice was low, but Sam could imagine his lips curling as he spoke. Remaining quiet the store owner looked around as the door opened.

A few women from the nearby hotel wandered in looking at some dry goods that had only arrived that morning.

"I wonder what made her change her mind about printing the *whole* story," The man continued talking, "What did you tell her Sam?" "Nothin'," Sam said as casually as he could.

One of the women glanced in his direction but paid no mind after seeing he was on the phone. "Now Sam, you told her somethin'. What did she tell you?"

"Only that she was sorry for my fall." Laughing softly on the other end the stranger took in a breath that was as sharp and concise as the knives used to cut him free of the binds the evening he was assaulted.

"I have to admit, you did good," The man stated, "You confirmed my suspicions all along, and you got her to keep quiet. Good work." Sam managed to find his voice, "I'm very sorry but I have to go now, customers."

"Remember," The man warned, "You keep quiet and we'll keep away." The line went dead, but in the back of his mind Sam Walker thought about what Irwin had said. Now, it was just a matter of time.

"Irwin?" Rash called from the foyer of the courthouse catching him before he turned into the interview room where Whitman and Lewis had their files. The deputy stopped short of the door and turned, "Did Wyatt arrive?"

"He did, but listen," Rash kept his voice low, "We were over at Four Oaks talkin', and you recall how the gentleman who reported that the carjacker tried to steal his vehicle was dressed like a minister?"

"Yes," Irwin answered, although unsure where Rash was going with the question. "Wyatt said there was a report in Yadkin County from last summer, a couple were carjacked on the mountain, but there was somethin' rather unique about it."

Irwin motioned for Rash to follow him into the Sheriff's Office. Henson looked up from the documents he was going over but said nothing as Walter closed the door. He continued to listen as his deputy and the Lieutenant officer spoke.

"Let me guess our car thief was dressed as a minister, or somethin' of the sort then too, am I right?" Irwin asked.

"Yes, and no," Rash paused, "he was dressed as a cop."

Henson watched as Irwin's expression shifted, "Just like the incident with Grace Roupe and Madison Smith."

Admittedly, Irwin quickly realized any concerns he had about Ridge's motives were blatantly made worse with this new piece of information.

"What are you talkin' about? What happened with Madison? Talber's girl?" Henson inquired.

"Short version, she and Grace Roupe were chased through Twin Oaks by a car with a siren. She believed it to be police, but he hit her bumper. He then proceeded to pay her for the damages, and apologized. She never saw a badge accordin' to Talbert," Irwin informed, "I asked Charlie if he could keep an eye out that evenin' which is why he didn't go towards Ashe—and when he arrested Seth Toliver for drunkin' disorderly."

"However he came about it, our guy has a uniform, and either way we look at it, that isn't good."

Irwin glanced at Henson who had a look of complete disbelief on his face. "Wish you would have informed me sooner, he said looking at Walter who nodded, "Honestly, I was not sure the two were connected at the time." "

Henson turned his attention to Rash, "What were Wyatt's exact words?"

"He said a few of the officers in Yadkin thought the couple was jokin', but they weren't. From hat to toe they saw the uniform and said it led them to believe he was an officer. And," Holden added, "They saw a second driver of an old pickup just like the latest report."

Before Irwin could make any further comments Holden continued, "Which leads me to think about the elephant in the room..." Irwin was suddenly seeing the combination of genius and madness behind the possibility of owning an officer's uniform and one hundred pounds of dynamite.

"The dynamite," Irwin said, "He could walk right into a department anywhere with a uniform and not be given a second glance." Rash did not say another word, which spoke volumes.

The remainder of his evening had been uneventful, and with his shift over Irwin dropped off the patrol car before heading back home.

As he opened the front door quietly removing the keys from the lock he made sure to catch the screen door before it smacked the frame. Unable to shake the feeling someone was watching he turned towards the sofa.

His wife Zora sat with her legs tucked up holding a book and staring at him from over the rim of her reading glasses.

"Kids asleep?" He asked. They had three boys, all between the ages of 11 and 15 years old. Zora removed her glasses while placing the book on a nearby inn table. "Yes, and now that you are home, I hope we can get some rest too."

"You didn't have to wait up you know."

"Are you sayin' you don't want my casserole?"

Smiling Irwin shook his head, "After the last few days I've had, I can't think of anythin' more I want than your casserole." Zora lead the way into the kitchen, as he followed, quietly glancing at the clock near the entryway. Irwin noted it read four minutes to four in the morning.

"Are you gonna tell me what it is you've been up to exactly the last few days?"

Irwin knew there was a price to pay for that casserole, and this was it. He would have to tell Zora what happened, but had no idea as to where to start other than with the stolen car report from Mr. Wagoner.

Between bites of her casserole and sips of water he managed to weave for her a picture of a man that had mostly gone unnoticed until Judge Carico's vehicle had been stolen across the state line in Virginia.

"My goodness," Zora raised the cup of hot tea she had made herself to her lips, its steam warming her nose. "And the mechanic is in the Yadkin lockup?"

"For now," Irwin answered, holding some of his casserole on the fork in his right hand, "Which means I have to be out of here bright and early."

"You're going back to Yadkin?"

"Yes," Irwin replied, "The BOI agent I mentioned, he will be coming with me." Zora took in a slow deep breath before sitting down her teacup and folding her arms, "Why do I still feel there is somethin' you are not tellin' me?"

He wasn't telling her everything, and as he liked to remind her from time to time, it might be in her best interest not to know.

"Do you suppose they'll hold the trail here, if you catch him?" Zora asked. Taking his empty plate Irwin walked over to the sink, "Yes. These boys, they hurt a lot of businesses and good folks round here. But first," Irwin added, "We have to draw their ringleader out into the open."

"What's his name?" Zora asked, turning sideways in the chair to look at her husband. "Ridge," Irwin said as he dried off his clean plate, "Connor Ridge." She could sense there was still something he was not saying, and while Zora often found it better to leave well enough alone when it came to her husband's line of work, she decided to speak up.

"There's somethin' else, isn't there? Somethin' you're not sayin'."

"Zora, you know I can't—."

"I don't think it's about the case per say," She admitted, "But I do think it has to do with *you*. You forget how well I know you Walter. You're tired, but I can still see your wheels turnin'."

Folding his arms and leaning with his back to the kitchen sink he quietly replied, "What would you say if I told you I may want to run for Sheriff?"

Zora Irwin's mouth formed a loving, knowing smile, "I would say it's about time."

CHAPTER 20

The loud sounds of doors opening and closing greeted Irwin and the others as they made their way into the Elkin City Jail. Lieutenant Holden Rash had been waiting for Irwin and Lincoln to arrive out front in the parking lot the better part of twenty minutes.

Sheriff Hayes wandered into the lobby just as they were heading to the desk, "Wanted to catch y'all up on what we learned the other night." The trio followed the Sheriff to his office closing the door.

The ceiling fan made a low hum above them as Hayes sat down behind his desk, "Had two individuals arrested and brought to me from the Wilkes County office. Officers there chased them over the county line and knew we were coordinatin'. Turns out they had an eventful evenin' at that race even busted a few bootleggers. However," He paused, "They brought me a husband and wife."

Holden folded his arms standing near a bookcase filled with various law books, while Lincoln sat down across from Hayes, and Irwin remained near the door, listening.

"Their last names were Faw," the Sheriff continued, "Anyway, one of them confirmed his wife is a cousin of Connor Ridge's wife. They know one another. Seems like he's a bit of a rounder. The gentleman said he won that race, and the pot."

Holden let out a breath and shook his head, "And he still got away."
"The car was too fast, a Model-A that had apparently been modified to
go well up to eighty miles an hour. Some of the Wilkes boys patrols
sustained tire and axle damages just chasin' down the one's they were
able to."

Frank Lincoln's expression remained calm, "And Joines probably
did the mechanic work?"

"Most likely," Hayes agreed.

"He'll be a fool to drive a vehicle like that into town, especially now
that he knows we're after him," Irwin spoke up, "What's Joines say
about the race?"

"Joines keeps sayin' he wants to talk to you," Hayes looked square
at Irwin. "Then let's go talk to him," Lincoln said, rising to his feet while
standing aside, allowing Hayes to lead the way.

As they reached the hallway Irwin noted that the lighting was much
dimmer than in the foyer.

The lack of light reminded him that most men who ended up in
prison hardly ever saw the light of day. In some cases that metaphor also
meant they would never find any hope in the darkness.

"Any idea what he wants to talk about?" Frank Lincoln asked
curiously. "Sounds like he wants to work out a deal," Hayes informed.
Irwin looked over his shoulder at Holden who added, "Depends on what
he has to say."

"Mr. Joines hasn't contacted a lawyer, yet," Hayes informed as the
three kept walking along the dimly lit hallway until they reached a
vacant meeting room, "However, I suspect he will, it's just a matter of
time. Have a seat," the Sheriff motioned to the fold out chairs, "I'll have
my deputy bring Joines down."

Moments later the door opened and Joines stepped through with an
officer behind him. As he was guided into the chair across from Irwin

and Lieutenant Rash, Joines's eyes were noticeably on Frank Lincoln who leaned on his left shoulder in the far-right corner of the room.

"Darrell," Irwin directed the prisoner's attention towards him, "The deputy said you wanted to talk."

"My family—are they safe?"

Irwin laid his hands out in front of him on the table, "I have Sheriff Hayes' word that they are." Letting out a long breath as if he had been holding it since having been brought to the jail, the mechanic leaned his head back.

Keeping their eyes on Darrell, Irwin proceeded, "Darrell, what more can you tell us about Connor Ridge?" "I can tell you he was at that race the other night. Overheard the family they arrested—they talked—And now he'll think it's me once he learns I'm here."

"We can offer you somethin' in exchange for information on Ridge," Holden spoke up, "But you have to tell us what you know."

"I thought it'd just be *you*," Darrell said looking at Irwin, "Didn't know you would bring friends."

"He's wasting our time," Frank Lincoln shoved away from the corner and started towards the door to knock for the deputy to return.

"Wait!"

"We've waited long enough already. What is it you want us to know?" Lincoln's voice was blunt but to the point.

Darrell's left leg started to jump up and down nervously, but he glanced over at Irwin with his dark eyes almost pleading, "I can't be in here for the rest of my life—." His breath caught at the sight of Lincoln moving to sit down adjacent to Irwin.

"Darrell you told me the name of this ~~man, but your case is not that~~ simple—." "I know—I know I can't get out now," Darrell stated seeming to rid himself of the nerves that had been holding onto him, "Before I can tell you anythin' I need to know what's in it for me?"

Lincoln spoke up, "We'll talk to the DA, get you a deal, and if you're lucky you'll be out in a year."

Satisfied with the answer, Darrell said, "Well I wanted to tell you I know where the money is."

"Money?" Irwin asked, "What *money?*"

Agent Lincoln's eyes darted between Darrell Joines and Irwin gauging each man's expression.

"What about his stills?" Irwin asked.

"Connor hid money somewhere near the stills."

Leaning forward Holden Rash's chair came down with a slight thud, "Let me get this straight, Ridge has money from his moonshine runs hidden somewhere near the stills?"

"That's what I just said ain't it?" Joines snapped while rubbing his eyes as if he were the one with the headache. "And how do you know where he keeps his money Darrell?" Irwin questioned.

"Because Whitaker and Shepherd told me."

Lincoln leaned back in his chair while Rash folded his arms and spoke up, "You talkin' about Thayer Whitaker? Who's this Shepherd?"

"Yeah, Thayer is one of 'em. Zane Shepherd," Darrell confirmed, "He's Connors right hand, his go-to. Whitaker and Shepherd took that sugar from Whitehead Grocery a few months back. Connor needed it for a large moonshine haul—."

"So you modified the coupe?" Irwin asked. Darrell nodded slowly, "And a few other cars too. The pay was more than I'd get workin' in a field—."

"Well at least we know our assumptions were correct. The sugar you boys stole from that store wasn't for making cakes." Lincoln commented, interrupting Darrell mid-sentence.

"Not in the least," Darrell Joines's laugh surprised the lawmen seated around him. "Cakes don't sell like shine. I know without a doubt, if you boys get Zane Shepherd, y'all know where they're hidden and more," He paused as Irwin felt a '*but*' coming.

"But they don't call it Devils' Ridge for nothin'. Rumor has it Connor covered that mountain in cottonmouths. If ya don't know where ya steppin' it may be the last one you take."

"Have you been to the stills?" Irwin questioned. "Only once, and only to deliver a car so I could get mine back. It's not the easiest place to find. In fact," Darrell added, "I swore I wouldn't go back. Too many snakes."

Irwin sensed there was a double meaning to Darrell's comment prompting Holden to give the deputy a look of concern. "One thing at a time Darrell," Rash said, "Where exactly are the stills?"

The mechanic smirked, "Give me a piece of paper and I'll draw y'all a map."

Lincoln rose, knocked on the door and ordered the officer who answered to bring back a piece of paper and a pencil. Less than ten minutes later, Irwin, Holden and the federal agent were staring at a crudely drawn map that would lead them to either buried treasure, or liquid gold.

Irwin stood outside the Elkin City Jail after having to listen to Darrell Joines for a solid hour detailing how one would both get to, and survive Devil's Ridge.

Holden Rash leaned on the passenger side of the patrol car, his eyes darting back and forth as the occasional resident eyed the pair, curious no doubt as to what had befallen their small town. As of late, it was a question Irwin was certainly asking himself.

Frank Lincoln appeared, holding the door for a pair of staff, and then turned towards the vehicle. Looking up he instantly recognized Irwin's pensive expression, "What's that look?" Stepping up onto the curb Irwin kept his eyes on the jail's entrance, "I've been thinkin'."

"About what?"

"Darrell, and how best to catch Ridge."

"And what have you come up with?"

"We take Darrell back to Alleghany."

Agent Lincoln cleared his throat, "What good will that do?" "He thinks he has outsmarted us right?"

"Right," Lincoln acknowledged, "But you think he's foolish enough to try and break out his mechanic?"

"And walk right into the county courthouse?" Holden added, sounding skeptical.

"He's not *that* smart. He's *arrogant*." Irwin replied.

Both the Highway Patrol and the Bureau of Investigations agent exchanged glances.

"Okay, I'm listening," Frank said.

"Arrogance is what will get him caught even Wyatt seems to think so." Rash nodded in agreement, "That he does."

"So, I am willin' to bet that he will try to break Darrell out if he knows he's there. I am also willin' to bet that he thinks he will be able to because, as we all know, he's in possession of an officers uniform. No one would give him a second glance."

"If we do this, we have to be smarter than Ridge, or his gang. There can be no room for error." After a brief silence between the three officers Holden Rash spoke up, "Well I'm in and I'm pretty sure we could get Henson in on this too."

Irwin's glance went from the State Highway Patrol officer to the BOI agent. "Let's do it," Lincoln turned back towards the jail and Irwin followed suit.

Mrs. Gambill noted a flurry of ringing telephones as she entered the courthouse after having lunch with Jenny. Over at Smithey's she had overheard snippets of discussions and whispers that a prisoner had been brought to Alleghany from the Elkin City Jail.

The two women glanced at one another and then approached the entry way towards the Clerk's office quietly.

"The first team should be Corporal Upchurch, Mr. Whitman, and Lewis. The second team will be me," Mrs. Gambill heard Irwin's distinct tone coming from the office, "Agent Frank Lincoln, and Holden Rash."

Jenny tugged lightly on Mrs. Gambill coat sleeve motioning for them to go back towards the stairs. Hesitating Mrs. Gambill whispered, "Go upstairs, I will speak with the Deputy, and see what's happenin'."

Her copy editor's cautious expression warned her not to overstep, as she headed back up the hallway.

Knocking on the door frame she stepped into view of the officers gathered all in that one room, "Having a busy afternoon gentlemen?"

"Mrs. Gambill," Holden acknowledged as he held the phone to his left ear. "Apologizes, I didn't mean to interrupt, just heard the phones ringin' and didn't see anyone round yet. Jenny and I just returned from lunch. Have you gentlemen eaten?"

"More like we've drunk a dozen pots of coffee," Adam Lewis replied as he worked on signing a form only to pass it off to Whitman. "I can drop into Smithey's while they're still open if you like," She offered.

Frank Lincoln answered before Irwin had the chance, "Appreciate the offer ma'am but we're going to be heading out shortly."

"Hey," Holden grabbed their attention, "That was the office, there's more."

"More?" Whitman asked.

"Excuse us Mrs. Gambill," Irwin stepped out into the hallway for a moment holding the door half closed, "I know you're wantin' details—."

"But you're not able to discuss it are you?" She answered, knowing full well what he was and was not capable of doing.

"Not yet," Irwin replied somewhat apologetically although she knew he had rather not say anything after the headline that morning.

"Can you at least confirm that Darrell Joines is now being held in jail here?" Irwin's expression remained stoic, he was not willing to let that news slip, not just yet.

"Deputy, a few people saw you bring back a man in cuffs, there was talk about it at Smithey's. I won't say a word but—."

Irwin took a quick glimpse into the nearby office wondering what was being discussed, thinking, *Every minute I'm out here is a minute I could spend getting closer to catching up to Ridge.*

"So, this prisoner has nothin' to do with your case?" Irwin did not so much as waver, but like his inaction had before, it told her she was spot on.

"You can't even give me the slightest hint?"

Irwin placed his free hand in his pocket, "Let's just say some of us are fishin'."

It was enough of a statement to both pique her interest yet keep her from asking further questions.

"Well, let me know what you catch," She said, heading back towards the stairs.

CHAPTER 21

After the third attempt to reach Darrell Joines, Zane Shepherd placed the telephone back on its cradle before glancing towards the living room where he could hear his wife, Connor Ridge, Jeb, and his grandson's talking.

Seconds later Connor was standing in the kitchen doorway holding a half drunk cup of coffee in his left hand and an unlit cigarette dangling from the corner of his mouth.

"What'd Darrell say?"

Zane shook his head, "Nothin'."

"What do you mean *nothin'*?"

"He wasn't home," Zane replied, "Must be in his garage."

"Well he better be if he knows what's good for him," Connor replied as he sat down facing the stove.

"We need to talk about this next haul," Zane said as he lowered himself onto a nearby stool, his eyes still focused on the telephone. Connor shrugged, "Nothin' to talk about."

"Thayer said police have been seen near the Yadkin line for weeks. He and his brother Erick have managed to dodge them, but it's only a matter of time."

Connor grunted, his usual response for whenever he thought he knew better.

Zane tore his eyes from the phone, "You best listen cause Roger Cheek lost his still two days ago," despite his tone it was the next portion of Zane's statement that caught Connors ear, "Rumor has it the Sheriff's Department is lookin' into car thefts on the mountain too."

There was a brief pause before Connor cut his eyes towards Zane, their gold outline burning like a ring of fire against the green backdrop that were his irises.

"Who have you been talkin' to?"

"Doesn't matter who told me," Zane snapped, "I am tryin' to help *us*."

Connor bolted from the chair catching Zane so off guard that he was in his face before his friend could blink.

The still runner's left hand came down on the wooden kitchen table fast and hard. The sound jarred the house to silence, and after that moment not a single voice carried from the living room.

"Who are you talkin' to..." Connor repeated slowly, his voice a low guttural growl.

"No one," Zane repeated firmly, being sure to keep his eyes locked on Connors. Standing up straight running a hand through his dark hair, Connors jaw sat in a tight line.

The cut throat bootlegger was just a few inches from Zane, "You listen to me, we are gonna to make that haul Friday. We're going to get that Model-A back in action. All I need is one part, and you're goin' to help me get it."

During their run from Wilkes County officers the Model-A had sustained some minor damage, but what they believed minor soon became serious when the vehicle would not stir to the left.

Deciding it was best not to give Connor any reason to suspect him of being a snitch, Zane relented.

"What do you need?"

"Part for the suspension and stirring," Connor answered redirecting his vision toward the phone, "And since Darrell isn't answerin', that means you and I are gonna repair that car if we're gonna to save that haul."

As Connor left the kitchen, his cigarette in hand and coffee cup on the stove, Zane could not help thinking, *but who's going to save us if we get caught?*

From the moment Darrell Joines had been brought into the jail Irwin was already hearing whispers of his detainment in Alleghany in connection with car thefts.

Frank Lincoln was standing outside the courthouse doors with a gentleman Irwin did not recognize. However, he too had the look of an agent with his black tweed coat and well shined shoes.

"Deputy," Frank greeted, "I want you to meet my partner, Agent Quinton Hollister. This is the Deputy I was telling you about earlier."

"Pleasure," Hollister offered his hand which was almost two sizes larger than Irwin's. He was a tall man, easily six-foot-five with a lean frame, dark eyes, and blonde hair.

"Nice to meet you too, Agent Hollister, when did you arrive?"

"Yesterday evening late, I stayed at the hotel down the street here—Four Oaks?"

"That's right," Lincoln replied, turning his attention back to Irwin, "Nice lady at the restaurant spotted right off I wasn't from here. Small towns like these, they like to talk." "You tell her you were from DC.?" Irwin asked.

Hollister shook his head, "Told her I was from Ohio, which I'm not lying, that's my home state. Buckeye through and through."

"Best if folks don't know everythin'," Irwin admitted. "Including the Editor in Chief?" Lincoln inquired holding up a copy of the *Alleghany-Times News.*

"I was sharing with Hollister why we decided to bring Joines here," Lincoln informed Irwin.

"If it works, it'll be ingenious," Hollister said. Sheriff Henson opened the entry doors. "Mornin', you fellas had coffee yet?"

"I have," Irwin said as Lincoln handed him the newspaper. Hollister, who decided it was time to break with Lincoln and Irwin, answered, "I could always use another cup." Irwin stayed behind as Lincoln and his partner went inside unable to take his eyes off the Headline of the newspaper.

"Alleghany Gang Being Pursued, Sought in Connection with Car Theft, One Arrested"

"*Gang?*" Irwin was unsure if he liked the use of the word, especially in Alleghany County.

Holden could be heard talking as he came walking up the steps with Wyatt, "I see Lincoln gave it to you."

"A *gang?*" Irwin sounded unsure but also uneasy about the term.

"That's what the newspaper is callin' them," Rash said as Wyatt motioned to see the edition and Irwin passed it to him.

The article had been written by Mrs. Gambill, but had not garnered any approval from the Sheriff's Office. "The good news is, now the word is out that Darrell's here. Right?" Rash asked.

"Could have done without the typical journalistic flourish but—I suppose," Irwin admitted as they continued through the courthouse doors.

"Any idea how she was able to obtain Joines' name for the issue?" Henson asked as Irwin reached the office. "Journalists have their sources." Irwin answered without further comment.

Frank Lincoln stood with his coffee in hand near the interview room door, "We're ready if you are."

"Ready," Irwin nodded with a glimpse in the Sheriff's direction.

Quinton Hollister lumbered after Lincoln with Rash and Wyatt following. Before Irwin could take his leave Henson stopped him, "Irwin,"

"Yes sir?"

"A moment," Henson motioned for Irwin to close the door.

"This is going to sound crazy, but I spoke with Darrell last night before heading out around four in the mornin'."

Henson placed his hands on the top of his desk as if bracing for a bullet to hit him square in the chest.

"What did he say?" Irwin asked. "He said that Connor Ridge did in fact have an officer's uniform, but that isn't all he has. I wouldn't have believed him except the incident with Seth Toliver and—."

"Didn't Charlie clear the Toliver issue up with Deputy DeBord?" Irwin interrupted, concern lacing his tone regarding the safety, if not for themselves, for the town.

"He did, but I'm afraid Joines dropped another bombshell on us, and it's more than the dynamite."

"Well what else is there to know?" Irwin was almost too afraid to ask, his words drawn out as he watched the Sheriff's expression shift, "He has keys."

For a moment Irwin was not certain if he had heard his boss correctly, "*Keys* to what?"

"The jail," Henson answered.

"And Darrell told you this?"

Raising his right hand momentarily expressing his wishes for his deputy to keep his voice down, Sheriff Henson explained, "It seems Ridge has been coming in and out of this building regularly as means of ransom. Major moonshiners get locked up like Toliver, he comes to their rescue for a price, and sets them free."

Irwin let the premise sink in as he tried to understand how someone like Connor Ridge was in possession of jail keys, "And that means he may very well try to break Darrell out after all."

"Walter, any idea how he could have gotten those keys?" Henson questioned, clearly beside himself with disbelief as to the circumstances this new information now put him and his deputies in.

Irwin had an idea, but there was one possible theory, one that Charlie had placed there. *Was Charlie right?* Irwin wondered.

Henson cleared his throat, "I know you and Charlie Shepherd too well; you're not gonna to be involved in somethin' like this."

"We're gonna need warrants for Connors home as well as Zane Shepherd's either before, or after, we catch 'em," Irwin said.

"Already workin' on them," Henson assured his deputy, "Which leads me to somethin' else."

The Sheriff lowered himself into his desk chair, "This theory of yours that Connor Ridge is arrogant enough to walk right in here and attempt a jailbreak, it isn't far fetched."

Irwin heard a knock on the door and opened it, "Sorry but Wyatt's party already left. Lincoln's waitin' for us."

"I'll be right out," Irwin closed the door, turning back to his boss. "We're all here tonight, and we make sure it stays quiet," Henson instructed. "All newspaper and court staff need to be out of here by 5 pm. We cannot have anyone in the crossfire if Connor Ridge does decide to show up."

"Agreed," Irwin admitted as he opened the door and headed out of the courthouse. Half jogging across the street he spotted Lincoln and Rash waiting, both leaning on opposite sides of the car parked just outside Harding's Store.

"Thought you were right behind us Deputy," Frank put out his cigarette with the heel of his shoe as Rash opened the back-passenger door.

Irwin climbed into the passenger seat of the Chrysler, "Apologies for the wait, but it turns out we have more to discuss than I thought."

Tommy Dalton came racing up towards his grandfather's back porch, his old worn out boots scuffing the first step as he headed towards the door. Jeb Dalton, already awake and having his twenty-two in hand opened the door slightly startling his grandson.

"Whatcha doin' here boy?"

"You haven't heard?"

Jeb put his twenty-two in the corner near the door and motioned for Tommy to come inside. The cool autumn air lingered as they stood for a few seconds in the living room.

Jeb Dalton had little but his home was his pride and joy. He had worked, alongside his wife, for many years to make it a real family home. They had raised five kids and watched several grandchildren grow up before their eyes there.

However, when the Depression hit Jeb lost money on the farm. Shortly after in 1930 he also lost his wife Nancy to Pneumonia.

"Who's up at Devils Ridge?" Tommy asked. "Matthew, or he should be. Why you askin'?" Jeb noticed the nervousness in his grandson and it did little to ease his own concerns.

"They arrested Darrell."

"What?"

"Folks s-saw him bein' taken into the c-courthouse,' ' Tommy stuttered, the words coming quicker than his tongue could move.

"Are you sure?" Jeb wanted to make certain there was no misunderstanding to what his grandson was telling him. Tommy nodded quickly, his hands firmly grasped around his hat.

"Who told you this?"

"Grandpa, it's in the newspaper. I was comin' home and saw Mr. Billings down the road," Tommy reached into his back pocket and pulled out the folded up newspaper hurriedly doing so, "See? Here it says Darrell Joines was arrested in connection with the suspected car thefts in and around the county, and he is in the county jail."

Jeb, who could not read a single word, trusted his grandson for all the schooling he had. Reaching for his coat Jeb threw it over his shoulders quickly turning into his bedroom across the hall looking for his extra ammo.

A few minutes later he emerged with a box of shells in his left hand and held out his right for the newspaper. Tommy turned it over watching his grandfather as he stuffed it inside his coat pocket.

"Zane said he couldn't get hold of him, been tryin'. I told him I'd ride down to see if Darrell's phone was off or if something happened, but after I saw this thought it was best to come straight here..." Tommy's voice trailed off as he watched his grandfather load his rifle.

Locking the barrel back into place, Jeb patted his grandson's shoulder then opened the front door, "You did good, now best get on home. You hear?"

"Yes sir, but what about—?" "Tommy, don't argue with me, just get." Jeb closed his front door swiftly behind his grandson, then made his way towards his pickup.

He waited to see if Tommy was in fact heading back towards his pa's and when he was satisfied his grandson was not coming after him Jeb pulled out of his driveway heading towards Devil's Ridge.

CHAPTER 22

Connor had assisted in the loading of barrels, filling jars, and putting out fires for the better part of three hours. Zane had yet to return from making a run for the stolen sugar hidden in his cellar.

"That's the last of 'em," Nathan announced as he made certain the stash was secure in the back of the modified Roadster.

"Whoa, where's the fire Jeb?" Issac Miller could be heard saying over the hilltop. Connor wiped his brow with the back of his sleeve upon hearing Jeb ask, "Where's Connor?"

"I'm right here," Connor strolled up the hill at a pace that told Jeb he was in no mood for nonsense.

By the time Connor reached Jeb he could tell the old timer was a bundle of nerves, "What's happened Jeb?"

"Did Zane get caught?" Nathan asked quietly.

"No," Jeb waved him off, "Where is Zane?"

"He's on a sugar run. What's gotten into you?"

"It's Darrell."

"What about Darrell?" Connor asked.

"He's been arrested."

Nathan cursed under his breath as he removed his hat, "Are you sure?" "You asked Tommy to head down and see him, well before he could he saw Lewis Billings down the road from me, he had a newspaper," Jeb pulled out the paper and handed it to Connor.

"Apparently they arrested Darrell and brought him to our county. He's sittin' in jail Connor—."

Taking the paper from Jeb a silence fell over the trio as Connor read over the headline and parts of the article.

"They're calling us a *gang* Connor," Jeb said, "A *gang*. That gets people like us locked up for life!"

"Do you think Darrell would sing?" Nathan asked.

"Not if he knows what's good for him," Connor replied, Jeb the only one who picked up on the hint of uncertainty in Connor's voice.

"If he sings—," Nathan was cut off by Connor's eyes, the afternoon shade from the trees made their gold rings almost appear ember. "Let's just say if he hasn't, we have to take care of him before he does."

Jeb kept his eyes on his shoes, "We have to move the still just in case—."

"That's three days work Jeb!" Connor snapped, not angry at the man but more angry with himself.

"If he has sung, if he has told them everythin'—we don't have three days, we may not even have hours."

Nathan looked up at Isaac, one of the other still hands who had remained silent the entire time, standing back in disbelief as to what he was hearing.

"The haul has to be delivered soon," Connor reminded them, "The simple fact is we can't afford *not* to run."

"We can't afford to either," Nathan stated, "If you get caught—."

Connor stared out into the woods, a little ways through the trees he could see the clearing he had come to when he had first climbed up the ridge. All that he had that was worth anything, was actually in that clearing. All the money he had saved from his hauls was buried there. All $8,000 worth.

"Nathan, get the boys together, Issac you help him get these stills movin', and Jeb," Connor pointed at the old man, "Make sure it's Darrell. If it is, I might just have a way of gettin' him out." Jeb wasted no time, he turned and headed back for his truck as Connor stared over his shoulder towards the clearing cursing loud enough to cause a flurry of birds above to scatter.

Before arriving back at Devil's Ridge, Zane had heard from neighbors about the arrest of Darrell Joines. The newspaper was making its weekly round in the county, and none of it was in favor of the mechanic.

Connor had several of the boys working to break up the stills as Zane arrived. He noticed they were leaving behind parts as they went, but it would take more than just parts of a supposed still to have revenuers on their trail.

"Good thing the last bit of liquor is in the Roadster," Connor motioned over his shoulder, "Did you hear?"

"About Darrell, I did," Zane removed his hat and looked around the woods, "Think he talked to them?"

"Knowing Darrell," Connor kept his voice low, "For the right price he may have. You know most lawmen here are lookin' to make a name of themselves, like that one out of Wilkesboro."

"Anything I can do?" Zane had noticed the boys putting out fires, and hauling what they could back to their pickups. "As a matter of fact, there is," Connor took a swig of moonshine from one of the nearby sampling jars, "We have to get Darrell out."

"How?" Zane asked.

"I sent Jeb to scout out the jail. He will go in, do his thing, and come back. When he gets here," Connor glanced towards the boys working on the stills, "We will walk him right out the front door."

"The place is going to be crawling with cops, you know that, maybe even revenuers if Darrell has talked."

"If that's true then they won't know me from Adam or pay me little mind with that uniform on."

"Connor, I don't think—," Zane hesitated but Connor cut him off. "That's right *you* don't think. *I* do. I think for all of us. Do you want to spend time in the joint behind bars for making nothin' more than a livin'?"

Zane shook his head, "Connor you know I don't, but I also don't want to see any of us be put in an early grave either."

With his hands on his hips, one no doubt on the revolver he always carried under his coat, Connor Ridge snickered, "That's why you got me Zane. That's why I do the *thinkin'*. We ain't goin' to get killed. We're getting' Darrell back and then we are makin' this haul. Now, go get that dynamite."

"What for?"

"Don't ask, just do it!" Connor growled his nerves on end. Without further discussion Zane headed toward the hidden cache in the thickest part of the woods while Connor headed to his own truck.

After driving for nearly an hour Irwin glanced down at the crude map outlined by Darrell Joines, his pencil markings beginning to fade, smudged around the outer edges.

He made a turn onto a dirt road he was unfamiliar with. Despite his reluctance Irwin drove the car cautiously forward, slowly scanning the treeline and road ahead for any signs of movement, vehicles, or residents.

Moments later and with another glance at the map Irwin announced, "This has to be it." Turning the wheel he pulled the car over into a grassy patch near some trees where it could not be well seen from above.

"Where are we?" Lincoln asked as he opened the passenger door and stepped out. "About mid-way to Wilkes County," Holden answered, "And by the looks of it, if we keep followin' that map, we will have no choice but to start hikin' through the woods."

Lincoln shielded his eyes from the mid-afternoon sun, "Only one way to find out," the BIO agent said, reaching for his sidearm, "Think we can do it?"

Rash shrugged, "Maybe, maybe not. How far did Darrell say the stills were from the road and ridge?" Irwin stared out at the mountains to their right, the hills in the far off distance still giving off their sapphire blue aura.

"Maybe a mile, a little less," He answered, turning his attention to Lincoln, "Worth a shot."

"Stay with the car and if you hear shots you know what to do," Lincoln instructed. Rash watched as the two climbed into the hills while placing a hand on his own weapon.

For someone like Irwin who had grown up hiking, hunting, and fishing in Appalachia Lincoln sensed he was out of his element.

Breathing heavier than the local deputy Lincoln took a moment once they reached the top of the hill, noticing the expanse before him on either side. A slight mist in the distance to his left gave off the impression that the mountains were exhaling, as if sighing in relief that someone had seen them for what they truly were. Captivating. Dangerous.

Irwin pressed on, his boots gripping the blanket of pine needles beneath them, crunching quietly with each step.

Lincoln followed suit, but when he slid the first time Irwin had quickly turned, offering him a steady hand, "Be careful." "Roger that," Lincoln admitted as he regained his posture and continued the track upward.

More than twenty minutes had passed before Irwin paused. Lincoln, hardly able to hear over his own heartbeat, asked, "Why did you stop?"

"Listen," Irwin instructed, holding up his left hand slightly, "You hear that?"

Lincoln's eyes cast upwards above Irwin's head, "Sounds like it is coming from up there."

"Sounds like it because it is. It's a waterfall," Irwin answered, "the water is rushing down the mountain just as Darrell said it did."

"So we're close?"

"According to this map we should be right under it."

"We have to hand it to Ridge, this is a great place to hide," Lincoln admitted. Irwin's eyes searched the trees, the sinking feeling that they were not alone rushed over him.

Lincoln seemed to sense the same as he gripped the hilt of his gun, "Why do I feel like we're being watched?"

"Because we probably are," Irwin answered, his own grip tightening on his weapon.

"Let's get back," Lincoln said, "I'll head out here at first light and we'll finish our search. No need to scare them off. We want to be alive to bust up that still and touch base with the others, let them know we found it."

Irwin kept searching the trees knowing full well at any moment someone might surprise them. The only surprise however, lay near the end of the trail when Lincoln had startled a buck from some nearby brush.

The agent stepped back and Irwin watched as the eight-pointer gracefully bounded through the woods kicking up leaves and twigs as he went.

"You might be good luck for someone to take huntin'," Irwin laughed passing Lincoln on the trail. The agent was had been amazed at the sight of the deer, "There is no denying this is a unique place you live in, hidden in these mountains." Irwin did not argue.

"Hey, what'd you two find?" Holden asked as he came into view. "A waterfall, just as Darrell said we would," Lincoln answered.

"You really think he was being honest about the money being somewhere near the stills too?" Holden questioned.

Irwin opened the driver side door to the patrol car, "Ridge has everythin' he needs here. He's secluded, well hidden, has water, cottonmouths, and the high ground. The real question is what makes you think he didn't hide money here?"

Jeb Dalton peddled past the open doors of the courthouse and made his way into the Clerk of Court office straight ahead, passing by the Sheriff's Office door which was closed. Jeb paused momentarily before continuing upon hearing voices inside the office signaling the Sheriff was most likely preoccupied.

Slowly he cautiously walked down the hall reaching the main desk "May I help you?" The woman behind the counter asked as she placed some papers off to the side. "Maybe," Jeb removed his hat respectfully, "Heard you folks had a prisoner? Might I ask what they're askin' for bail?"

The young woman did not answer, instead she inquired, "Are you a relation?" "Kind of, more like a family friend," Jeb kept his voice low and approached the desk in an attempt to keep hear her better due to the hum of the fan overhead.

"We honestly do not have that scheduled as of yet sir, but if you're willing to wait..." "Might I see him?" Jeb interrupted wondering silently, *How close will they even let me get?*

"If you're not immediate family or his legal representation, they will not allow me to let you see him."

"It's his ma," Jeb decided to lie, "She isn't well and asked me to come down to check on him. It'd break my heart to have to go back and tell her I couldn't lay an eye on him."

The young assistant empathized, "We understand but—." "I just want to let him know how she is and that he has an attorney comin'."

Jeb saw a flicker of emotion in the young lady's expression, and realized his words had appealed to her good nature despite rules and regulations she had to follow.

The young woman slowly walked around the desk, "Follow me." Jeb stayed a little ways behind her as she approached the back of the courthouse and knocked on a door. She stuck her head inside a hallway, her voice muffled through the door with a murky glass window.

A moment later a Sheriff's Deputy appeared wearing a crisp white shirt, blue and gray colored striped tie, and matching dark blue slacks. His shoes were scuffed from what Jeb ascertained was from farm work. "Charlie Shepherd," The man extended his hand kindly.

Jeb shook it, "Afternoon."

"Shelia here tells me you know the prisoner's family?"

"Yes sir, his mother, she sent me up here to have a word. Won't be but five minutes then I'll be on my way."

"How do you know his mother?" Charlie asked, just seeming to make conversation but Jeb knew how this could play out.

"I'm a neighbor, and we've lived next to one another a good while."

"That right?"

"Yes sir," Jeb said without hesitation, trying to sound as matter-of-fact as he could. "And where do you live Mr...?" Jeb swallowed before speaking, "Just above Darrell's there in Yadkin, his home is just a stone's throw from mine on the right."

Charlie grunted, although the deputy seemed somewhat appeased Jeb realized he would have to be quick.

"Step in here, the door will remain open and I'm right outside," Charlie made the instructions sound more like a cautionary statement.

Partially speechless Jeb was only able to take a few steps closer to the door where he could see two jail cells. The walls were brick, the bars were solid cast iron and aged. Blacker than black, with hints of copper colored rust around the key holes. Sitting in the second cell nearest the window that overlooked the back side of the courthouse was Darrell Joines.

"Darrell?"

The young man's head lifted, his eyes shot up to Jeb, his face turning a pale shade of white. "I came by to say your ma has a lawyer comin', and she wanted me to check on you before I headed back. You alright? They treatin' you okay?"

Glancing momentarily towards the door Darrell quickly turned his attention back to Jeb, "I'm all right, how is everyone else?"

"Worried, as usual," Jeb managed, trying to keep things between the lines. "And brother? Does he know?"

Jeb knew this was Darrell's nickname for Connor whenever they were drinking. Shrugging he replied, "He will be better when things are settled with the lawyer."

Jeb watched as the realization of what he was saying sunk in. Darrell shook his head, "No need for that, they are gonna to send me off, no two ways bout it. Tell 'em to come next Tuesday, and I'll say goodbye then."

"They won't hear tell of it," Jeb replied, "No talkin' them outta this. I'll try and come Tuesday too, all right?"

Darrell frowned as the deputy reappeared, "Times up." "Thank you sir," Jeb said looking back at Darrell, "Take care you hear?" Jeb proceeded out of the cells and back into the hallway of the courthouse.

After quietly thanking the deputy again he was back in his pickup, his heart racing as he realized what he had just done. And although it was not the worst thing, he knew that whatever Connor was up to, could make it seem a lot worse.

CHAPTER 23

Nathan had spotted the movement just as he was making his way towards one of the trails leading back to his car. He sank down behind a large oak tree and peered out through the branches of a nearby mountain laurel at the two men as they walked diligently up the side of the hill.

From here the waterfall nearby could be heard, but only slightly. Although he could not make out what they were saying, he watched as they paused, hearing the water.

Darrell talked, Nathan thought quietly as he saw the glimmer of an unmistakable badge on one of their belts. *Revenuers? Local police?* Either way, Nathan decided it was time to get back to the still to warn the others. After a few minutes more Nathan watched as the two turned, heading back in the direction they had walked, but not before gripping their weapons.

Definitely revenuers, Nathan groaned inside as he climbed back up the steep embankment trying to remain as quiet as he could.

When he reached the top he raced down a narrow trail hardly visible from a distance, and followed the sound of rushing water. As the waterfall's roar became louder Nathan almost felt it become part of him, like the very blood that flowed through his veins.

"Connor?" Nathan said over the rushing water, "You still here?" "What are you doing Nathan? Thought you were gone." Connor leaned on a nearby tree lighting a cigarette. All around him were remnants of jars, smoldering fires left to flame out in their pits, and a few stray pipes here and there.

"Revenuers, they're at the base of the road just east of here. If you want out you can't go that way. Thought I'd warn ya." Connor shook out the match he had struck to light the cigarette, "Seen Jeb?"

"Not yet, thought he would be back by now," Nathan looked around half expecting to see the old man emerge from the surrounding trees.

"Wonder what's takin' him so long," Connor muttered as if speaking to the nearby water that moved quickly past them from atop the bank.

"It has to be Darrell they got. He talked to Connor," Nathan stated, "You know it and I know it. The good Lord knows Jeb probably knows it too by now. That's the only way they would've ever found us out here—."

"Nearly found us after that race in Wilkes," Connor replied, "Zane and I were chased a good ways."

"You never said—," Nathan started but Connor cut him off with a wave of his hand, "Doesn't matter, we weren't caught." "Anyone else you know who might've been?" Nathan asked. The question lit a fuse inside Connor, and it was visible from the outside as Nathan stepped back. Connors's eyes with their coppery outline turned a shade of dark red in the late afternoon shade that Nathan could only compare to that of an ember.

"What'd you say?"

"I didn't mean nothin' by it Connor—."

"No, what did you say?" Connor asked, his voice even, sounding more like a curious child than a dangerous moonshiner.

"Just wondered if anyone was at the race you knew?" Nathan understood it was not his exact words, but it was what he had meant. Connor arched his left eyebrow, his eyes traveling back to the water, "Matter of fact there was. A couple of people."

"Any of 'em get caught?" Nathan posed the question again. Connor remained quiet until he heard something behind them. Reaching for his revolver he kept a hand on it and stayed behind the tree, Nathan stepped into the shadows that were starting to form as the sun waned over the ridge.

"It's me," Jeb whispered loudly, "Don't shoot!" Connor peered around the tree, cigarette hanging from the corner of his mouth, "Took you long enough." The older man made his way over to the pair, his hat in his hands.

"Well," Connor urged, "What'd you learn?"

"It's Darrell. Easy to see he hasn't had much sleep, and now he knows we're comin'."

Noticing Nathan's expression Jebs eyebrows crinkled upwards, "You got somethin' to say Nate, say it."

Connor raised his hands to silence the two, "Revenuers are sniffing around, they're gettin' close, but they won't get any closer."

"I don't think he told them anythin' willingly," Jeb defended, "Probably got threatened."

Nathan took in a deep breath, "Speakin' of threats, where is Zane?" Connor walked ahead of the two men, "Zane went to get some things we're going to be needin'. Best be movin' the sun is goin' down and we have things to do before sunrise."

After waiting a while in Connors pickup with Nathan sitting in the bed, Jeb had decided it was time for him to head back. Connor dropped him off at his own truck and cautioned his old friend to be careful.

Ten minutes later Nathan tapped the window notifying Connor to pull over. "My car's not far from here," Nathan replied as he leaned into the passenger side window, "You all right?"

Connor nodded, "I'll be better when we get that haul takin' care of. Where you headin'?"

"Home," Nathan said, "For now. Listen, you need me, call." Connor acknowledged Nathan's offer to assist but knew he, like himself, was a father of young children and did not wish to put any more of his boys at risk than necessary.

"What about Darrell?" Nathan asked curiously, "What's the plan?" "We already moved the stills, but I plan to get him out of there." Nathan took a step back from the pickup, "How?"

"Like I told Zane, just leave it to me."

Without another word Connor put the pick up in drive and coasted away from Nathan leaving him standing along the side of the road. Looking back through the rear view mirror Connor watched as Nathan's image nearly vanished in the dust kicked up from the tires.

Thayer Whitaker paced the length of the new still. He watched as Matthew Jones checked for any cracks in the barrels from their recent move. Thayer had been searching the unfamiliar territory for wood.

The fires would need to be kept to a minimum at first but in a few weeks they might be able to burn at capacity. "Who's land we on?" Matthew questioned as he put down the barrel and went to work on the piping.

"I suspect it's Lonnie Caudill's side of the ridge, but don't hold me to that."

"He friendly?"

"For the right price anyone can be friendly," Thayer retorted as he took a cigarette from his overall pocket and lit it.

The sound of a car off in the distance drew both men's eyes from their tasks and towards the southern end of the embankment.

A thick line of trees bordered the edge of the hillside. Thayer reached for his weapon as a whistle came up through the wind, slick and high pitched. It was a sound Thayer was all too familiar with, "It's Zane."

"Good grief," Matthew sighed, taking his hand off the revolver he had stuck in his back pocket.

"That mash won't make itself," Zane's voice carried for a few feet as he walked towards the others. "Can't help ya there, that's not my specialty," Thayer replied, "Where's Jeb?"

"He'll be back later, had to run on and talk to his son." "Where's Connor and Nathan?" Matthew inquired without looking up from his work.

"Connors behind me."

"Jeb learn anything?" Thayer questioned.

"It's Darrell. Jeb told Connor he looks pretty exhausted." "No doubt they ain't kept him up day and night tryin' to get him to talk about the still."

"I don't think it's the stills they care about," Zane muttered keeping his voice even. "Then what is it?" Matthew asked.

Outside of Connor, Zane, and Jeb no one really knew what Connor had to do over the years to get deliveries, or money to pay them with.

Plenty of things bordered on illegal, moonshine being one of the worst. Zane knew Connor often stole farming equipment or tools to friends or neighbors who would pay him in return. Some of them were even in debt to Connor for helping them, and not just monetarily.

Seth Toliver was a good example. He was just one of a handful of moonshiners since Connor had received the keys to the jail that had been broken out. Some owed Connor money, others a favor. Zane had noted at one point that even those who did not owe Connor felt it best not to cross him.

"We'll worry about that," Zane tried to sound reassuring but he knew that the words were empty, especially if they were to get caught. "Worry about what?" Connors asked.

Zane shrugged, keeping his cool, "The details of the delivery." Connor smirked, "We're makin' that haul, and the sooner the better."

"Zane says Jeb saw Darrell," Thayer put out his cigarette and noticed Connor was clutching something under his left arm. "Don't worry about Darrell, he'll be out before dawn."

Matthew snickered, "How you figure that?"

"Because Thayer here is gonna to help us."

Thayer Whitaker shifted his weight from one leg to another, "What do you mean *help*?"

"Listen up Thayer," Connor motioned to the road, "Get your truck. In fifteen minutes we're pullin' out and headin' into town. By the time we get there the courthouse should be empty. I'm goin' in, armed, but I need you outside to make sure Darrell and I both walk out of there. You hear me?"

"We're doin' what—?"

Connor reached into his right pocket dangling a set of keys. Thayer stared at them in disbelief. "We're gettin' Darrell out," Connor explained, "Now go get your truck, we ain't got all night."

Zane glanced into the back of his cab at the cache of weapons. A forty-four caliber, a couple of sawed off shotguns, and riffles lay in back.

Connor emerged from the thick trees straightening his jacket. The cigarette in his hand left a transparent trail, an invisible chain that might pull him back towards the woods.

Having the stills set up elsewhere for the time being was just a precaution until things settled down. In the meantime Matthew was asked to stay with them making sure no one came along to bust them up.

Connor decided he would look into who owned the property as soon as their current haul was delivered. If it was who he suspected, he knew he might have a shot at keeping them quiet for the right price.

Looking down at the tires on the truck Zane said nothing. "Get in," Connor instructed as he opened the driver side door and cranked the engine. Once Zane was settled in the passenger seat Connor could not help but to notice his friends needing to speak.

"What?"

"Just wonderin' if you really believe you can carry through?" Tilting his head towards his friend Connor replied confidently, "If I had any doubts do you think I would be here?"

Pulling the cigarette away from his lips Connor stared over the steering wheel into the early evening, "We have the uniform right?"

Zane said nothing but as the truck backed up he could sense something foreboding about Connors silence. "What else?" Zane asked. Connor tossed the cigarette butt out the window of the truck, "We have insurance that we're walkin' out of that courthouse with Darrell."

The words escaped Zane's mouth before he could stop them, "Guns are no insurance we walk out of there *alive*. If they catch us—."

Connor snickered, "You forget, guns aren't the *insurance* I'm talkin' about."

Glancing over his shoulder Zane peered down into the truck bed where he saw the old crate he had brought down from the ridge. Connor had covered it with an old worn sheet.

"We're not leavin' that courthouse without Darrell," Connor explained, "Because when I get him where I want him, we're goin' to have a heart to heart about loyalty."

Lincoln, Irwin, Wyatt, and Rash made their way to Four Oaks just a few minutes from the courthouse to speak with the others. The three of them had decided the best course of action was to split up into search parties.

Whitman, Lewis, Morris, Wyatt, and Upchurch were all waiting in Whitman's room on the top floor of the hotel. Irwin accepted a cup of coffee from Whitman as the others started asking about the exhibition into the woods.

"Did you find anything? Anything close to what Mr. Joines mentioned?" Wyatt inquired. "We believe so, and tomorrow we will get the chance to prove Mr. Joines' worth." Lincoln answered as he leaned on the nearby wall with his hands in his pockets.

"What about you, deputy?" Upchurch asked, "You seem awfully quiet." "I meant to ask back at the courthouse if anyone had been to see, or tried to see, Darrell."

Rash took a sip of the dark coffee, "They didn't mention anything when I went to the back to check in."

"Who was there?" Irwin asked, wondering if the shifts had changed and whether or not Shepherd was still guarding the prisoner.

"Short guy, brown hair, wore a plain shirt and tie with slacks. Seemed nice enough, never met him until now." "That's Taylor," Irwin said, realizing Charlie Shepherd had most likely gone home by the time they arrived.

"We will have backup here in the morning," Frank Lincoln assured the men, "Then we'll split up and start searching Mr. Ridge's residence for missing car parts, vehicles, and maybe learn more about his bootlegging operation."

Whitman cleared his throat, "Still believe bringing Joines here was a good idea?"

Rash replied, "Good idea or not, it will cause them to make a mistake, and when they do we will be able to catch all of 'em—not just Ridge." "It's more than likely he will," Irwin spoke up. Everyone stared at him from across the room.

"What are you implin' Walt?" Rash asked. "Before I went with you and Lincoln on the hunt for the still this mornin', Sheriff Henson received some news from Darrell concernin' the jail."

Lincoln sat down in a nearby chair beside the window, "That's why you got held up?"

"Yes," Irwin replied.

"What sort of news?" Rash questioned.

"We know Ridge has a uniform, a badge, and a patrol siren. What we didn't know," Irwin hesitated, "Was he also has keys." "Keys to what?" Whitman inquired. The room was silent as the realization of what Irwin was saying sunk in.

Rash shook his head, "No, no, no."

"Afraid so. We had a prisoner go missin' after a drunkin' disorderly charge. Charlie Shepherd had brought him in, but he never got booked for a hearin' date, and no bond was set."

"So you think Ridge or someone who works with him broke out this drunk and disorderly detainee?" Lincoln asked, sounding skeptical for the first time since they had been investigating. Irwin nodded, "I do, and it might not have been the first time."

CHAPTER 24

M rs. Gambill reached the stairs leading towards her vehicle that was parked alongside a dusty gray pickup.

As she opened the Chevy car door a pair of headlights flickered to her right drawing her gaze down the length of main street.

Mrs. Gambill felt the thickness in the air as she gripped her keys. The cool metal against her warm palms forced her to glance downward, away from the direction of the lights.

The vehicle pulled out heading towards the intersection before making a left and leaving town in the direction of Laurel Springs.

Slowly she lowered herself into the car and from peering out the windshield noticed Sheriff Henson staring out one of the windows nearest the front of the courthouse. His silhouette was unmistakable as he removed his glasses and headed back into the hallway of the building.

As she looked up into her rear view mirror, if not for the lights of the nearby Spartan Theater she may not have noticed a pickup slowly pulling in across the street directly behind her.

Watching she witnessed a tall gentleman with what appeared to be sandy colored hair climb out of the passenger side and stare in the direction of the courthouse.

The driver, who was slightly shorter emerged, closed the door, and reached down into the truck bed pulling out what appeared to be a rifle. Remaining observant Mrs. Gambill was careful not to move or draw attention to herself. Within view of the rear view mirror she perceived the man placing something she could only assume was ammunition into his pockets.

Careful that neither man saw her she slunk down in the seat, locked the vehicle door, and drew her purse close to her. In the darkness they would not have spotted her, nor thought twice about looking inside the car.

Watching as a shadow snaked its way over the car seats, then up towards the dashboard and out over the hood, she waited, trying as best she could to keep her breathing calm.

Slowly Mrs. Gambill rose from her spot near the floorboard and peeked over the steering wheel to see one of the men confidentially approaching the courthouse doors.

She quickly realized the man she was seeing was wearing a uniform, *Another officer?* She questioned, *Where is he from?*

The uniform looked familiar, standard issue, but the man was not familiar. Having been working around the courthouse Mrs. Gambill knew everyone there. In fact she knew all deputies, and the Sheriff included, wore their badges when out on patrol. The shiny copper emblems were always visible either on their belts, their coats, or shirts.

A wave of panic overcame her as she realized that this man was not an officer at all. He was the exact opposite. He was the figure from the police reports, he was the man who carjacked residents on the nearby mountains, the one who had outwitted the departments of neighboring counties. Yet even more worrisome, he may have more than guns with him. This was the ghost of a man everyone had been hunting, especially Irwin.

Having emerged from the dark corners of the mountains she sensed he and his accomplice were there to do nothing but cause chaos. At that moment she knew she had to be careful, but she also had to get to the Four Oaks hotel. Looking back in the rear view she saw the passenger in the pickup smoking a cigarette, his eyes angled towards town.

Glancing back at the courthouse Mrs. Gambill thought about the prisoner who had been brought there by Irwin and Lincoln. *If their intention was to lure this man out of hiding,* Mrs. Gambill thought, *it appears to have worked.*

In a split second she made the only decision she knew she could. Keeping an eye on the man in the pickup she opened the car door, stepped out into the street, and started walking as casually as she could towards the hotel.

Irwin had followed Rash downstairs into the lobby where the Highway Patrol officer took out a pack of *Lucky Strikes,* "Want one?" Shaking his head, Irwin glanced at the doorway, noticing slight movement near the parking lot, "I like tobacco every now and then, but I'm not a big smoker."

"Really?" Rash lit his and stuffed the pack back in his coat pocket, "After that bombshell back there about the keys, thought news like that would've changed your mind."

Irwin could not keep his eyes off the parking lot. Walking towards the door the deputy saw the pale expression of a familiar face through the freshly cleaned glass.

It was starting to rain, the air had been thick with humidity most of the afternoon. The smell of fresh cut grass and earth rushed to greet him as he opened the door, "Mrs. Gambill? What are you doing—?"

A few feet away Mrs. Gambill's eyes shifted from Irwin to Rash. "Deputy, Lieutenant Rash" She said as her heels clicked the last couple of steps towards the door.

"Ma'am," Rash stepped aside, allowing her access inside the lobby.

"There's something wrong at the courthouse."

"How so?" Irwin asked.

"I just made it to my car, got in, when another car pulled in behind me a few seconds later. Two men got out. One was carrying a gun—." Her breath caught in her throat, but she collected herself quickly, "An officer I think, but I couldn't be certain—."

"What did she just say?" Lincoln's voice carried from behind Rash on the stairs. Irwin glanced over the newspaper editors' shoulder, a sinking feeling taking hold.

"Rash, tell the others to stay here, but get Wyatt, we're gonna need his car. Tell him to hurry."

"He reached into the truck and put something in his pockets—," Mrs. Gambill said, "It wasn't a gun—I don't think—."

Lincoln checked his weapon, "You either know or you don't, so which is it?"

"What makes you believe it wasn't a gun?" Irwin understood that from the angle at which Mrs. Gambill saw these men she might not have had the best view of their weapons. The lights from the theater were blinking after all and the effect alone could be disorienting especially when staring through a mirror in reverse.

"The way he was holding it, not by a grip," Mrs. Gambill explained as quickly as she could. Lincoln motioned for her to have a seat inside the lobby, "Who else is in the courthouse?"

"Sheriff Henson, Charlie maybe..." Her voice trailed off as she realized all four officers were ready to leave. Motor Vehicle Investigator Adam Lewis appeared on the staircase, "Mrs. Gambill, I'll stay with you here in the lobby."

Irwin shot her a glance that suggested she listen. Although she appreciated their concern for her safety, she knew if it meant missing out on a front page news story for the *Times*, sitting idly by in a lobby was not something she was about to do.

Connor had left Zane sitting on the haul not far from the courthouse. The evening was hotter than it had been all afternoon, the humidity caused him to nearly sweat through the light fitting uniform. "Think it's my new color," Connor joked as he had parked his pickup just below the theater.

Having done this a few times already, Connor knew that the courthouse was seldom locked with just one deputy on call. He had also taken into account that it was very likely that the Sheriff was still inside, but took his chances.

"Where'd he get these anyway?" Zane had asked jingling keys to the jail before they got out. "Someone owed Thayer a favor," Connor explained. "Some favor, and a nice set up too if you ask me. Did this have somethin; to do with how easy it was to still that haul from the Fortner's a few months back?"

Connor said nothing, knowing full well that the deal between him and Lucas Fortner had insured runs and money in their pockets. A door at the end of the hallway just past the entrance squeaked open slowly and Connor could hear someone clearing their throat.

Quickly he drew the forty-four from his holster leveling it directly at the man's head as he came into view.

Sheriff Dean Henson shifted his gaze towards the intruder, his eyes locking with that of Connors. "Evenin' Sheriff," the gunman grinned broadly. Henson raised his hands, sure to keep his right away from his holster, although every instinct in his body told him to grab it.

Speechless, Connor realized Henson had a good idea as to who he was, "Don't mind me," Connor continued, "I'll be out of here in a matter of seconds. Let's go get the prisoner, shall we?" Henson's eyes narrowed in quiet disbelief. He thought about the conversation Irwin had with Rash earlier in his office, and realized their worst possible fear had in fact come true.

"Move!" Connor shouted, his voice echoing through the hallway, the rain outside becoming heavier and more steady.

Henson turned around and walked towards the jail door, the gunman was cautious, careful not to stay too close behind, and just far enough out of the reach of Henson making it impossible to turn and simply disarm him. "Open the door Sheriff," Connor instructed, seeing the keys Henson had on his left belt loop.

"Where'd you get that uniform?" Henson asked as he placed the key inside the lock to the jail opening the door.

"Suits me doesn't it?" Connor laughed as he spotted Darrell. The mechanic was lying stretched across a thin mattress with his hands folded beneath his head, "What in the blazes—!"

"Get up Darrell," Connor exclaimed as he tossed him his spare keys. Darrell sat up, a look of sheer shock on his face as he lifted the keys from the dusty floor. "Are you crazy?" He bellowed.

"It's time to go Darrell, now get out of there!"

"I ain't goin' anywhere!"

"Darrell!" Connor shouted, "Get out here now!" He was keeping the forty-four level and aimed straight at the Sheriff, careful not to get closer than he needed to.

"Or what?" Darrell questioned.

"Or I shoot the Sheriff, and leave you here to burn with this place."

"Burn?" Henson's voice was not just loud, but full of concern. The realization of what the bootlegger aimed to do was almost unimaginable.

"You heard me," Connor seethed, "Now, get out!"

Tired of the bickering, Connor motioned for Sheriff Henson to head towards the cell, "Keys!"

Henson reluctantly handed Connor his jail keys, stepping into the spare cell, his inability to do much else turning his face a blistering red.

"Listen," Henson tried to reason, "Clearly Darrell here doesn't want—." "I didn't ask what he *wanted*," Connor shot back his voice low, a growl. He opened the cell with the Sheriff's spare keys and walked into the cell pulling Darrell out by the shirt collar nearly throwing him into the wall, "We're leavin'!"

"And keep your head down."

"What you goin' do?" Henson shouted.

"What I told you I would," Connor answered.

Stalling, Henson insisted, "That's not an answer."

Connor glared at the Sheriff, the copper edges of his eyes reminding Henson of a snake just before it struck. Giving a disgusted smirk Connor leaned closer to the bars, hissing, "This isn't personal Sheriff. This is about survivin'."

"When you break the law, that isn't survivin'." Henson retorted unapologetically.

"For some folks that might be true, but I ain't one of 'em and neither are some of the folks here."

There was nothing more Henson could say before Connor shut the outer door disappearing then locking it with the heavy thud of the key as it turned.

Standing in the hallway Darrell looked down at Connor's left hand knowing immediately that the bootlegger was about to send the entire town a message.

"Let's go!" Darrell's eyes caught sight of the thin tubes, his complexion turning as pale as the tubes were yellow. "We can just leave Connor, we don't need to—."

"Go on," Connor said calmly, his mind reserved to the fact of what was next. "Broth—." "Before Darrell could plead any further Connor left him standing outside the Clerk's Office.

CHAPTER 25

Agent Quinton Hollister had not expected to arrive back in the county as early as he did. The weather had held up just long enough for him to make it back from Yadkin County.

Turning the Chevy into a spot his white wall tires were the only distinguishing marks between his and Lincoln's vehicles.

They were the same make, same model, same year, but Hollister had insisted on the white wall tires. Closing the door he noticed four silhouettes in the distance, two on either side of the street inching their way cautiously towards the courthouse.

"Agent Hollister?" A man's voice asked quietly from the doorway of the hotel. Hollister's first instinct was to place his hand firmly on his weapon, his second was to examine the gentleman standing in the only strip of light for several feet, "Who's asking?" "It's me, David Whitman, we met briefly a few days ago. I work with the Underwriters' Detective Bureau."

Hollister grunted, "You're the one tracking the cars?"

"That's the idea," Whitman paused, "Look, the newspaper editor saw a gentleman enter the courthouse that she didn't recognize. He was wearing a uniform and carrying—." Before Whitman could utter another word the sound of gunfire ripped through the silence of the otherwise quiet town.

It was enough of a distraction to draw Rash and Wyatt's attention away from the vehicle they were coming up on. The driver was slumped down, gripping the wheel, his eyes focused on the courthouse lawn. The gunfire was loud enough to suggest a high caliber weapon, something much more powerful than the standard twenty-two Rash was used to hearing.

"What in the—?" Both men found themselves crouched down, careful to keep their images hidden from the driver. Within seconds two men emerged racing across the lawn.

"Freeze!" Lincoln shouted raising his weapon and coming into view of Darrell Joines and a man he could only assume was Connor Ridge.

"That's Joines," Sergeant Wyatt whispered to Rash as he checked his weapon and pulled back the hammer. The Sergeant had jumped in to assist the moment he heard from the stairwell in the hotel what was happening at the courthouse.

From his viewpoint Rash could see Irwin leveling his weapon in the same direction as Lincoln, but instantly sensed something was not right.

"Come on boys," the gunman said loudly, "You know you're going to let us walk clean off this courthouse lawn." "If you say so," Lincoln scoffed.

"Hands up Ridge!" Irwin shouted.

Connor's identity was clearly unveiled and he turned his attention towards Irwin, "You shoot either of us and your Sheriff dies." Rash felt a sudden heaviness settling atop his rib cage.

Irwin's expression did not waver, nor did his weapon, "Hands where we can see them Ridge, that's my last warning!" Lincoln took a step or two back towards the curb, "You ain't gonna to shoot me," Connor remarked, his hands still not visible. Darrell Joines glanced back and forth between Connor and Irwin's gun.

"We're leavin',' Connor proceeded down the steps towards their getaway vehicle. The click of the hammer on Lincoln's gun was just barely audible through the rain as Ridge inched closer, "On the ground!" His voice was unrelenting, but Connor did not stop, instead he pushed Darrell forward.

Darrell, seemingly having had enough turned and shoved Connor, but not as hard as he might have had he been closer, "Get off me!"

"Then move!" Connor shouted angrily.

"Sheriff's in the jail! They've got dynamite!" Darrell shouted just before squealing tires raced around the corner near Farmers Hardware and a burst of gunfire ripped through the street. Irwin caught sight of the gunman from the moving vehicle and noticed he was aiming squarely for Lincoln.

Irwin and Rash both reacted at the same time. A rapid return of bullets once again broke through the night, muffled only by the rain and random cracks of thunder as lightning lit up the sky.

From the pick up came a swift and no-holds-barred reaction that left Irwin and Lincoln diving for cover among the storefronts and a couple of parked vehicles. Just before reaching cover Irwin witnessed a bullet strike Lincoln, his blood flying into the rain landing in a puddle under his boots as he crouched behind a Ford.

Rash and Wyatt both emerged firing into the blinding rain attempting to stop the gunfire, but upon firing they too were bombarded from the car that had raced to the middle of Main Street.

The sound of glass shattering and light bulbs bursting took over as bright orange and red sparks danced above the theater, only to rise seconds later as vapors of smoke.

It was as if their weapons were on swivels and capable of spraying back and forth in a rapid session. Irwin recognized the faint sound of a Winchester twenty-two being fired in the mix. Lincoln looked towards the street where Connor and Darrell had been standing, only to see them both gone.

Darrell Joines was in the truck, Connor behind the wheel, but the man who had swapped places with Connor was standing on the street keeping Irwin and the others distracted.

In a split second one of Rash's bullets caught the gunman in his left side, Irwin watched as he collapsed. Having watched Ridge's accomplice fall, Lincoln cursed under his breath shouting to Wyatt and Rash, "Hit the tires!"

Irwin spotted Rash first, his outline a dark silhouette against the remaining lights of the Spartan Theater as he kept himself low. The car that had remained parked in the center of the street had raced off towards Whitehead. Irwin took that as a sign they had either ran out of ammo, or completed their task of distracting officers while damaging the street.

Rash fired off a shot towards Connor's truck. The bullet could be heard slapping the tailgate but ricocheting into one of the windows at Smithey's.

Heart racing Irwin stood up, "Rash, Wyatt, get to a car! Go after 'em!" "Already on it," Agent Hollister said as he rolled up in his vehicle, "Get in boys!"

Rash and Wyatt jumped at the chance to get out of the stinging rain, Hollister laid his foot to the gas and they were off heading towards Cherry Lane.

Lincoln turned his attention back to Irwin and there was no mistaking the deep graze across the right side of the agent's neck. It was not lost on Irwin that if the bullet had been any closer, agent Lincoln would have been dead.

"You all right?" Irwin asked.

Lincoln reached up, touched his neck and let the rain wash the blood away, "I've been worse, let's go."

Throughout their endeavors Thayer had been stuck by Conner. Although he felt laying low would have been a safer solution given Darrell's arrest he also knew Connor was never one to run from a fight, nor was he someone who liked to play it safe.

Having been dropped off at the back of the courthouse, he was let in by Connor who insisted he finish the job. Connor then turned over the spare keys so Thayer could unlock the safe inside the Clerk's office. Neither man had been willing to pass up the chance to obtain extra cash.

A small ring of smoke slithered into the air. Glancing over his shoulder he saw no movement from the street wondering, *Did Connor killed them all?*

Taking in a deep breath Thayer realized that if that were the case he had to be leaving, and in a hurry. Placing the keys in his blue jean pants pocket he headed for the exit, and what he hoped would be a clean getaway.

A quiet but very present '*click*' stopped him inches from the foyer. It came from just inside the Sheriff's office where he turned his sights on a very tall, very broad shouldered deputy. "Goin' somewhere?" Irwin inquired curiously. Thayer noted the man was drenched, his coat soaked through.

Another *'click'* came from across the hall on the opposite side. Looking to his left Thayer smirked, "Well isn't this a fix." "You could say that," Lincoln stepped forward and put his gun in his holster, "Hands up, now."

Thayer did as he was instructed without much fuss. Irwin looked towards the jail cell door and then back at the intruder, "Where's Sheriff Henson?"

Thayer said nothing, but Irwin already knew thanks to Darrell.

"You have keys?" Lincoln asked as he removed the copies from Thayer's pocket. "I do now," Irwin took the keys and rushed to the cells.

"Dean, you in there!"

"Irwin?" Dean sounded relieved and frustrated at his circumstances.

Opening the door that led to the cells Irwin could smell something burning.

"What are you waiting' for, get me out of here!" Henson shouted. Irwin tossed him the keys, turning his attention to the Clerk's office.

"What's the matter?" Lincoln could see the urgency in Irwin's movements while he held onto a handcuffed Thayer. "Smoke," Irwin replied, searching the office at the lower end of the hall.

Towards the back of the Clerk's office Irwin spotted a twinkling red and gold light worming its way across the hardwood floor.

The next three words escaped his mouth one at a time, "Oh. My. God." Irwin quickly realized there was more than one light. There were several.

"Get out now!" Lincoln shoved Thayer towards the exit, Dean Henson having finally freed himself was right behind the agent and the prisoner. Irwin quickly worked to close the office's heavy oak doors in the hopes of holding off part of the energy from the oncoming blast.

Halfway down the hall the first explosion tore through the back of the courthouse shaking the ground and causing Irwin to stumble just before the door.

Lincoln and the others were outside, well into the street when the second eruption happened, blowing the oak doors off their hinges and propelling them into the hallway just as Irwin made it past the first few steps of the courthouse.

The force was so great behind him that the deputy had hardly enough time to cover his head as his body slammed onto the edge of the lawn.

CHAPTER 26

Mrs. Gambill cried out as the second blast seemed to propel Deputy Irwin across the courthouse lawn and towards the rock wall in front of the vehicles.

Whitman, Morris, UpChurch, and Lewis all stood stunned in the middle of the street along with several other Four Oaks guests. The rain was coming down in sheets as flames in the back of the courthouse started to lick the sky.

"Get Doc!" Mrs. Gambill shouted at the Four Oaks owner W.C. Fields who quickly darted out of sight.

"Mrs. Gambill don't—!" Before Mr. Lewis could protest she was running towards the courthouse.

Lincoln reached Zane Shepherd and once he determined the man was still breathing a few bystanders assisted him in moving to the curb in front of the drug store.

Zane clenched his teeth as sharp pains radiated up his side and into his shoulders.

Lincoln locked eyes with Thayer whom he still had a grasp on despite the ordeal, "Stay there!" He ordered shoving the bomber against the hood of one of the cars.

"He isn't goin' anywhere," William Hawks' voice rose from the rain and smoke. Hawks had arrived moments after the blast, his men were working to keep everyone calm near the theater. "Caption, glad you made it," Lincoln acknowledged before heading back to aid Irwin.

Mrs. Gambill and him met at the same time, "Doc's on his way, Mr. Fields went to get him." Irwin was beginning to sit upright. The violent explosion tore through his eardrums making it impossible to hear anything other than muffled shouts and disorienting voices.

Gazing up at the courthouse, the flames stretched higher as the wooden floors burned, the building's walls groaning from the lack of stability. Irwin knew it would take only minutes before shelves, desks, and the courtroom on the second floor would give way under the heat.

Instead of lingering on what was about to be lost, Irwin knew he had to salvage what could be gained. He stood up, straightened his coat and looked to Lincoln, "Where's the prisoner?"

"Over there but Irwin—."

Irwin came off the last few steps and Mrs. Gambill stepped aside letting him pass by her. The agent knew that Irwin was determined and watched as the deputy reached out and grabbed Thayer pressing him up against the solid brick wall of the drug store. Clearly surprised the prisoner did not have time to react.

"Where is he?"

"Long gone," Thayer said, feeling slightly relieved.

"I want you to take a good look around," Irwin stood so close that there was no way for Thayer to avoid the deputy's eyes, "You are left holdin' the bag on this one. He doesn't care how you fair, or how your friend down there is doin'," Irwin motioned behind him to the man struggling to sit up against a nearby car.

"If you think he does, or ever *did*, you're as big a fool as you look right now!"

Before Irwin could press him further Mrs. Gambill approached, "Why don't you boys tell the deputy your names?" Thayer grinned, "Don't have to, reckon he already knows mine."

"I do, but who's your friend?" Irwin questioned.

"Zane Shepherd," Doc Choate announced as he looked down at the injured man from the gunfight earlier. "Shepherd?" Irwin turned, not quite ready to release his grip on Thayer, "Any relation to Nolan Shepherd?"

"Who is Nolan Shepherd?" Lincoln asked, trying to keep up. Irwin explained, "Another local moonshiner who has been in the jail a few times, although not recently," looking at Zane Irwin added, "Now I know why.

Irwin kept hold of Thayer's arm, "Where is Ridge goin'?" The young man took his eyes away from the deputy letting them drift down to Zane who was being lifted into a car.

"We know more than you think we do," Lincoln commented.

"Not that it matters," Thayer said, "But he was headin' to Yadkin tonight on a haul. Probably already there."

"Where bouts in Yadkin?" Irwin questioned.

"Place called Harper's Farm Rd."

"I know where it is," Irwin said, "Who's he meetin'?"

"I don't know, he didn't say. Connor never tells us the details."

"No, but he sure showed you how to use that dynamite," Lincoln shot back while motioning for Irwin to follow him. "You're under arrest," They heard Henson say before racing to Lincoln's vehicle.

Hollister's vehicle gilded around a curve near Glade Valley before a strong vibration ripped through the moving vehicle.

"What was that?" Duncan asked as he craned his neck to look at Rash.

Staring out of the rear windshield Rash's eyes could barely make out the faint glow of what appeared to be fire.

"Whatever it was, we can't turn around now," the Lieutenant Highway Patrol officer said in a tone that worried Hollister.

The BOI agent momentarily glanced in the rear view to see Rash checking his weapon. "Hang on," He instructed as he shifted the vehicle's gears and both men braced themselves for another curve.

"He's heading to Yadkin," Duncan muttered, "Should've called ahead before we took off, should have had the cavalry backing us up."

"Too late for '*should haves*'," Rash remarked.

The taillights of Ridge's truck were just slightly within view. "Besides rain is gonna make this mountain a beast to go down. The good news is he isn't going to fly," Rash stated as he noticed the visibility waning. Hollister grunted in agreement but kept his eyes on the road ahead.

Suddenly Connor gave his truck a burst of speed and the fog swallowed the truck's dark outline just like the blue ridge mist did the mountains any given morning.

An arrogant grin swept across Connors face as he launched the Ford into the fog. The thick atmosphere made it easy for them to lose their tail, and even easier to hide.

"What are you doin'? Are you crazy?" Darrell shouted, "Can't see one curve after another—!" Connor lifted his revolver wrenching back on the hammer, aiming it at Darrell's temple. The mechanic swallowed hard, "Connor, listen—."

"No *you* listen," Connor didn't take his eyes off the road nor his hand off the gun, "When this is over, you and I are gonna to have words."

"I ain't told 'em nothin' Connor—I swear!"

"They knew where the still was Darrell," Connor lowered the gun, keeping it close to his side as he gripped the steering wheel, sifted gears, and then pulled into a side road Darrell had not even seen until just a second before.

Connor flipped the car around making sure the back lights were not showing, cut the headlights, reached into his shirt pocket and pulled out a cigarette.

Darrell knew he had been caught in a lie, and part of him thought it would be best to jump out of the truck and start running for his life. The other part of him knew he would never make it. Connor would as soon kill him than let him survive knowing he had sung like a canary.

"You could," Connor took a long drag on the cigarette tossing the match out of the driver side window. Darrell recalled how perceptive Connor could be at times, it was as if he had read the mechanics mind.

"I could *do* what?

"Run."

"What for?" Darrell sounded amused.

"I know you told 'em about the still Darrell," He exhaled a ring of smoke, "but the real question is what else did you tell 'em?"

"Nothin'—I told 'em nothin'—I—."

"Own up Darrell."

"Connor you know me—."

"I know I've been the one paying you, and this is how you repay me?"

"It isn't like that—!"

"Then what is it like Darrell?"

"It's—."

Before Darrell could utter another word a car going close to forty miles an hour zipped by in the fog, its white walled tires easily spotted.

The passengers had been incapable of seeing the truck due to the heavy fog and angle of the vehicle. Connor gave it a moment more and then eased himself back into the road.

Darrell's heart sank slightly as he realized Connor Ridge had outfoxed the law again, making it Darrell's last hope of stepping out of that vehicle alive.

CHAPTER 27

Floyd Crouse, Doctors Leff and Burt Choate, Mr. Harding, Mr. Fields, and countless other men were rushing to fight the flames. Mrs. Gambill stood off to the side, watching with the others as her office, the courthouse, the nearby buildings, all went up in smoke.

Nearby she could hear someone calling her name, but she could not seem to take her eyes off the destruction before her.

"Floyd got some of the papers out," Rebecca Mitchell from Floyd's office could be heard saying. Mrs. Gambill felt someone touch her shoulder and as she spun around she was greeted by her husband, Robert.

"What happened here?" Her husband asked as she wrapped her arms around him, "How did the fire start?" Looking up at him Mrs. Gambill shook her head, "It's a long story."

"Dynamite," Kirk Billings answered as he pushed through the crowd, "We need the commissioners together tomorrow mornin'. Would you be available Robert?"

"Of course," Robert Gambill stared down at his wife in disbelief, "Dynamite? Were you in there?" She shook her head, "No, thankfully not."

There was nothing left to say at that moment. Instead he held her close for a moment and then started to move her towards the cars, "Where did you park?"

"It's in the rubble," She looked back at the courthouse.

Robert saw the pained expression in her eyes, "As much as I hate to hear that, I would have hated it a lot more if somethin' had happened to you. We will take care of the car tomorrow. Lets get home."

Mrs. Gambill held her husband's hand as he guided her through the crowd towards his car parked a few feet from Smithey's.

As she sat down in the passenger side and he closed the door she wondered how he had known about the fire. "Who told you about the courthouse?" "Doughton, he was home this evening when Floyd rang him. Said the place was ablaze. He knows you work on the top floor so he called me, asked if you had made it home."

"That was kind of him," Mrs. Gambill acknowledged, "I am sorry Robert, I should have called——."

He held up his hand cutting her off, "It's all right, I am just glad you're okay and no one was seriously injured. Looks as though this could have been a lot worse."

"It will be if Irwin and the BOI don't catch who did this," She said without realizing she had done so aloud. "Who *did* do this?" Robert asked.

"A moonshiner." Mrs. Gambill answered. It took Robert a few minutes before he spoke, finally admitting, "Now I definitely want to hear this long story."

"Whoa," Walter saw the dim glow of brake lights against the fog. Lincoln's car was just close enough so the two could make out the Ford lettering on the back tailgate.

The truck's lights had been barely visible as Lincoln's car rounded one of Elkin mountains blind curves. "I see 'em," Lincoln slowed his vehicle, careful not to lose the lights but cautious enough to stay several lengths behind.

"Where is Hollister?" Irwin asked, noticing they appeared to be the only two cars on the mountain at that hour. "My guess he's at the bottom," Lincoln replied, "Connor probably pulled out somewhere, ducking them."

"A few months back my cruiser got a radio, I'm inclined to believe every car needs them. Would be helpful to communicate during moments like this," Irwin explained.

"Couldn't agree more," Lincoln acknowledged as he rounded a curve and shifted gears. Irwin glanced out of the passenger side window, the night pitch dark, the fog overtaking what few lights were below.

"Sorry about the courthouse," Lincoln offered, "It's a shame." "Yeah, it is," Irwin's mind turned back to the explosion, and then to his wife. *What will Zora think? Had she been told?* Taking a deep breath he held on as the fog started to lift and the Ford pick up ahead of them raced on.

"Do you remember where Shepherd said Connor was heading down here?" "Harper's, I know the way."

Lincoln glanced off to the right, his eyes spotting a dark vehicle with white walled tires sitting between heavy bushes on an old dirt road that seemed to lead to a nearby house. Irwin followed the agent's gaze and spotted the car too. "Told you so," Lincoln said as he pulled off the road.

Hollister cursed under his breath as he continued to weave his way down the steep incline finally coming to a flat stretch of road just outside of the county limits.

"He dodged us," Wyatt shook his head in disbelief.

"In that fog, it's easy done," Hollister said as if scolding himself. Rash sat quietly in the backseat, his brain working, "Let's just hope Irwin and Lincoln have caught up to him."

"Did you think it odd that Darrell told us where the Sheriff was?" Wyatt questioned.

"Nothin' unusual if Darrell wants to keep his deal," Hollister said, "Seen it before especially when there is too much heat on them."

"And we know where their biggest operation is," Rash added.

"They've probably already set it up elsewhere," Wyatt answered, "So that doesn't matter."

Hollister grunted, "Where?"

"Wherever they like. These moonshiners place stills on other properties, some even on their neighbors. They've been known to pay a cut from their hauls to the land owners so they don't threaten to report. Money isn't good for much these days but here," Wyatt added, "It sure does keep some folks nice and quiet."

Rubbing his eyes Rash glanced back up in the distance to see a dark Ford pick up slowly making its way out of the fog and turn off onto a side road just past Hollister's patrol car.

"Well I'll be," Wyatt smiled back at Rash, "Patience is a virtue."

"Amen to that," Hollister said as he motioned to the car that appeared behind the pickup, "Looks like you were right, Lieutenant."

Rash nodded, "Told you, Walter isn't bout to let him get away."

Opening his vehicle door Hollister ran up to Lincoln's car. Irwin lowered the passenger window making it easier to talk.

"You fellas are right on time."

"Good to hear," Lincoln said.

"Just saw him turn up that road there past the field," Hollister pointed without looking back, "We're gonna be right behind you," the agent assured them and stopped before turning back.

"What happened back there? We almost got to Roaring Gap and felt something."

Lincoln frowned, "Dynamite happened."

Hollister arched his eyebrows in surprise, "How much we talkin'?"

"Enough to level the courthouse," Irwin replied. The BOI agent ran a hand through his dark hair, "Let's get this guy." He tapped the top of the car three times before heading back to his cruiser and climbing inside.

Irwin reached for his weapon, checked the rounds and nodded, "You heard the man." Lincoln glanced around the car to ensure no one was coming and pulled out. Moments later Hollister was behind them as they turned onto Harper's Dairy Rd.

Through the passenger side mirror Darrell noticed the headlights slowly creeping along the darkened treeline of the dirt road a good 200 yards behind the pickup.

Deciding it was in his best interest he said nothing, and drew his eyes back to the front of the car. Neither he nor Connor had spoken a word to one another since coming off the mountain.

"Tell me what you told 'em," Connor finally spoke as he tossed out another withered cigarette from the driver's window.

"Connor I didn't—'," Darrell started to insist but Connor interrupted, "You told them somethin'. They knew about Devils Ridge, they knew where to come lookin'." "They got lucky," Darrell scoffed, "They've got the BOI with 'em."

Connor pressed down on the accelerator and shifted gears so fast the pickup jolted forward, "The BOI?" Darrell did not blink as he stared at Connor, "That man back there, the one Matthew and the others shot at, who ordered you to stop, he was BOI."

A simmering sense of dread washed over Connor Ridge for the first time since he had hauled moonshine. Having started at the age of seventeen he was bold, and maybe a little too arrogant for his own good.

An hour into his first haul he had found himself being flagged down by the Johnson City Sheriff. It was then Connor realized he had a knack for lying and quite convincingly.

That night had been the only time Connor had felt an epic rush of sickness, dread, fear, and self loathing.

After he watched the Sheriff's car disappear into the rainy evening, he vowed to change the rules of hauling.

His rules had worked. He had established loyalty among his drivers, his mechanics, and his fellow bootleggers in northwestern Appalachia.

Whenever he hauled there was always another car, maybe two, close by watching and ready to take over if trouble arose.

Tonight, he had broken that rule for the first time in years, and he suddenly realized the cost it might ultimately have.

"Tell me Darrell," Connor cleared his throat, "This BOI agent, is he the only one?" "I don't know," Darrell admitted. "Who else is with the Deputy?" Connor suddenly wished Jeb had asked him more questions, or at least had been given the privacy to.

"I told Jeb you shouldn't come back for me," Darrell said quietly, "They were countin' on it."

Connor glanced into the rear view mirror before replying, "They didn't count on me bringing friends though, did they?" Falling silent again Darrell looked out the passenger window.

"Did you tell them where the haul was goin' Darrell?" "No, of course not—I didn't even know you were still gonna—."

"Shut up," Connor gripped the gun at his side, "Well *someone* did." Before he could threaten to aim the weapon Darrell quickly rambled off, "What makes you think Zane or Thayer didn't talk! These cops, the G-Men, they offer deals for snitches, and you know Thayer as soon snitch as sit in a jail cell any day."

Connor kept his eyes on the dirt road, without warning he took a turn to the right and darted midway between a split wood fence and what appeared to be a small out building where tools were kept.

Putting the car in park Connor turned his attention back to Darrell, "Get out."

"Connor I—."

"I said—GET OUT!" Connor shouted, the force of his voice alone enough to shake Darrell to his core. Fumbling for the door handle the mechanic did as he was told. Not even half a second later he heard Connor climbing out of the vehicle, his boots crunching above the crushed gravel followed by a loud crack.

CHAPTER 28

The gunfire echoed down the road where Lincoln had paused, cutting his lights after seeing the pickup dart off towards a nearby field. Through the semi-darkness Irwin spotted the silhouette of a figure running, stumbling, and then falling to the ground, "That's Darrell."

Lincoln accelerated their speed and with Hollister close behind they reached the small roadway just barely squeezing between the tool shed and a wooden fence. With his window rolled down Irwin heard another fiery crack cut through the sounds of cicadas.

As the deputy started to get out of the patrol car, he spotted Connor Ridge climbing effortlessly back into the pickup and heading straight for the road again. The pickup flew around Lincoln's Chevy leaving Darrell Joines to fend for himself laying in the field.

Dust, gravel, and leftover mud from an evening rain flew up smacking the patrol car's hood and Lincoln's side window.

"For heaven's sake—!" Irwin noticed the agent's patience was wearing thin.

"Hold on," He instructed the deputy as he kicked the car back into gear and spun the back tires, the vehicle slightly lifting into midair as its tail caught the gravel.

"Whoa!" Irwin felt the car kick forward and a second later forced him to put out his right leg to keep himself from being launched into the dashboard.

"I said hang on," The fluidity of Lincoln's motions as he turned the wheel, pressed the gas, and shifted gears, made Connor Ridge's stock car skills seem stale.

Part of Irwin wondered what all law enforcement might be able to accomplish if their vehicles were as high-powered as some of the bootleggers, and what training that would require.

Hollister and the others were at a standstill back at the field, and Irwin momentarily caught a glimpse of Rash rushing form the car to apprehend Darrell Joines.

A loud thud brought Irwin's attention back to the road ahead of them, Connor was weaving from side to side. Irwin could sense his desperation, fearing it might cause more damage if he was not stopped.

The sun was starting to creep up over the mountains, "Come on sunshine," Lincoln muttered as he watched Connors bumper. Irwin knew any amount of daylight at the moment would be a gift.

The bootlegger slung the pickup around a sharp curve, the incline afterwards slightly steeper than Lincoln had been prepared for. When they hit the bottom the front of the patrol car scraped then bounced jarring the agent and deputy for several seconds. Lincoln cursed under his breath before shouting over the roar of the engine to Irwin, "You trust me?"

Nodding Irwin replied, "What do you have in mind?"

"We're gonna have to shoot out his tires." Irwin knew the maneuver Lincoln was talking about all too well, "All right."

"You think you can?" Lincoln asked.

"Right now, that's our only option," Irwin gripped his weapon, pushed on the door and placed his right foot on the runner below, steadying himself as the outside wind worked against him.

Connor was not in the habit of looking back. He kept his eyes front and center, none too concerned with what the two lawmen behind were doing.

It was just simpler to press forward, but it was also nerve wracking as he could still hear their engine gaining on him in the pickup. Part of him wished he had taken the Chevy Darrell had modified for the stock race.

Finally he got the nerve to glance over into his driver side mirror, "What in the name of—?"

Is that deputy serious? He wondered part of him in disbelief, the other part of him trying not to panic.

Pressing the gas while daring a quick glance at his gauge, Connor decided to toggle back and forth. The deputy had stepped out onto the patrol car's runner and was aiming straight at his back driver side tire.

"He won't make that shot," Connor whispered to himself aloud, *Or will he?*

Irwin took a deep breath, steadied his grip on the door and his left leg that grounded him to the inside of the patrol car. His heart was racing as fast as the wind. Surrounding them he noticed the sun streaking a brilliant crimson red against the silhouetted mountains, reminding him of fire.

Lincoln shifted gears, the car bolted closer to the pickup making it possible for him to take the first shot. The bullet could be heard smacking the bumper just above the tire.

"Try again!" Lincoln called over the rush of the current. Irwin relaxed his grip, waited for the patrol car to fall back another few inches, and fired for a second time.

The pickup weaved this time, preventing the shot, and Irwin bit his lower lip. *Third time has to be a charm,* he thought as he pulled back the hammer on his thirty-eight and took aim once more.

Without hesitation Lincoln swayed the car to the right, near the shoulder of the road, having anticipated Connors move. Irwin had sensed the shift, adjusted, and the third shot ripped through the back passenger tire of the pickup. Lincoln called out, "Nice shot!" Irwin ducked back into the car, closing the door and falling back into the seat, "Maybe that'll stop him."

It didn't. To Irwin's dismay Connor kept going, swaying, and depending on the three good tires he had remaining. Looking in the backseat Irwin reached for the one of Lincoln's rifles, "Is this thing loaded?"

"Of course it is," the agent answered, "What are you thinking?"

"We end this," Irwin checked the chamber, closed it back and pushed open the passenger side door again.

Lincoln did not argue, he was ready for this to be over as much as Irwin. He watched as the country deputy took aim for a fourth and final time at Connors rear driver side tire.

There was no need for a second try, Irwin had mastered the shot and Connors truck skid, the rubber shredding against the metal rims giving way to a plum of black smoke from the exhaust.

Just missing the smoke, Irwin slid back into the patrol car and took a deep breath, "Watch out!" Lincoln put the brakes on to avoid what might have been a collision if the pickup had not started to roll towards the hillside on the right shoulder of the dirt road.

The outline of a barn rose in the distance the closer Lincoln inched to the pickup.

"He's gonna to run," Irwin said, knowing full well what was coming next. Men like Connor Ridge did not get caught, and if they did— things never ended well.

"Wait," the word just barely escaped the agents mouth before he saw Connor jump from the pickup with a shotgun in his hand, and a bundle of something else."

CHAPTER 29

Irwin kept the rifle low, but he kept his finger on the trigger, carefully approaching Connor Ridge.

"Ridge?" He called out, the man, who could not have been more than thirty, wearing a deputies uniform glared, keeping his rifle aimed at Irwin.

In his left hand was a sawed off shotgun, but it was what he held at the trigger that was all too frightening. Lincoln emerged from the car, his gun up, his stance just past the driver's door.

"Connor, put the gun down," Irwin ordered, "It's over." "It's over when I say it's over," Connor adjusted his grip on the shotgun, waving it towards Irwin.

The deputy kept his eyes locked on Connor's. How this man had eluded them for so long had been more than baffling, but now that Irwin finally got to see him up close, he understood.

Connor Ridge's features were solid, stubborn, and uniquely average. His dark hair and green eyes with their yellow trim slightly gave off a gold appearance while his overall features appeared worn, even weathered. Instantly Irwin thought about his own boys.

"Look, Connor, I know you have a family. I know you have a wife, kids, I'm sure you want to see them. I know they'll be wantin' to see you. Moreover," Added Irwin, "they'll want to see you alive rather than dead, and that's where this is headin' if you don't put that gun down."

Lincoln's gaze went back and forth for a moment between the deputy and the fugitive standing with his hand firmly on a shotgun and a cluster of rusty yellow colored cylinder tubes that could only be one thing.

"I have a family too, and I would not want to see them hurt. Not the way you want to hurt folks Connor. Leavin' in a hail of gunfire, or an explosion, that does your kin no good. They depend on you."

Connor scoffed, "You think you know me deputy?"

"I do," Irwin said without hesitation, "I know where you're comin' from. More than you know."

"Then you should've left my business alone." Connor tossed the tubes into the back seat of the pickup and Lincoln immediately knew what was about to happen,

"Drop the gun!" Lincoln fired but the bullet was only a warning shot, not knowing what other items the bootlegger may have been hauling. Connor had already expected the warning shot, and fired into the backseat the single bullet striking the dynamite cylinders.

Hollister, Rash, and Wyatt rolled up just as Lincoln fired the warning shot at Connor. "Stop the car!" Darrell shouted as he kicked the back of Hollister's seat. The agent was both annoyed and angered by the action at first, but a second later he found himself glad he listened.

A thunderous roar erupted from the pickup just a couple hundred feet up the road, and the passengers watched as Irwin and Lincoln dove into opposite ditches on the road to avoid the hail of glass, metal, and flames that launched into the air.

"Holy cow!" Rash shouted as he opened his door and raced out. Wyatt did the same leaving Hollister with Darrell Joines who remained ducked down in the back seat.

"Walt!" Rash shouted.

"Agent Lincoln!" Wyatt exclaimed as he raced by Rash on the opposite side of the road. The smoke and smell of moonshine smothered the air as the two closed the gap between Hollister's car and the pickup.

Irwin uncovered his head and looked up coughing, "Where is he?" Before Rash could respond Irwin was back on his feet, his rifle in hand, cautiously walking towards the burning vehicle.

"Be careful!" Lincoln shouted.

Rounding the front of the pickup, careful of the flames and the popping of hot glass, Irwin brought the rifle up, searching for any sign of Ridge. Movement on the embankment above in some of the brush and thin pines caught Irwin's attention, "There!" He shouted to Rash who bolted up the side drawing his weapon.

Lincoln sprinted up the embankment, his breathing steadier than it had been the first time he had climbed such an incline.

Circling a few oak trees Lincoln thought he caught sight of Ridge's jacket a few steps ahead until he heard a click and felt cold metal touching his left temple.

Chastising himself, Lincoln knew there was no easy way out of this situation.

"Give me your gun," Connor Ridge instructed in a hushed voice, "And not a word." Lincoln clinched his jaws together in defiance. "I said," Connor repeated each word slowly, "Hand over your gun." The cold metal pressed against Lincoln's skin. "Fine."

Lincoln turned his gun barrel towards the sky preparing to hand it over, but before he could, a powerful crack deafened him.

Irwin lowered the rifle, smoke still steaming from the barrel as he handed it off to Rash. Wyatt kept his own weapon drawn and followed the deputy towards Lincoln who had stepped back and rubbed his ear.

"Sorry about that!" Irwin shouted so the agent could hear him over the ringing he was undoubtedly hearing.

Lincoln looked down to see Connor Ridge bleeding, his gun flung a good several feet lying on top a mix of leaves, pine needles, and dew covered earth.

The sunrise had reached over the peaks of the trees, their dark outlines and the fiery red clouds caught the gold in their captives eyes.

Connor Ridge gripped his wounded hand, and struggled to stand up. Before he could attempt another step Irwin grabbed his arm, spun him towards the nearby oak tree and took out his cuffs, "Connor Ridge, you are under arrest."

Sheriff Dean Henson and Deputy Charlie Shepherd stood outside Four Oaks hotel talking as the cars had rolled up. Many of the highway patrol officers that Hawks had brought into town were still there too, and the clean up on Main Street was underway.

The smell of smoke, wood, and burnt concrete hung in the air as shadows of the rising sun began to crept over the shell of the building.

"Wow," Hollister's voice rose from the solemn silence that had gripped the officers.

"You weren't foolin'," Rash said as he walked around the car where Irwin was standing, "Looks like the fire got more than just the courthouse."

"It did," Henson approached with his hands in his pockets, a look of both defeat and disgust on his face as he stared down the street towards the damage. "All that remains are the pillars."

"Goes to show buildings can be burnt down, but the community is still standing. People still want to help," Irwin stated, acknowledging the challenges that lay ahead.

"Sheriff, we're sorry about the courthouse, about Ridge, all of it," Lincoln said, "But we do have some good news amid the ashes."

Henson looked at Irwin who motioned towards the back of Lincoln's car, "Recognize him?" Henson and Ridge locked eyes for a moment, "Gentlemen, you're right, that's the best news I have heard in a long while. How'd you catch him?" "Ended up havin' to shoot him," Irwin admitted.

The Sheriff leaned on the car and looked over at Lincoln, "Doc patched up Shepherd. He's in lock up down in Yadkin until we can figure out where we're gonna to be pendin' a new courthouse. Take this over to Doc, and Rash's men can escort him back down to River Hayes."

"I'll go with you," Irwin offered, opening the passenger door as Henson stepped aside.

"What happened to the hood?" Charlie Shepherd asked to examine Lincoln's Chevy from the steps of Four Oaks. "Long story," Lincoln called as he sat back down behind the wheel of his car.

Ridge had been dead silent since his arrest and Irwin was glad of it. Doc Choate met them in the waiting area of his office, "What happened?"

"Gunshot to the hand," Irwin explained.

Examining the injury for a moment, Doc took in a deep breath, "Follow me." Irwin stayed behind letting Lincoln accompany the injured prisoner into one of the three examining rooms.

"Hannah?" Irwin removed his hat as he approached Doc's secretary Hannah Blevins. "Deputy," She smiled. "May I use your telephone?" "Certainly," She lifted the phone from the far side of the desk towards him and stepped away to gather some things for Doc.

Removing a folded up piece of paper from the inside pocket of his jacket Irwin lifted the receiver, "Operator, get me Mr. Roger Wagoner please."

In a few brief rings Mr. Wagoner answered his phone, "Hello?" Irwin glanced up to see Hannah heading towards the exam room with fresh supplies and answered, "Mr. Wagoner, this is deputy Irwin. Do you remember our conversation at the courthouse in Sparta a few months back?" "I do," Roger answered, "What may I do for you, deputy?"

"If I recall correctly Mr. Wagoner you told me you were good at rememberin' faces."

"I did."

"Might I trouble you to come down to Doc Choate's office for a moment? There is someone here I need you to identify." "I'll drop by," Wagoner replied, ending the call.

CHAPTER 30

6 Months Later

Pulling over onto a patch of grass Walter Irwin climbed out of his patrol car and stared up at the familiar hillside before him. Connor Ridge was sitting in the Yadkin County jail along with Darrell Joines and a few other gang members the team had been able to round up.

Ridge was patiently awaiting his hearing, pending the completion of the new courthouse.

Parts of Main Street had also caught fire that evening from the explosion, stores suffered damages, and the town was certainly different. Although temporary, many offices had to move and this included the newspaper office, the Sheriff's Department, the Register of Deeds, and the Clerk of Courts office.

Doc Choate had been kind enough to even offer up a room on the main floor of his practice to the Deeds Office while the Sheriff's Department operated out of a room or two at the Four Oaks Hotel down the street.

The night of the fire, county attorney Floyd Course had managed to salvage several boxes of files from the courthouse, but not all of them, and sadly those were irreplaceable.

Turning to have a look over the mountains Irwin saw the small buildings that belonged to the town he called home below.

Pulling out his pocket watch he noted the time and proceeded to climb the embankment where he could once again make out the sound of a waterfall. The hillside was spotted with large pines and oaks, the occasional squirrel darting in and out of view among the brush.

Irwin paused a moment to look out over the mountains, standing in almost the exact spot as agent Lincoln had months earlier. The man had been right about one thing. This was a beautiful part of the country, and one Irwin hoped would stay that way for his children and his grandchildren.

Remaining content in the moment he moved towards a narrow path that was well worn between pines and laurel. Following it the noise of the thundering water rolled downward somewhere to his left. Pausing every few steps Irwin took note of the landscape, watching the water glisten as it glided over rocks effortlessly in an attempt to reach the bottom.

As he stepped towards a clearing the deputy heard a soft ping that drew his gaze downward. A wound up, partially rusted copper pipe was sticking out from under his boot. Reaching down he lifted the piece of coil knowing it had once belonged to part of a still. Crouched down he spotted the clearing off to the far side of the waterfall, just before its rapids—and something else.

Leaning against a nearby longleaf pine was a small shovel. The handle was well worn and slightly loose. Someone had dug with the instrument often, giving Irwin reason to glance around. The money Darrell Joines had mentioned, it was hidden all right, and Irwin suspected he knew where.

Taking a step closer to the clearing he saw a very familiar motion to his right.

Stepping back, Irwin soon realized he had nearly crossed paths with numerous snakes. The long slithering creatures were easily camouflaged against the dark green shadowed earth. Angling the shovel downward Irwin got a good look at the type of snakes lurking about. *Cottonmouth moccasins.*

In that moment he recalled the questions posed to him by Rash a few days prior after Connors arrest. Silently Irwin said to himself, "*That's why he called it Devil's Ridge.*"

Having made his way safely back to the other end of the clearing where there were no further snakes in sight, Irwin grasped the shovel and out of habit tried to stake it in the ground. However, when the ground did not give way he tried again. The second attempt forced Irwin to stare at the ground as something hard made it impossible for him to push through the dirt and moss.

Slowly he worked the shovel around the object until he began to see silver. Stepping back he removed more dirt from around the base of the object until it came into view just enough for him to make out what it was.

Leaning on the shovel Irwin shook his head, "Well I'll be." There, still partially buried in the ground, was the slot machine from Twin Oaks General Store. Knowing full well that Connor and his boys had probably already emptied it, Irwin made a note to ask Charlie or even Sheriff Henson to come back with him at some point to retrieve it.

Placing the shovel back against the tree, Irwin headed out of the clearing as carefully as he could, still mindful of the slithering devils along the ridge. He had things to do before the sun sat, and one of them required a stop by the local board of elections.

People stood watching the activity at the newly built courthouse from across the street as Irwin spoke with Ben Reeves and a few others outside the theater.

"Have you heard anythin' new about the Ridge case Walt?" Ben asked. "Only that they bring 'em all back before the first session on Tuesday mornin'. It seems Mrs. Gambill is projecting standing room only," Irwin motioned to the *Alleghany Times* the store owner Harding was holding in his left hand.

"So she is," Ben replied, "What does Zora make of you runnin' for Sheriff?"

"I bet she was surprised," Burt Choate chimed in from behind Harding.

"Actually she told me it was about time," Irwin smiled, recalling her expression when he had first mentioned it.

"When was this decided?"

"Few months back, Walt went up to the board of elections and filed," Ben answered. "I keep tryin' to get him to do an ad in the paper," Mrs. Gambill said as she came from the direction of Smithey's.

"Mrs. Gambill," The men each said her name in unison with Burt removing his hat. "No harm in advertisin' a good cause," She replied. "Oh I agree," Ben nodded, "We should donate one." "Donate what" Sam Walker from Twin Oaks Store called as he headed over from his pickup.

"An ad for Irwin, he's runnin' for Sheriff," Burt explained. "That's right, I heard it down at the store," Sam grinned, "An ad is a great idea, it's the least we could do." "I agree," Mrs. Gambill said firmly, "And if anyone wants to purchase one they may come visit me this afternoon in my new offices."

"*Offices?*" Irwin asked.

"We got word they are giving us two spaces on the top floor of the new courthouse. Didn't you know?"

Irwin looked at the courthouse and for a moment considered backing out of the election, "I do now." The other men could hardly keep straight faces.

"Who's cuttin' the ribbon?" Mrs. Gambill asked as she admired the new structure.

"Henson and some of the County Commissioners, I believe your husband is involved," Irwin informed. "Would you gentlemen like to give comments about the new courthouse for an upcoming edition?"

"Sure," Harding motioned for her to follow him back into the store and out of the late morning sun.

A few minutes later the street was filled with onlookers and to Irwin's surprise a few very familiar faces.

"Holden?" The Lieutenant Highway Patrol approached and offered his hand, "Good to see you again Walt."

"It's been a long few months uh?" Irwin greeted.

"Sure has, and we cannot wait to get this started."

"No one is more ready than I am," Irwin replied as he also spotted Wyatt, Lewis, Whitman, Upchurch, and Hollister.

"The lawyers have been selected to represent the state, and they'll be here tomorrow to go over the charges. They do want to add the charge of impersonating an officer among the arson, illegal liquor operations, and car thefts. I was told by Hawks they feel it will really drive home the lengths Ridge went to in order to make a dollar."

"Agreed," Irwin nodded. The ceremony started and after the ribbon was cut the community was allowed to do a walk through of the new building.

It was hard to believe that just a few months ago the space had been reduced to ash. Irwin still heard the thunderous explosion that tore through his ears and the force that propelled him onto the lawn outside. It was an experience he doubted would altogether leave his memory.

Stepping through the main doors he noticed the similarities and the differences to the former building. The staircase leading up to the second floor was gilded with a dark iron banister that caught the sun coming through one of the nearby windows. Mrs. Gambill branched off, heading up the incline eager to inspect her new space.

Reaching the center of the building he could see the new Clerk's Office straight ahead, just where they should have been and the Deeds office off to the left. The Sheriff's office and the meeting room were now side by side to the right, but one major change was the addition of the judges chambers.

Rash whistled, "They did a great job rebuilding." Irwin decided to head to the courtroom, curious to see where Connor Ridge would be tried. The irony was also not lost on Irwin that the very building the bootlegger had sought to destroy was the very one he would be brought to justice in.

Mrs. Gambill was standing in the center of the courtroom between the newly important dark wooden benches. "It's beautiful," Mrs. Gambill said without turning around. "It is perfect," Irwin acknowledged sitting in the back just before the doors.

"Wow," Whitman gasped as he came up the stairwell, "This is really somethin'. Isn't it somethin'?"

"It is," Irwin answered, "By they way I heard the prosecutors have been selected."

Whitman nodded, "Hollister has more information on that, and Frank said hello by the way. He is takin' some much needed time off before the trail."

"How's his neck? Heard he had a number of stitches."

"Like Humpty Dumpty he got sewed back together," Hollister answered as he emerged from the stairwell landing.

Mrs. Gambill folded her arms in an attempt to force down a smile, "I'll leave you all to it, I have some arrangements to make before our next edition, excuse me gentlemen."

They watched her disappear into the back rooms. "Shepherd, Joines, and Ridge will get the maximum sentences allotted," Hollister said clearing his throat, "But the DA is willing to go easy on Shepherd because in the end, he tried to warn us, and he gave up the location of the still operation."

"Did you ever find the still?" Whitman inquired looking at Irwin. The deputy stared straight at the county seal, "I found it, but there was no still there. Only some pipes, and a slot machine." Neither man said a word, but they did exchange curious glances.

"When they threatened Sam Walker at Twin Oaks, they stole a slot machine from the back room."

"Was it full?" Hollister asked. "Don't know, probably never will," Irwin replied.

"They just left it out in the open?" Whitman asked. "No, they buried it." Whitman stuck his hands in his pockets. As he turned away Irwin could sense the Underwriter Bureau agents further disbelief of the case.

"What was it he was callin' the place? Devils Ridge?" Hollister said, "And wasn't there some mention of actual money, not a slot machine, but legal tender?"

Irwin stood up as he answered, "If there was any legal tender on that mountain I wouldn't go lookin' for it. The place is crawling with cottonmouths on one side, which is probably why he called it Devil's Ridge in the first place."

CHAPTER 31

The lock on the door beyond the cells gave a click and opened, "Your wife wants a word," One of the two deputies who had been rotating shifts announced.

Connor took in a deep breath, "Fine."

"You have five minuets," The deputy reminded and allowed Lizabeth to enter the holding cell.

Connor stood up, "How are the kids?" Her expression was much changed from the first time she had walked through the door to visit him after his initial arrest. She appeared more resigned to the idea of him being locked up, possibly for good.

"They're with your mother, and they're fine. She sends her love."

"Listen to me," Connor leaned on the bars, folding his arms in front of him, "I don't want you here tomorrow. Understood?"

"Connor you know I—."

"I know, I know," He raised his hands in mock surrender, "But showin' up will not change the outcome." "I saw Mr. Warren downstairs, has he come to talk with you yet?"

"No, not yet."

"You need to listen to what he has to say, they take you away for a decade—that's long..."

"Listen to me," Connor reached out for her hand, although wary she took it, "Whatever the outcome, this will be alright. I have somethin' that will set us right."

"And what do you have to set us right?" She implored seemingly unaware that her husband had not only run the largest bootlegging operation in western North Carolina, but that he had also prepared for a moment like this.

"You, the kids, and our families, we are all going to be fine. Can you trust me Lizabeth?"

There was a long silence but she finally said, "All I've done is trust you since we met Connor Ridge, and look where it's gotten me—gotten us!"

"I know you're angry," He admitted.

A look of contempt passed across her face, "How are we going to be taken care of with you in jail? Rumor has it that Jeb's grandson left here for Tennessee, and Jeb hasn't been seen hide nor hair of since that night."

Connor squeezed her hand, "Jeb's stayin' low, and he should. Just know, this is a promise I can deliver on, and if you wait for me, it will be worth it."

Lizabeth held onto his hand for a moment longer and then stepped back, "Fine, but I'll still be here tomorrow."

Before he could protest the guard opened the door, "Times up, and your attorney is here." Lizabeth Ridge gave him a faint smile, something for him to hold onto until morning, and left without another word. The deputy opened Connors' cell door and motioned for him to turn around.

Hands in cuffs Connor was led to the meeting room across from the holding area in the newly built courthouse. The smell of wood and fresh paint still lingered in the air the moment the door leading into the hallway opened.

At first glance Connor thought the deputy was all alone, but then noticed several other officers, agents, or officials walking about.

Toward the exit stood a familiar presence, with copper colored eyes and a set of scars. Frank Lincoln's stare could have burned a hole straight through Connors soul.

Looking away the door to the meeting room was opened by the deputy allowing him to step inside. As he sat down at the table across from defense attorney Mick Warren, he was offered a cigarette. The deputy closed the door giving them a moment of privacy, but did not venture far.

Connor Ridge took the cigarette offered by his attorney, but did not bother to ask for a light, not yet.

"Mr. Ridge, as you know we have been in communication with the prosecutors in your case. The judge presiding tomorrow is McElroy, and he has tried many a bootlegging case, but none such as this. While we hope for the best, we also need to be prepared for the worst."

Remaining silent Connor eyed the cigarette. Clearing his throat the attorney started again, "Now, it seems we have come to an understanding with the prosecution and the state in this case. One that may be to your favor."

Connor cut his eyes upwards, "Get to the point Mick." "Put plainly, if you give the prosecution something they can use to convict the individual or individuals who provided you with the uniform, keys, or even the siren, they'll cut you a deal."

"What kind of a deal?" Connor asked, not sounding overly convinced. "They'll remove a certain number of years from your sentence, and you may be looking at less time."

"But they're still going to try me?"

"No, they'll have to accept the plea. Tomorrow is more about formality, as the judge will determine what charges you may face." Mick answered keeping his eyes trained on his client for any sign of acceptance.

"No."

"No?"

Part of Connor knew that if he betrayed this individual, life could be made very hard for him on the inside. Another part of him heard his wife's voice pleading with him to do what Mick asked. The pause was enough to give Mick Warren reason to ask again.

"In all my years being a lawyer I have never once lied to a client about their chances and I won't lie to you now Mr. Ridge. You are looking at 10 to 15 years. That's a decade or decade and a half away from your family, you have children—."

"They're cared for," Connor replied without so much as a hint of concern in his tone. The lawyer's mouth hung open for a moment eager to protest, yet he decided against it a second later.

"Well that's all I have to offer in the way of hope Mr. Ridge," Mick stated as he lifted his briefcase from the floor, "I'll see you in the morning."

He started to stand up when Connor held up the cigarette, "Can I get a light Mick?" Seemingly agitated Mick Warren withdrew a match for his pocket, struck it on the side of the pack and lit the cigarette. After a couple short draws Connor motioned for him to have a seat.

Mick reluctantly returned to the chair preparing for whatever his client had to say. "I did favors for a lot of people along the way Mick, you understand? Good thing about doing favors is that sometimes someone owes you a favor too. Maybe now is the time to call in one of those favors."

Without a word Mick Warren felt he was about to receive a bombshell of a confession.

"Here's what you're going to do," Connor leaned forward, "You're going to tell them I gave up the person who gave me those things, and in exchange I want at least five years knocked off the sentence. Deal?"

Mick took in a slow steady breath, "I will do my best to get them to agree to it, but you're going to have to tell me who this person is."

"No one will believe you, but you tell 'em I have a witness and they can ask Zane," Connor leaned back in the wooden chair exhaling a ring of smoke, relieved he had one final card to play.

Irwin and most other local candidates stood in the hall of the courthouse waiting for the numbers to be made official. The counting had ended just before ten in the evening.

Robert Gambill strolled over with his hat in his hands, "Always amazes me how nervous I am every election cycle. Despite having held the office for eight years now, I still feel I might get kicked out."

Irwin laughed softly, "You're too good at your job Robert, you're gettin' back in." The farmer placed his elbows on his knees and looked out the doors into the night. Lights on main street were brighter than they had seemed the last few months.

The sound of heels clicking the staircase signaled that Mrs. Gambill had been called by the office. Per directions she would have been the first to know the results for the mornings special edition of the *Alleghany Times*. "Gentlemen," She greeted as she walked past, giving her husband a gentle touch on his shoulder. "Mrs. Gambill," Many of them respectfully replied or nodded in her direction.

From the narrow glass windows on the doors the men could see her scribbling numbers onto her notepad. "What do you think?" Robert inquired, "Good news?" "Fingers crossed for you Robert," Irwin said leaning back on the new wood bench.

Moments later the doors opened and Mrs. Gambill began to head back to the staircase. "Mrs. Gambill," One of the men stopped her, "What did they say?" "Mr. Caudill, you are going to have to pick up a copy of the newspaper tomorrow morning if you want to know the results."

A few of the men groaned, but Robert and Irwin laughed. "Come on Mrs. Gambill," One of the others spoke up, "We've been here all night." Smiling, Mrs. Gambill looked to the Clerks door, one of the volunteers emerged holding a long piece of paper, "No need, they will," She motioned before heading back upstairs.

Irwin, Robert, and the host of others who had been waiting all gathered around the paper after the volunteer finished fixing it to the wall with a piece of tape. Robert's mood lightened as he saw he was indeed back in office along with others. Irwin however, waited until the last few people remained before daring to glimpse at the list.

"Congratulations Walter," Robert called as he proceeded down the hallway toward the staircase. Irwin glanced up at the sheet and noted he had won the Sheriff's office over Henson by more than three hundred votes.

"Congratulations Sheriff Irwin," A familiar voice commended, causing him to turn around. There standing in her evening coat and a dark emerald colored dress was the one person he knew supported him no matter the outcome.

"I told you it was about time," She smiled as he wrapped his arms around her lovingly. "I couldn't have done it without you Zora. I just couldn't."

He could not recall the last time he had a really good burger. Smithey's store was buzzing with activity as he approached the front, opened the door and stepped inside. The counter, the shelves, the restaurant, all of it was just as he had recalled.

"What can I get for ya hun?" The young woman behind the counter asked politely with a smile. Despite the fact that she had no idea who he was, he smiled in return, "How about one of those good hamburgers you're fryin' up?"

"Want the works?" She asked scribbling his order on a small faded green notepad. "Sure."

Of all of life's lessons, the one lesson he had never forgotten was to indulge once in a while because life was too short. He shook his head as he stared down at the counter thinking about what a farce that was. Too short? It was *too* long.

Like the days he had spent in a ten by ten cell in Raleigh for close to five years. He could hardly believe that his sentence was anything less than ten, seeing as how most would have wanted him gone for good. But the way he saw it, he had done what he had to in order to survive.

Just shy of five years Connor Ridge emerged from his cell and from the NCDOC a 'reformed' individual. *Reformed,* he scoffed quietly. What he was was ready to move on.

A week earlier he had made up his mind to come into town, show his face, and leave. His wife and family were ready for a fresh start and so was Connor. The only way to get that was to head to Tennessee where Jeb's grandson had set up his own operation working stock cars by day and running shine by night.

Thayer Whitaker had not yet been released, nor had his brother who remained locked up in West Virginia. Erick Whitaker had murdered a woman in Johnson City just a month before Connors' trial in Alleghany.

The bootlegger had caught wind of the account through mutual friends in Wake County corrections.

Erick was sentenced to life imprisonment. Both boys had been heading for trouble most of their lives, but it had all caught up to them sooner than anyone realized it would.

Jeb Dalton passed away shortly after Connor had been sentenced. Zane however, had served time just like Connor. His three and half year sentence had left his wife nearly destitute, but in the end they had been able to pick up the pieces working their farm.

Zane had stayed far from moonshine according to most who knew him, however, Connor had learned his old partner and friend was looking at starting a dealership down near Boone. Connor doubted he would never speak to Zane again.

"Here you go hun, anythin' else I can get you?" The young woman sat down his burger and drink, giving him a look that spoke of concern. "This will do, thank you," Connor acknowledged and then stopped her, "Wait—I have a question and maybe you can help me." She lifted a nearby glass coffee pot and placed it in front of her, "I'll try."

Connor picked up his hamburger holding it steady with both hands, "What can you tell me about the Sheriff now? Is Henson still in office?"

"The Sheriff? You mean Walter Irwin? He's a good man, and if you're having any issues he's the one to go to." Her answer made Connor wonder if his ears were deceiving him.

"Did you say Irwin?"

"That's right," She said trying to sound cheerful, "Would you like for me to ring him or—?"

"No, no, I was simply askin', heard Henson was in last time I was around.

"Oh yeah, Henson retired, never ran again," She paused looking out over the store, "And it's such a shame, they're all looking for that girl—," She stopped upon seeing his inquisitive expression. "I'm sorry, I'll let you enjoy your food while it's hot. Mamma always said I had the gift of gab."

She walked away heading to a nearby table full of teenagers before Connor could inquire any further.

When he finished he took out a five dollar bill and laid it on the counter top, patted it for good measure, and headed out onto the street.

For half a decade he had been waiting for this moment, and for half a decade he had kept this very detail to himself. Not Zane, not Shepherd, not even Jeb, had known what he had done that night before they broke Shepherd out of the jail. In all honesty it had been one of his better moves.

The Parkway project had changed the road leading up the embankment to where his stills had once been. Connor would never forget the angle or the route it took to get there. Sure enough in a little over thirty minutes he was right where he needed to be. The only change was an overlook, a nice, smooth, easy to pull over space that afforded him the ability to safely park.

Climbing out he looked over the ridge at what the Parkway people had named, Bullhead Mountain. Dusk was starting to set in as daylight was becoming increasingly shorter. Reaching into the back of his truck bed Connor took out a shovel and proceeded to walk the familiar hillside.

Although he was not as agile as he had been at the age of twenty-five, he was still well acquainted with the mountains, their strength seemingly part of his resolve.

Climbing for several minutes he reached the summit, looked down and took in a long deep breath. He had thought it a million times before, but in that moment, if he were to die, Connor knew he would have preferred to die on this ridge than anywhere else.

Peering through thick overgrown trees he struggled to gain his bearings, deciding whether or not he had come too far or not far enough on the hillside.

Taking a few more steps, cautiously trying to avoid any fallen limbs or large rocks, he began to hear the roar of water. Smiling faintly he let the sound rush over his memory like moonshine down into a mason jar.

Once he reached the clearing where he had leaned his old shovel he noticed the instrument was on the ground. He had imagined it would be gone given the time that had passed. Yet, what remained clear to him was someone had found Devil's Ridge, and Connor believed he knew exactly who.

Where the shovel lay he distinctly recalled a slot machine having been buried, and although he was not surprised, it was gone. The hole left by its presence in the earth had been partially filled leaving a slight dip near the bottom of the nearest tree.

For years he had hidden his money in this clearing, just so, for the snakes to guard.

While his men had been busy moving still parts and taking care of the weapons stashed on the ridge, Connor had been busy ensuring his nest egg remained hidden and well guarded.

Now as he reached the patch of poison ivy, weeds, and wildflowers he kept a watchful eye for any signs of movement that could spell disaster around his boots.

Behind him the sun was starting to set to the west, making the ridge glow a brilliant burnt red.

Sticking the shovel into the dirt Connor heaved up four or five good shovels full of dirt and tossed them to the side. After the eighth he stopped, looked down, and recognized the bag he had placed there all those years ago.

Reaching down he pulled the bag up, its weight as he remembered, the scent of damp earth rushing up to greet him.

Crouching Connor untied the thick rope that had been used to make sure nothing penetrated the bag. The moment the folds turned back to reveal the contents Connor Ridge knew he would never have to worry about merely surviving again.

"We are here and this is now. Further than that, all human knowledge is moonshine."

~ H.L. Mencken

THE END

ACKNOWLEDGMENTS

Thank you to my editor Jorge Arena. Without his assistance I could not possibly have pulled this book together so beautifully.

Thank you to Brenda Irwin Frizzell, granddaughter of Sheriff Walter Irwin, and Caroline Taurus, her Godmother. Their stories, photos, and time lent to interviews about Irwin and his wife are deeply appreciated. Moreover, I wish to thank them for giving me the opportunity to make him part of this novel.

To Debbie McMillan Yopp for speaking with me about her grandfather, former Sheriff Bruce McMillan and the history of Alleghany County.

To Jerry Brooks who took time to discuss all things cars, moonshine, and the history of the Alleghany-Elkin Railroad, thank you does not seem like enough.

Also want to thank the Mount Airy Police Department and Detective Justin Stirewalt for providing information on the history of sheriffs who held office in Surry, and for providing research assistance.

Thank you to G.W. Plain, poet, friend, and gifted writer for composing the poem for this novel. It is something both I and readers will forever treasure.

To my friends, family, and volunteers who took the time to read this novel your efforts have not gone unnoticed. I want to say how truly grateful I am for each one of you. Without your support this second book would not have been possible.

Additional Acknowledgments:

Alleghany Register of Deeds

Alleghany News

Alleghany Public Library & the

North Carolina Board of Elections

Photo*: Sheriff Walter Irwin (right) standing with officers at a moonshine bust. Photo credit to Brenda Irwin Frizzell*

On September 5, 1939 former Sheriff Walter Irwin of Alleghany County, North Carolina was sworn in as a U.S. Deputy Marshall. One newspaper stated he was assigned an office in neighboring Wilkes County. Wilkes is also known as the county that gave birth to NASCAR & the Moonshine capitol of America. Even after the Depression, moonshining was still big in Alleghany County, as it continued to be in parts throughout the state.

ABOUT THE AUTHOR

Stacy Hawks is a resident of Alleghany County, North Carolina.

A graduate of Alleghany High School she holds an Associate of Arts Degree in History from Wilkes Community College, a Bachelor of Arts in History from Brevard College, NC having graduated Cum Laude, and a Masters of Education Teaching & Learning from Liberty University.

Stacy's first novel, *Dividing Ridge: the Unsolved Murder of Elva Brannock* is a North Carolina Literary Map book and may be found in the Library of Congress.

In her spare time she enjoys reading Presidential biographies, photography, and spending time with family and friends.

She is also the author of three poetry collections, and a fourth due out in early 2022. Follow Dividing Ridge Books on Facebook or Instagram for books, gifts, and events.

Social Media
www.facebook.com/dividingridge37
www.instagram.com/dividingridgeauthor

Website
https://dividingridgebooks.webador.com

Made in the USA
Las Vegas, NV
15 December 2021

37959492R00171